the perfect veneer

(a jessie hunt psychological suspense—book 26)

blake pierce

Blake Pierce

Blake Pierce is the USA Today bestselling author of the RILEY PAGE mystery series, which includes seventeen books. Blake Pierce is also the author of the MACKENZIE WHITE mystery series, comprising fourteen books; of the AVERY BLACK mystery series, comprising six books; of the KERI LOCKE mystery series, comprising five books; of the MAKING OF RILEY PAIGE mystery series, comprising six books; of the KATE WISE mystery series, comprising seven books; of the CHLOE FINE psychological suspense mystery, comprising six books; of the JESSIE HUNT psychological suspense thriller series, comprising twenty-eight books; of the AU PAIR psychological suspense thriller series, comprising three books; of the ZOE PRIME mystery series, comprising six books; of the ADELE SHARP mystery series, comprising sixteen books, of the EUROPEAN VOYAGE cozy mystery series, comprising six books; of the LAURA FROST FBI suspense thriller, comprising eleven books; of the ELLA DARK FBI suspense thriller, comprising fourteen books (and counting); of the A YEAR IN EUROPE cozy mystery series, comprising nine books, of the AVA GOLD mystery series, comprising six books; of the RACHEL GIFT mystery series, comprising ten books (and counting); of the VALERIE LAW mystery series, comprising nine books (and counting); of the PAIGE KING mystery series, comprising eight books (and counting); of the MAY MOORE mystery series, comprising eleven books; of the CORA SHIELDS mystery series, comprising eight books (and counting); of the NICKY LYONS mystery series, comprising eight books (and counting), of the CAMI LARK mystery series, comprising eight books (and counting), of the AMBER YOUNG mystery series, comprising five books (and counting), of the DAISY FORTUNE mystery series, comprising five books (and counting), of the FIONA RED mystery series, comprising five books (and counting), of the FAITH BOLD mystery series, comprising five books (and counting), and of the new JULIETTE HART mystery series, comprising five books (and counting).

An avid reader and lifelong fan of the mystery and thriller genres, Blake loves to hear from you, so please feel free to visit www.blakepierceauthor.com to learn more and stay in touch.

ISBN: 978-1-0943-8177-0

BOOKS BY BLAKE PIERCE

JULIETTE HART MYSTERY SERIES
NOTHING TO FEAR (Book #1)
NOTHING THERE (Book #2)
NOTHING WATCHING (Book #3)
NOTHING HIDING (Book #4)
NOTHING LEFT (Book #5)

FAITH BOLD MYSTERY SERIES
SO LONG (Book #1)
SO COLD (Book #2)
SO SCARED (Book #3)
SO NORMAL (Book #4)
SO FAR GONE (Book #5)

FIONA RED MYSTERY SERIES
LET HER GO (Book #1)
LET HER BE (Book #2)
LET HER HOPE (Book #3)
LET HER WISH (Book #4)
LET HER LIVE (Book #5)

DAISY FORTUNE MYSTERY SERIES
NEED YOU (Book #1)
CLAIM YOU (Book #2)
CRAVE YOU (Book #3)
CHOOSE YOU (Book #4)
CHASE YOU (Book #5)

AMBER YOUNG MYSTERY SERIES
ABSENT PITY (Book #1)
ABSENT REMORSE (Book #2)
ABSENT FEELING (Book #3)
ABSENT MERCY (Book #4)
ABSENT REASON (Book #5)

CAMI LARK MYSTERY SERIES
JUST ME (Book #1)

JUST OUTSIDE (Book #2)
JUST RIGHT (Book #3)
JUST FORGET (Book #4)
JUST ONCE (Book #5)
JUST HIDE (Book #6)
JUST NOW (Book #7)
JUST HOPE (Book #8)

NICKY LYONS MYSTERY SERIES
ALL MINE (Book #1)
ALL HIS (Book #2)
ALL HE SEES (Book #3)
ALL ALONE (Book #4)
ALL FOR ONE (Book #5)
ALL HE TAKES (Book #6)
ALL FOR ME (Book #7)
ALL IN (Book #8)

CORA SHIELDS MYSTERY SERIES
UNDONE (Book #1)
UNWANTED (Book #2)
UNHINGED (Book #3)
UNSAID (Book #4)
UNGLUED (Book #5)
UNSTABLE (Book #6)
UNKNOWN (Book #7)
UNAWARE (Book #8)

MAY MOORE SUSPENSE THRILLER
NEVER RUN (Book #1)
NEVER TELL (Book #2)
NEVER LIVE (Book #3)
NEVER HIDE (Book #4)
NEVER FORGIVE (Book #5)
NEVER AGAIN (Book #6)
NEVER LOOK BACK (Book #7)
NEVER FORGET (Book #8)
NEVER LET GO (Book #9)
NEVER PRETEND (Book #10)
NEVER HESITATE (Book #11)

PAIGE KING MYSTERY SERIES
THE GIRL HE PINED (Book #1)
THE GIRL HE CHOSE (Book #2)
THE GIRL HE TOOK (Book #3)
THE GIRL HE WISHED (Book #4)
THE GIRL HE CROWNED (Book #5)
THE GIRL HE WATCHED (Book #6)
THE GIRL HE WANTED (Book #7)
THE GIRL HE CLAIMED (Book #8)

VALERIE LAW MYSTERY SERIES
NO MERCY (Book #1)
NO PITY (Book #2)
NO FEAR (Book #3)
NO SLEEP (Book #4)
NO QUARTER (Book #5)
NO CHANCE (Book #6)
NO REFUGE (Book #7)
NO GRACE (Book #8)
NO ESCAPE (Book #9)

RACHEL GIFT MYSTERY SERIES
HER LAST WISH (Book #1)
HER LAST CHANCE (Book #2)
HER LAST HOPE (Book #3)
HER LAST FEAR (Book #4)
HER LAST CHOICE (Book #5)
HER LAST BREATH (Book #6)
HER LAST MISTAKE (Book #7)
HER LAST DESIRE (Book #8)
HER LAST REGRET (Book #9)
HER LAST HOUR (Book #10)

AVA GOLD MYSTERY SERIES
CITY OF PREY (Book #1)
CITY OF FEAR (Book #2)
CITY OF BONES (Book #3)
CITY OF GHOSTS (Book #4)
CITY OF DEATH (Book #5)
CITY OF VICE (Book #6)

A YEAR IN EUROPE
A MURDER IN PARIS (Book #1)
DEATH IN FLORENCE (Book #2)
VENGEANCE IN VIENNA (Book #3)
A FATALITY IN SPAIN (Book #4)

ELLA DARK FBI SUSPENSE THRILLER
GIRL, ALONE (Book #1)
GIRL, TAKEN (Book #2)
GIRL, HUNTED (Book #3)
GIRL, SILENCED (Book #4)
GIRL, VANISHED (Book 5)
GIRL ERASED (Book #6)
GIRL, FORSAKEN (Book #7)
GIRL, TRAPPED (Book #8)
GIRL, EXPENDABLE (Book #9)
GIRL, ESCAPED (Book #10)
GIRL, HIS (Book #11)
GIRL, LURED (Book #12)
GIRL, MISSING (Book #13)
GIRL, UNKNOWN (Book #14)

LAURA FROST FBI SUSPENSE THRILLER
ALREADY GONE (Book #1)
ALREADY SEEN (Book #2)
ALREADY TRAPPED (Book #3)
ALREADY MISSING (Book #4)
ALREADY DEAD (Book #5)
ALREADY TAKEN (Book #6)
ALREADY CHOSEN (Book #7)
ALREADY LOST (Book #8)
ALREADY HIS (Book #9)
ALREADY LURED (Book #10)
ALREADY COLD (Book #11)

EUROPEAN VOYAGE COZY MYSTERY SERIES
MURDER (AND BAKLAVA) (Book #1)
DEATH (AND APPLE STRUDEL) (Book #2)
CRIME (AND LAGER) (Book #3)
MISFORTUNE (AND GOUDA) (Book #4)
CALAMITY (AND A DANISH) (Book #5)

MAYHEM (AND HERRING) (Book #6)

ADELE SHARP MYSTERY SERIES

LEFT TO DIE (Book #1)
LEFT TO RUN (Book #2)
LEFT TO HIDE (Book #3)
LEFT TO KILL (Book #4)
LEFT TO MURDER (Book #5)
LEFT TO ENVY (Book #6)
LEFT TO LAPSE (Book #7)
LEFT TO VANISH (Book #8)
LEFT TO HUNT (Book #9)
LEFT TO FEAR (Book #10)
LEFT TO PREY (Book #11)
LEFT TO LURE (Book #12)
LEFT TO CRAVE (Book #13)
LEFT TO LOATHE (Book #14)
LEFT TO HARM (Book #15)
LEFT TO RUIN (Book #16)

THE AU PAIR SERIES

ALMOST GONE (Book#1)
ALMOST LOST (Book #2)
ALMOST DEAD (Book #3)

ZOE PRIME MYSTERY SERIES

FACE OF DEATH (Book#1)
FACE OF MURDER (Book #2)
FACE OF FEAR (Book #3)
FACE OF MADNESS (Book #4)
FACE OF FURY (Book #5)
FACE OF DARKNESS (Book #6)

A JESSIE HUNT PSYCHOLOGICAL SUSPENSE SERIES

THE PERFECT WIFE (Book #1)
THE PERFECT BLOCK (Book #2)
THE PERFECT HOUSE (Book #3)
THE PERFECT SMILE (Book #4)
THE PERFECT LIE (Book #5)
THE PERFECT LOOK (Book #6)
THE PERFECT AFFAIR (Book #7)

THE PERFECT ALIBI (Book #8)
THE PERFECT NEIGHBOR (Book #9)
THE PERFECT DISGUISE (Book #10)
THE PERFECT SECRET (Book #11)
THE PERFECT FAÇADE (Book #12)
THE PERFECT IMPRESSION (Book #13)
THE PERFECT DECEIT (Book #14)
THE PERFECT MISTRESS (Book #15)
THE PERFECT IMAGE (Book #16)
THE PERFECT VEIL (Book #17)
THE PERFECT INDISCRETION (Book #18)
THE PERFECT RUMOR (Book #19)
THE PERFECT COUPLE (Book #20)
THE PERFECT MURDER (Book #21)
THE PERFECT HUSBAND (Book #22)
THE PERFECT SCANDAL (Book #23)
THE PERFECT MASK (Book #24)
THE PERFECT RUSE (Book #25)
THE PERFECT VENEER (Book #26)
THE PERFECT PEOPLE (Book #27)
THE PERFECT WITNESS (Book #28)

CHLOE FINE PSYCHOLOGICAL SUSPENSE SERIES
NEXT DOOR (Book #1)
A NEIGHBOR'S LIE (Book #2)
CUL DE SAC (Book #3)
SILENT NEIGHBOR (Book #4)
HOMECOMING (Book #5)
TINTED WINDOWS (Book #6)

KATE WISE MYSTERY SERIES
IF SHE KNEW (Book #1)
IF SHE SAW (Book #2)
IF SHE RAN (Book #3)
IF SHE HID (Book #4)
IF SHE FLED (Book #5)
IF SHE FEARED (Book #6)
IF SHE HEARD (Book #7)

THE MAKING OF RILEY PAIGE SERIES
WATCHING (Book #1)

WAITING (Book #2)
LURING (Book #3)
TAKING (Book #4)
STALKING (Book #5)
KILLING (Book #6)

RILEY PAIGE MYSTERY SERIES
ONCE GONE (Book #1)
ONCE TAKEN (Book #2)
ONCE CRAVED (Book #3)
ONCE LURED (Book #4)
ONCE HUNTED (Book #5)
ONCE PINED (Book #6)
ONCE FORSAKEN (Book #7)
ONCE COLD (Book #8)
ONCE STALKED (Book #9)
ONCE LOST (Book #10)
ONCE BURIED (Book #11)
ONCE BOUND (Book #12)
ONCE TRAPPED (Book #13)
ONCE DORMANT (Book #14)
ONCE SHUNNED (Book #15)
ONCE MISSED (Book #16)
ONCE CHOSEN (Book #17)

MACKENZIE WHITE MYSTERY SERIES
BEFORE HE KILLS (Book #1)
BEFORE HE SEES (Book #2)
BEFORE HE COVETS (Book #3)
BEFORE HE TAKES (Book #4)
BEFORE HE NEEDS (Book #5)
BEFORE HE FEELS (Book #6)
BEFORE HE SINS (Book #7)
BEFORE HE HUNTS (Book #8)
BEFORE HE PREYS (Book #9)
BEFORE HE LONGS (Book #10)
BEFORE HE LAPSES (Book #11)
BEFORE HE ENVIES (Book #12)
BEFORE HE STALKS (Book #13)
BEFORE HE HARMS (Book #14)

AVERY BLACK MYSTERY SERIES
CAUSE TO KILL (Book #1)
CAUSE TO RUN (Book #2)
CAUSE TO HIDE (Book #3)
CAUSE TO FEAR (Book #4)
CAUSE TO SAVE (Book #5)
CAUSE TO DREAD (Book #6)

KERI LOCKE MYSTERY SERIES
A TRACE OF DEATH (Book #1)
A TRACE OF MURDER (Book #2)
A TRACE OF VICE (Book #3)
A TRACE OF CRIME (Book #4)
A TRACE OF HOPE (Book #5)

PROLOGUE

Grover Nix was behind schedule, and it irritated him to no end.

He was supposed to knock on the bedroom door of Mr. and Mrs. Booth with breakfast at exactly 7:30 a.m. Depending on whether they were ready for him to enter or not, he would bring it into the bedroom suite or simply leave it on the table outside the door. Either way, he was supposed to be knocking at 7:30.

With a full tray of food, it took a good five minutes to walk from the kitchen, through the mansion, up the stairs, and down the long hallway to the bedroom. But it was already 7:26 and he was only now putting the metal covers over the plates.

The chef had let Mr. Booth's eggs teeter beyond over easy to over medium and had to redo them, pushing everything back. In addition, Mrs. Booth's cantaloupe was sloppily cut. It had been a disaster of a morning.

Grover finally gripped the handles of the tray and turned to the kitchen door, ready to make haste, when a loud, piercing alarm sounded, echoing throughout the grounds. Unlike the main alarm for the estate, this was one he'd never heard before. Rather than guess what it meant, he did what he was trained to do: he put the tray down and immediately began running toward his employer's bedroom.

Grover wasn't just a valet. Before entering the world of hospitality, he'd been an SAS soldier in the British Army, serving in both Iraq and Afghanistan. While he hadn't worn the uniform in over fifteen years, his time in the military was what had earned him multiple private security and bodyguard positions. And it was what had gotten him his position here at the Booth Estate.

Grover sprinted as fast as his suit and his forty-six-year-old legs would allow as he shot through various first floor rooms and reached the stairs. Part of the reason he'd taken this job was that his body could no longer stand the rigors of daily, nonstop, public-facing security scenarios. Protecting a sixty-four-year-old billionaire who rarely moved outside the bubble of mansions, limos, high-rise office buildings, and private jets was supposed to mean an end to all the physical stress. And yet, here he was, about to bound up three flights of stairs.

"All units," he huffed into his comm as he leapt up the stairs two at a time, trying to be heard over the shrill alarm siren, "this is Prime. I am approaching the Principal's nest. I need unit one to meet me there. Unit two, secure the estate perimeter. Control room, get me eyes."

He had to stop talking as he reached the top of the stairs. He was out of breath, and he wanted to stay quiet as he approached the bedroom. He carried a sidearm but was reluctant to remove it from its holster. The likelihood was that this was an unintentional activation of some alarm, and he didn't want to escalate the situation by inadvertently shooting someone, especially his boss. So, instead, he pulled out his retractable nightstick as he jogged toward the Booths' bedroom door. When he saw that it was open, he knew something was wrong. They never just left it open.

Stepping inside, he scanned the room. There was nothing overtly unusual. The bed was unmade. Neither Mr. nor Mrs. Booth was anywhere in sight. He slid along the wall, his back pressed against it to support his slightly shaky calves as he neared the giant barn door that led to the bathroom.

He was about to spin around the corner when he thought better of his choice of weapon. Whatever was going on, he was now dubious that it was just an accidental tripping of an alarm. He replaced the nightstick, unholstered his gun, took a deep breath, and rolled into the open doorway facing the bathroom.

The space was larger than most other bathrooms, with a marble vanity that stretched fifteen feet across, two farmhouse-style sinks, and separate his and hers toilet stalls and closets. No one was visible in those darkened areas, though he noted that there was a dim light coming from the back of Mr. Booth's closet.

He got to his feet and was just moving in that direction when he heard footsteps behind him and swung around, ready to fire. Staring him in the face was Rufus, aka "Unit One," in the four-person security team. The younger man with the dark buzzcut looked stunned to have a weapon pointed in his face and seemed about to gasp when Grover held the index finger of his free hand to his lips to indicate silence, then pointed at the closet.

He mouthed the words "cover me." Rufus nodded and removed his own weapon. Grover indicated what he planned to do next. Again, Rufus nodded. Lying to himself that it wouldn't hurt, Grover knelt at the edge of the closet, took a step, and did a somersault into the closet, popping up onto his knees with gun pointed in the direction of the light.

It took him a second to process what he saw. The back wall of the closet, which had several long coats draped on hangers, appeared to actually be a door, leading to another, hidden room. It was slightly ajar. That was where the light, and the ear-splitting noise, was coming from.

Grover stood up and dashed over. There was just enough room to get through the opening. Once he'd passed through, he realized he was in a high-tech panic room, one that Mr. Booth had never informed him of. But that fact became secondary almost immediately.

More pressing was the fact that his employer, billionaire Lowden Booth was lying on the floor with a giant indentation in his forehead where it had clearly slammed into the corner of the nearby safe on the floor. The safe was bloody. His head was bloody. The cement floor around his head was quickly pooling with blood from the gaping wound. And Booth's wide-open eyes were proof that he was beyond help.

Grover turned his attention to Booth's young wife, Devon, who was seated, slumped on the floor beside him, her head resting against the wall of the room. She was either dead or unconscious. Her hands were tied behind her back.

"Jesus," muttered Rufus from behind him.

Grover walked over to the control panel, studied it for a second, and then pushed one of the buttons. The alarm went quiet.

"Control room," he said into his com, "we have a home invasion. The intruder or intruders may still be on the property. Make an announcement alerting all staff to lock themselves in secure rooms. Monitor all CCTV cameras for suspicious movement. They can't have gotten far. Unit two, have your weapon ready. The intruders have violently attacked the Principal. Assume they're armed and dangerous. Unit one will be coming to assist."

He was about to give Rufus further instructions when a soft moan escaped Devon Booth's lips. He felt like an idiot for not having immediately checked her status. He was getting sloppy in his old age.

"And control room, call LAPD. Use the private emergency number we were given. Let them know who's calling and alert them that we need immediate assistance. Tell them that we have an assault victim with a head injury and another victim who is deceased. Do this now."

CHAPTER ONE

"You do realize that you are the only patient I ever allow to go over time."

Jessie Hunt couldn't help but smile when she heard the words.

Dr. Lemmon had said them with what was clearly intended to sound like exasperation but, despite her best intentions, affection had slipped in ever so slightly. Jessie looked at her therapist on the screen of her laptop and batted her eyes flirtatiously.

"Why Doc, does this mean that I'm your most favoritest patient ever?"

The doctor stared back at her impassively behind her thick glasses. The sixty-something psychiatrist with aggressively permed blonde hair and a reputation as the best in the business wasn't about to let Jessie get the upper hand.

"Nope," Lemmon said, "I think your little sister has stolen that title from you lately. And your friend Jamil is starting to close the gap too."

"Speaking of Jamil, how's he doing?" Jessie asked, dispensing with the playfulness. Even though the conference room was locked and soundproofed, she glanced around just to be safe. After all, she was having this early morning tele-therapy session with her psychiatrist at the very police station where she and Jamil Winslow worked. It wouldn't be appropriate for him to walk by while she discussed him. But apparently even Lemmon thought the question was out of bounds.

"You know I can't discuss Jamil's sessions with you, Jessie," she said disapprovingly. "You should be ashamed of yourself for even asking. What I *can* say is that he's putting in the hard work. That reminds me, there's a group being run out of the hospital that I think could benefit all of you—Jamil, Hannah, and yourself. It's focused on survivor's guilt and the moderator is fantastic. Her name is Clea Masterson. She trained with me briefly, so I know her well. You've each been meeting with me privately, but I think that sharing your stories in a group setting could be equally productive at this point in your recoveries. They meet on Saturdays."

"I'll think about it," Jessie said noncommittally.

"Good," Lemmon replied. "I'll send you the details and you can pass them along to the others. Please don't conveniently forget, Jessie. This is about more than just you, okay?"

"I'm afraid we're out of time, Doctor," Jessie said, mimicking the tone Lemmon used so often at the end of their sessions, "and I've got some crimes to solve."

"Goodbye, Jessie," Dr. Lemmon said tolerantly.

"Bye," Jessie said.

She ended the call and sat quietly at the conference table. She didn't actually have any pressing cases to solve. Just yesterday, she and Detective Jim Nettles had managed to wrap up a situation involving an escaped mental patient who was stalking a popular TV actress. They found him hiding in her pool house with electric tape and a cattle prod. The guy had since been returned to his facility and Nettles managed to leave for his vacation to Cabo on time late last night.

That left Jessie with no official case today and too much unfilled space in her head to contemplate what Dr. Lemmon had said. Did she really want to go to a group session centered on survivor's guilt with Jamil and Hannah? It was hard enough to address her issues in private with her psychiatrist. But in a group setting?

She wondered how Jamil would do. Jamil Winslow was the genius head of research for Homicide Special Section, the elite LAPD unit they both worked for, which investigated cases with high profiles or intense media scrutiny—typically involving multiple victims or serial killers.

But he was also a twenty-four-year-old kid who was haunted by one of those recent cases. The case involved twenty-seven people who were poisoned by the deranged acolyte of a woman obsessed with Jessie. It was all part of an elaborate plan called Operation Z.

Jamil felt responsible, as if he should have been able to uncover the clues that would have prevented those deaths. He didn't listen when told that his brilliance was essential in ensuring that only twenty-seven people had died in Operation Z and not thousands.

Jessie stood up and stretched after an hour of sitting at the table staring at a laptop screen. As she did, it occurred to her that Jamil might have the same reservations about sharing his guilt with a group of strangers that she did: regular people just might not get it like the two of them did. After all, the deranged acolyte who had poisoned all those people, Zoe Bradway, did it at the behest of Andrea "Andy" Robinson, whose obsession with Jessie started Operation Z in the first place.

But that uncomfortable personal connection wasn't where Jessie's guilt came from. Hers stemmed from the night that Andy kidnapped her from her own wedding and locked her up in an abandoned mineshaft in Arizona. In a moment of weakness after the abduction was complete, Andy had revealed that her own uncle had raped her as a teenager in that very mineshaft.

Later, Jessie used that knowledge, along with her awareness that Andy's obsession with her had mutated into something romantic, to manipulate and confuse the woman when trying to escape. Just before her death, Andy had called her on it. The accusation had rung in Jessie's head ever since. She had used someone's childhood sexual trauma to get the upper hand on her. Yes, the person was unhinged and planned to kill her, but still.

And then there was Hannah. Her younger, half-sister, Hannah Dorsey, had been there the night Jessie tried to escape. Hannah, along with Jessie's best friend, Kat Gentry, and retired Detective Callum Reid, had rescued Jessie from the crumbling mineshaft where Andy had taken her to either be her forever plaything or to die.

Unfortunately, when they fled the collapsing mine, Andy wasn't the only one who died inside. Callum Reid had returned inside the mine to get a bag with a burner phone essential to stopping Operation Z. He was able to retrieve it but got trapped on the wrong side of a giant chasm. Hannah, just eighteen years old and already having seen far too much death in her life, watched as the ground crumbled underneath Callum and he disappeared from sight.

She had been struggling with the guilt of knowing that his choice to help them save Jessie left his two young children fatherless. Even Jessie's decision to set up college scholarships for them didn't completely assuage the pain she felt when she thought of them growing up without him. Would discussing that pain with strangers in a windowless hospital meeting room ease that guilt?

Jessie closed the laptop and put it in her backpack as she pondered the other factor that lingered over everything. No amount of group therapy would matter if Hannah was dead.

The thought was only mildly hyperbolic. After all, it was just two weeks ago that Jessie received a phone call from Zoe Bradway, who was currently incarcerated in a psychiatric prison, saying that Operation Z was still very much active.

According to Zoe, only the first part of the operation—the attempt to murder thousands of Angelenos by poisoning the popcorn butter flavoring at a major movie theater complex—had bene thwarted. The second part—torturing and killing the people closest to Jessie to make her suffer—was still a go. Zoe reminded her who was at risk: Hannah, Kat, and Jessie's husband and boss, Captain Ryan Hernandez.

Ever since then, they'd been on high alert. At Jessie's insistence, Ryan had passed the threat along to their former captain at Central Station and the current Los Angeles Chief of Police, Roy Decker, who had assigned protective units for Ryan, Hannah, and Kat.

Initially, that wasn't overly complicated. Ryan spent most of his time at their workplace—downtown's Central Station, surrounded by other officers. Having a squad car escort him and Jessie home and remain there overnight wasn't a huge burden.

And since Hannah was spending the summer interning with Kat at her private detective agency, only one squad car was required to keep tabs on their whereabouts most of the time too. At the end of the day, a second car would arrive to follow Kat home, while the first one dropped Hannah back with Jessie and Ryan.

But while the logistical burden wasn't overwhelming, the stress of constantly being on guard was starting to weigh on them. Plus, after a couple of weeks of this, Jessie could sense that Ryan was getting anxious about the plan. He'd been dropping hints that he thought the outlay of financial and human resources for their personal benefit was becoming increasingly onerous.

Just then, almost as if he was reading her mind, her husband appeared outside the conference room door, his brow furrowed in consternation. She smiled as she approached the door and unlocked it. Even looking worried, Ryan Hernandez was impossibly handsome.

His shirt was tucked in, casually highlighting his muscular frame. He ran a hand nervously through his short dark hair and offered her a half-smile that couldn't hide his concern or his adorable dimples. His big, brown eyes, always filled with warmth and compassion, were currently clouded with uneasy thoughts.

"Your session with Dr. Lemmon is over, I gather?" he asked.

"Just finished," she said. "What's up? You look troubled."

"More frustrated than troubled," he replied, holding out the file he'd been gripping in his left hand. "The Marina del Rey Sheriff's Station issued their final report on the Woody Garnett killing yesterday while you and Nettles were working that stalker case. So I asked Karen Bray and Susannah Valentine to review their findings for any discrepancies."

"And?" Jessie asked, though she could already tell from his tone what the answer would be.

"Nothing," he said, unable to hide his skepticism.

She tended to share the feeling. Woody Garnett was a recent murder victim who had been stabbed in the stomach on his own boat in the marina two weeks ago. Alone, that wasn't especially interesting. But a few months back, Garnett was also nearly the victim of a serial killer, a young woman taking vengeance on cheating spouses. She had stabbed him in the stomach in a Marina del Rey hotel room and he would have died if Jessie and Ryan hadn't arrived to stop her and save him. The nature and location of his death seemed *awfully* coincidental.

"Really?" she said, incredulously.

"They couldn't find any connection to the prior case. Harper Grey, who stabbed him the first time, was locked up at the time of his murder. His ex-wife, who had the strongest motive to try to kill him this time around, was out of town. His ex-girlfriend—the one he left his wife for—had an alibi. No one else seemed to give a damn about him. There's no motive. There's no evidence to tie anyone to the scene. Nothing to go on at all. You're welcome to review the file, but Karen and Susannah went over it pretty thoroughly and said the sheriff's people did a solid job. No corner cutting. We may just have a strange twist of fate here."

"Okay," Jessie said, sensing an opening as she gently pushed the file back toward him, "I guess that means I can focus more energy on Zoe and this whole Operation Z thing."

Ryan sighed heavily and she knew what was coming. But she said nothing. She wasn't going to make it easy for him. She was going to make him speak the words.

"About that," he said, motioning for her to take a seat at the conference table as he closed the door, "I've been doing some thinking. I know what Zoe told you. But I just don't see how she could make this threat a reality. Think about it. She spent months strategizing that attack on the movie theater. Then she was arrested. Do you really think she had the time to plan this alternative Operation Z? Or the resources? Andy is dead. She's not writing any checks these days. This sounds like a young woman who is frustrated that her big operation got short-circuited and is lashing out by making collect calls to you, trying to scare you into thinking the people you love are still in danger."

Jessie was far less certain. There was no reason that, during all those months that she planned the movie theater attack, Zoe couldn't have also been planning something else. And who was to say that Andy Robinson didn't provide Zoe with all manner of financial resources through back channels that they had yet to uncover?

Still, she couldn't deny that Ryan might have a point. This could just be an unstable, resentful woman attempting to create anxiety for her mentor's nemesis in whatever pathetic way was still available to her. Either way, she knew they couldn't have officers providing security for them forever. It wasn't tenable and it wasn't fair.

She knew that Chief Decker had a soft spot for her and would authorize the cost of the protective units in perpetuity, but she couldn't put him in that position. He'd only just been named permanent chief. He didn't need the press asking questions about preferential treatment for people from his old station and their civilian loved ones, even if there was legitimate cause.

And Ryan had only been the captain of Central Station for a few months now himself. Even though he'd never say it, every additional day that he had a protective detail was a day that he looked weak to the rank and file.

Finally, there was Hannah and Kat. When Jessie had first learned of this threat, she'd gone straight to her best friend and said that her little sister's safety was in her hands, regardless of how many LAPD officers were around. Kat hadn't batted an eye. That was because Kat Gentry hadn't always been a private detective.

Prior to that, she was in charge of security for a psychiatric facility for mentally unwell criminals. More importantly for Jessie's purposes, before taking that position, she'd served in Afghanistan as an Army Ranger, where she engaged in everything from special reconnaissance to close combat missions, until she was injured in an IED explosion that left her with scars both internal and external. Despite that, or maybe because of it, Jessie knew that Kat would be on high alert every second that she and Hannah were together.

"When are you dropping the protective details?' she asked Ryan, not even attempting to argue with him.

"I put in the order this morning," he said. "The unit assigned to meet Kat and Hannah has been alerted and I will tell them in person momentarily."

"Okay," Jessie said, standing up and starting for the conference room door. "I would have preferred more of a heads-up, but since it's a done deal at this point, I guess we'll just have to trust that Zoe is full of crap."

"Yeah," Ryan said, following close behind her, "at some point, it becomes a 'crying wolf' situation when she keeps making all these idle threats."

Jessie stopped in her tracks at the conference room door and turned to face him. She could tell from his guilty expression that he knew he'd screwed up.

"What do you mean, '*keeps* making all these threats,' Ryan? She only called me once. What aren't you telling me?"

CHAPTER TWO

For a second, it looked to Jessie like Ryan might try to squirm out of it.

Then his whole body slumped, and he leaned back against the glass window of the conference room.

"That call you got from Zoe wasn't the first time she made a threat like that," he muttered under his breath.

"When *was* the first time?" Jessie asked, trying to control the volume of her voice.

"The night we stopped Operation Z, when I arrested her at the movie theater," he said, his eyes focused on a spot on the carpet between them. "She said something very similar as I was cuffing her."

Jessie swallowed hard before responding, again trying to fight off the urge to yell.

"Why didn't you think to mention that?"

"In part, for the same reason I mentioned earlier. I thought she was blowing smoke after getting caught, trying to puff herself up. Also, after everything you'd been through, I didn't want to worry you. I thought that after the kidnapping, along with the concussion you suffered and Callum's death, it was one more thing you didn't need."

Jessie felt her whole body tense up. The only thing that prevented her from blowing up completely was the sight of two uniformed officers rounding the corner and walking down the hall past them. Once they had gone by, she leaned in and spoke through gritted teeth.

"That wasn't your call, Ryan! A woman who just tried to kill thousands of people tells you her next order of business is to go after you, my sister, and my best friend as a way to make me suffer and you make the command decision not to share that with me?"

"In the moment, it seemed like the right decision," he protested. "You were struggling with headaches, dizziness, memory issues. You were consumed by guilt over the circumstances of Andy's death. I didn't want to pile on."

"But that was almost two months ago," she countered, not having any of it. "You've had ample time to tell me at any point since then. And Zoe's call to me was two weeks ago. You could have come clean after that, when it was obvious that it wasn't just a one-time threat. But even then, you said nothing. You kept me in the dark all this time, when the three of you were in danger and I could have been doing something. I cannot fathom why you kept this from me."

"That's why," he said, struggling to keep his own voice under control, "that mentality. Because 'we're in danger' and you could have been doing something. That's what I was trying to avoid. And it's not like I haven't been looking into it. I have people keeping tabs on Zoe as a precaution. But I'm still not convinced that we *are* in danger. It could all be talk. And even if we are, what could you be doing, Jessie? You already demanded that Decker put units on us 24/7. Were you going to hire private bodyguards? Were you going to have someone go undercover at the Western Regional Women's Psychiatric Detention Center to win Zoe's trust and get her to reveal her secret plan? Were you going to ask your FBI friends to run a forensic analysis on Andy Robinson's offshore bank accounts? What? Where does it end? You would never get a good night's sleep again."

Jessie listened to his arguments, waiting for the one that might convince her that she was overreacting. But none did. In fact, they only hardened her resolve.

"Actually," she replied, "every single one of those sounds like a great plan. I've got the financial resources so why not hire a bodyguard for each of you? Maybe you wouldn't go for it, but I could have hired them for Hannah and Kat and they wouldn't have even needed to know. You don't think Jack Dolan at the FBI would have run Andy's accounts for me after learning that a woman who killed over two dozen people had threatened the lives of my husband, sister, and best friend? He wouldn't have batted an eye. Getting someone into Western Regional PDC might have been harder but it's a damn good idea. If I'd have known about Zoe's intentions two months ago, I could probably have someone in there by now. The point is, underestimating crazy is almost always a mistake. We need to be prepared to defeat it. And that requires sacrifice. So what if that means losing sleep? I've dealt with sleepless nights before. I've dealt with stalkers and serial killers and sociopathic ex-husbands. I can deal with a lot. What I *can't* deal with is the man I married keeping things from me to 'protect' me from myself. That's not love, Ryan. That's control."

He opened his mouth to respond but before he could, a loud knock on the glass made them both jump. It was Beth Ryerson, the unit's junior researcher. The anxious expression on her face told them that whatever she needed to say couldn't wait.

Jessie unlocked the door and opened it.

"Sorry to bother you," Beth said quietly, "but Chief Decker is on the phone. He says he's been trying to reach both of you."

"Oh damn," Ryan said. "I put my cell phone on silent when I came in here."

Jessie realized she'd never taken hers off silent after her session with Dr. Lemmon ended.

"What is it?" she asked.

"I don't know," Beth said. "But he said to get you and tell you he's waiting on line one. He also said it's urgent."

***

Thirty seconds later, after they both sprinted to the office marked "Captain Hernandez" and locked the door, Jessie gasped for air as Ryan hit the button to put the call on speaker.

"Hi Chief," he said, clearly trying to hide his shortness of breath, "sorry to keep you waiting."

"I hope I'm not being too much of a pain," Decker said drily, 'but I was eager to have a word with you and Ms. Hunt, if you could spare a minute or two."

Jessie was glad that she wasn't the one who had to reply to that. She might be pissed at Ryan, but she didn't envy his position right now.

"Of course, Chief," Ryan said, sitting down at his desk as Jessie took a seat in a chair opposite him. "Jessie is here with me now. What can we do for you?"

"First of all, briefly before I get to the point of my call, I understand that you requested that the protective detail I approved for yourself, Ms. Dorsey, and Ms. Gentry be suspended as of today. Care to tell me why?"

"Yes, Chief," Ryan replied, visibly wincing. "At this point, I just don't think we can justify the departmental resources when there's no tangible evidence to suggest that Zoe Bradway's threats are anything more than bluster."

"Do you agree with that assessment, Ms. Hunt?" Decker asked.

Ryan looked over at Jessie nervously. She was at a genuine loss. Until two minutes ago, she would have reluctantly agreed with his assessment. Now she didn't know what to think.

But she didn't want to throw her own husband under the bus, not under any circumstances, and especially not when she had no credible evidence that he was wrong. Plus, she didn't want to put Decker in the vulnerable political position of continuing to pay for officers to protect them.

"I defer to Captain Hernandez's judgement in this matter, Chief," she said.

There was a long silence on the other end of the line, after which Decker finally responded.

"Very well then, let me get to the point of my call. We received notification on our private alert line about five minutes ago about a death at the Booth Estate in the Hollywood Hills. Are you familiar with Lowden Booth?"

"The pharma billionaire?" Ryan asked.

"That's correct," Decker replied. "Details are scarce so far but what we know is this: he was found dead by a member of his security team in a panic room on his estate just before 7:30. His wife was apparently also assaulted, though she seems to have survived. It appears that the murder occurred only minutes earlier."

"Are units on the scene yet?" Ryan asked.

"As I said, the call came in through our private alert line via their security team rather than over the traditional 911 channel. Units are en route, as are the crime scene unit and the medical examiner. But this case was called in literally six minutes ago now. My first call was to the captain of Hollywood Community Station to have him send units to the estate and to tell him that Homicide Special Section would be handling the case. My next call was to your cell phone. And then to Ms. Hunt's. And when those were unsuccessful, finally to the Central Station detective line. So we're pretty fresh here."

"Apologies again for that, Chief," Ryan said.

"Regardless," Decker told him, "this obviously fits HSS's case profile, but not just because this guy is well-known. Booth isn't just a celebrity. He's the CEO of a massive corporation. His murder could move economic markets and have national implications. I'd like Hunt and a detective of your choosing to be there in the next twenty minutes. We have a rare chance to get on this from the get-go. Let's not waste it."

"Yes sir," Ryan said, before hearing the dial tone that indicated that Decker had hung up on them.

"Well I guess we know where he stands," Jessie said, standing up. "Who are you pairing me with?"

"That may be a problem," Ryan said, punching at his keyboard as he stared at his computer screen. "As you know, Nettles is in Cabo. Valentine and Goodwin are working a case that came in late last night. And Karen Bray is scheduled to testify in court at ten. I could pull someone from another unit, but I don't think Decker would approve of that on something this big."

"Maybe just pair me with a detective from Hollywood Station until Karen is done in court," Jessie suggested. "Then she can join me when she's through."

Ryan shook his head.

"With possible delays, we don't know how long she'll be stuck there. It could be all day. I have another idea."

Jessie didn't love his tone.

"What?"

"I'm going to work the case with you."

Her jaw dropped.

"You're going into the field?" she asked. "What about all your captaining responsibilities?"

"I can multi-task," he said. "Besides, I don't want my investigative skills to atrophy. It's important that I get out there every once in a while. Plus there's an added bonus for you."

"What's that?" she asked.

"It will give you an opportunity to ream me out some more. I got the sense that you weren't done yet."

He was right. She wasn't done.

"Are you sure you're not just coming so you can be my secret protector without telling me about it?"

"I can tell this day is going to be fun," he said, throwing on his sports jacket. "We should head out."

Jessie had a comeback in mind but bit her tongue. After all, if they were going to solve this crime, her focus needed to be on the job at hand. Her personal life would have to wait.

CHAPTER THREE

Hannah was in the corner of the downtown coffeehouse, stirring sugar into her coffee, when the cop walked up to her.

She tried not to act surprised, but it was hard. This was the first time in the two weeks since patrol units had been following her and Kat that an officer had directly approached her other than to drive her home at night. That could only mean something bad had happened.

Was he coming to tell her that Ryan had been attacked? That Kat, supposedly up in her detective agency office a half block away, had met some awful end? That it had all been a ruse and Jessie was Zoe Bradway's real target all along?

"Hey," the young, brown-haired officer with the nametag reading Cormier said.

"What happened?" Hannah asked quickly. "Is someone hurt?"

"Oh God, no," he said, seeming to realize that his presence had given the wrong impression. "I'm sorry. Everything's okay. I'm just supposed to let you know that your protective detail has been pulled as of this morning. My partner is informing Ms. Gentry right now. I'm to escort you back up to the office, but after that, I guess you're on your own again."

"Do you know why?" Hannah asked. "Has the threat been neutralized?"

Officer Cormier shrugged helplessly.

"They don't really tell me stuff like that," he answered sheepishly. "All they said was that we were being pulled, that I should inform you, and escort you to your place of business for the day. That's the detective agency, so that's what I'm doing."

"Well, okay then," she replied, realizing she wasn't going to get any more details from the guy.

Hannah grabbed her coffee in one hand and Kat's in the other and headed for the door. She caught her reflection in it just before Officer Cormier opened it for her and was surprised by how much she looked like every other downtown office worker. No one would have guessed that she was just two weeks removed from her high school graduation.

Part of that was intentional. Her shoulder-length blonde hair was done up in a casually professional bun. She had even invested in a pair of unnecessary glasses, which currently dangled from the top button of her shirt, but could be worn in a pinch to add a little bookishness to her bright green eyes—the same shade as her sister's—when she needed it.

She wore tan slacks and a baby blue button-up shirt. Her shoes, black sneakers that looked like loafers at first glance, added an extra inch to her already respectable five-foot-nine height. The entire ensemble gave the impression that she was closer to her mid-twenties than eighteen, which proved extremely useful when working as an intern at a detective agency.

They made the short trip down the block to the building that housed Kat's office. Hannah noticed that Officer Cormier, despite almost being off bodyguard duty, was still on high alert. His eyes darted around constantly, and he made sure to keep his body between hers and anyone else walking by.

She guessed that he was in his mid-twenties and silently wondered where he'd be in his career twenty years from now. Would he be married, with children, and on the verge of retirement, like her friend Detective Callum Reid had been at that age? Would he even make it that long? Would he, like Callum, leave his family to fend for themselves, sacrificing himself to save another family who would carry the guilt of that sacrifice every day afterward?

"Are you okay?" Cormier asked, snapping her out of her thoughts as they took the elevator to Kat's office.

"Yeah, sorry," Hannah said, as the elevator dinged, and the door opened. "Just daydreaming, I guess."

They walked down the hall and stopped at the door with the frosted glass window reading "Gentry Investigations." Hannah pushed the button on the retro speaker box beside it and a moment later Kat's voice could be heard.

"Yeah?"

"It's me and your coffee," Hannah said.

The door buzzed. Cormier opened it and they stepped in. Hannah was startled to find that they weren't alone. In one of the two chairs in the tiny waiting room was a petite woman who seemed to be hugging herself for comfort.

She looked to be in her mid to late-thirties. She was wearing blue jeans and a gray sweatshirt that read simply "Reba," with a photo of the iconic country singer below the word. Her pale face was thin and angular, and she had an arched nose that had clearly been broken at some point. Her eyes were brown but currently flecked with red, as if she'd been crying recently.

She had a bruise under her left eye and another one on her right cheekbone. Her black hair was loosely tied back in a bun. It had clearly been done in a rush and multiple strands hung dejectedly around her neck, which was exposed and vulnerable looking. She looked like she'd been borderline pretty about a decade ago, before whatever unpleasantness she'd clearly gotten involved in had started to take its toll on her.

Kat came out of the back office with Officer Cormier's partner, an older man with a slight paunch, in tow. She took the coffee from Hannah and smiled at the two cops without acknowledging the presence of the other woman in their midst.

"Well thanks, gentlemen," she said. "It's been interesting. I hope your next assignment offers you a little more action."

"You take care," the older officer said and started for the door.

Cormier glanced at the apprehensive woman in the chair, clearly wondering if perhaps her situation required their intervention. But then, seeming to sense that if she wanted the help of the police, she would be at a police station and not a detective agency, he gave his patented shrug and followed his partner out the door. Once they were gone, Kat turned to the woman.

"I'm sorry about that, Violet," she said. "I know it had to be a bit of a shock to have so many unexpected visitors show up."

"A little bit," the woman said meekly, her voice barely audible.

"Why don't you come into the back office, and we'll continue our conversation there?"

Hannah stood by silently as Violet got up and followed Kat into the back. The woman even walked timidly, like a dog who'd been beaten by its owner so often that it was afraid to take a wrong step. That impression wasn't altered by the fact that she topped out at about five-foot-four and 120 pounds.

She was the antithesis of Katherine Gentry, whose bearing and build exuded sturdiness. About five-foot-seven and 140 pounds, she was powerfully built, with arm muscles that bulged without even flexing. She was attractive, in a casual "I don't give a crap" way, which was reinforced by her lack of makeup and the loose ponytail in which she tied her dirty blonde hair.

She and Violet *were* similar in one way however: their scars, though Hannah doubted that the terrified woman standing before her got hers the way Kat had. Back when she was an Army Ranger in Afghanistan, Kat's encounter with an IED had left her with multiple facial burn marks and a long scar that ran vertically down her left cheek from just below her eye.

Once Kat was behind her desk and Violet was seated across from her, Hannah chose to take a spot leaning against a wall. She still wasn't sure what this was all about and wanted to have a bit of distance to get a read on the situation. Kat looked over at her, then back at Violet.

"Violet, please allow me to introduce Hannah Dorsey," she said, using a warmer tone than she ever did when the two of them were alone together. "She's interning with me over the summer and has been an invaluable resource in a number of cases. I'm sure that she'll prove very helpful in yours as well."

"Hi," Violet said, raising her hand in a quick, half-aborted wave, and making brief eye contact before looking away.

"Hi," Hannah replied.

"Hannah," Kat continued. "This is Violet Sheridan. She arrived while you were on the coffee run. She read a news story about our involvement in the Riley Stroud case a few months back—how we helped rescue the little boy—and apparently it stuck with her. Do I have that right, Violet?"

The woman nodded hesitantly.

"Do you want to tell Hannah what you told me, or should I explain, and you jump in where you feel comfortable?" Kat asked, still using her most gentle professional manner.

"Maybe the second?" Violet suggested.

"Okay, I'll try my best," Kat promised before turning to face Hannah. "Violet needs our help. Her husband just got out of prison a few days ago…"

"Common law husband," Violet corrected apologetically.

"That's right," Kat said, flipping through her notepad as she spoke, "An important oversight on my part. Her common law husband, Hank Keene, was just released late last week after serving a four month stint for…what was it again, Violet?"

"Assault with a deadly weapon," Violet explained. "He got in fight in a bar and beat a guy up with a pool cue."

"Wow, that's a detail you didn't mention before," Kat muttered, shaking her head in disgust. "So anyway, he gets out and the first thing he does is get drunk, then go find Violet for a good time. But she wasn't in the mood, which he didn't appreciate. You can see the results of that."

Kat pointed at the woman's face.

"That's not the worst of it," Violet said, lifting up her Reba sweater to reveal multiple black and purple bruises running along her ribcage. "This is what he did *after* he had his way with me. And he said I was getting off easy."

Hannah saw Kat cringe slightly and wondered if her boss was regretting letting her be an intern at this moment, imagining what Jessie would say if she knew that her little sister was being exposed to this kind of horror. But the truth was that Hannah had already seen far worse in her life.

"What do you mean 'getting off easy?'" she asked, trying to sound professional even as she felt the indignation rise in her chest. If there was one thing that set her off, it was physically powerful people abusing those who happened to be weaker.

Violet looked at Kat as if to indicate that she couldn't go there herself and needed help.

"Apparently Hank threatened that if she wasn't more compliant the next time he came around, he was going to kill her; so after he left, she took off and has been on the run ever since."

"I gathered what I could carry in a backpack and just bailed," Violet said, finding a strength in her voice that Hannah hadn't heard before. "I've been staying in cash-only fleabag motels ever since. I knew I couldn't go to the cops. I tried that before—getting a restraining order—and they said that because California doesn't recognize common law marriages, there was nothing they could do."

"That's not actually true," Kat told her. "When it comes to domestic violence restraining orders, you can file for one in California even if you're just dating the person or *used* to date them. So common law marriages vs. legal ones are irrelevant. You were intimately involved. I suspect that the cops who told you that just didn't want to deal with the hassle."

"I didn't know that," Violet said. "But either way, we're past that point. If I tried to get one now, it wouldn't stop him. It would just make him angrier. He doesn't care about going back to jail. He's out for blood. That's why I came to you. I need to get away from him, for good this time. I was hoping you would help me."

“And just as Violet was making that request,” Kat explained to Hannah, “our friend in blue arrived at the door. So we had to put our discussion on hold. So now that L.A.’s finest have left, why don’t you tell us what it is you’re hoping we can do for you?”

Violet looked at them both with uncertainty in her eyes, as if she didn’t know if she could truly trust them with what she had to say next. But then she seemed to cross some line in her head and nodded silently to herself.

“I have an idea,” she said. “Like I said, I just want to get away from him for good. Whether that means moving to the east coast, to some little town in Iowa, or going to Mexico, I don’t care. But I can’t go anywhere unless I know it’s safe to move around. And I can’t feel safe unless I know where Hank is. It would be great if he was back in jail for a few weeks or even days so I could skip town without worrying about him hunting me down. But even if I just knew where he was, then I could steer clear of him, and get out of town, out of the state.”

“So you want us to track him down?” Kat asked.

“Yes,” Violet said. “Find out where he is at the very least. If you can get him picked up for doing something illegal that will get him tossed behind bars for a while, even overnight, that’s even better. But if you can just locate him, that’s good too. I’ll take whatever I can get. I just need time. Also, I was hoping you could help create a new identity for me. Maybe a new birth certificate or driver’s license. I don’t know if that’s even legal. I just want to start fresh but I’m worried that he’ll be able find me again. He might not seem like it, but he’s really good at that sort of thing.”

Hannah didn’t say a word. She was curious to see how Kat would respond to a request that skirted such legally dubious terrain, even if it was on more morally stable ground.

“We can certainly look into where he is right now,” she said. “As to those other requests, we’ll have to see.”

“If it’s a matter of money…” Violet started to say.

“That’s not the issue,” Kat interrupted.

“Oh,” Violet said, “well speaking of money, that’s the other reason I came to you rather than some other detective. After reading about what you did for that little boy, I knew I could trust you with this.”

She stood up, unbuttoned her jeans, and tugged them down slightly to reveal a money belt hidden below.

“I’ve had some money stashed for a while,” she said, unclipping the belt and handing it over. “Part of it is from some antique furniture I sold that my mother left me when she died. Also, Hank gave me some jewelry a while back, including this one ring with a big emerald in it. I think he might have gotten it all in a robbery. I never asked. But I pawned all of it after what happened last week. And I had a little bit of my own saved here and there over the years. Anyway, it's all in this belt—everything I have in the world. It comes to just over $30,000. I don't want it on in me in case he finds me. I figured I could trust you to hold on to it for me. You could take out what I owe you for the case and maybe for the identity papers if you do that kind of thing, and then you can give me back the rest once it's safe for me to leave town."

Hannah said nothing. It wasn't her decision to make, although she knew what she would do if it was. She couldn't help but notice that the money belt had flecks of blood on it.

"I'm not sure about this, Violet," Kat said uneasily.

"Normally, I would never give somebody I'd never met all my money, but I'm out of options," Violet pleaded. "I'm not getting out this city on my own. I have to trust someone, and I figured it might as well be you, Kat. And if you trust Hannah, then I'll trust her too."

Kat looked over at Hannah, as if her approval mattered. Hannah knew that it was a formality, that Kat Gentry would do what she wanted whether her intern agreed or objected. But as long as she was given the opportunity to make her opinion known, she figured she might as well get it on the record.

She nodded her support for helping Violet. Half of her wanted to get the woman safely out of town. The other half was more interested in in seeing Hank Keene pay for what he'd done. But she kept all that to herself.

"We'll do it," Kat said. "I can't make any promises on the false documents front. That's not my area. But here's what I *can* promise: we'll keep you somewhere safe until we can move you permanently. While you're out of the picture, we'll do everything we can to locate Hank."

"Where do you plan to stash her?" Hannah asked.

Kat smiled.

"Mitch's," she said. "He owes me."

"Who's Mitch?" Violet asked, confused.

"He's my boyfriend," Kat said. "He has a cabin in the mountains up near Lake Arrowhead. He also happens to be a sheriff's deputy in that area. So you'd be out of town *and* with a law enforcement professional I personally trust. And since he's been staying with me the last few days, you've got a ready-made ride, who is currently just a fifteen-minute drive away. Sound good?"

Violet almost mustered a smile.

"If you trust him, then so do I," she said shyly.

"Good, I'm going to call him," Kat said. "After that, you're going to tell us everything you know about Hank Keene—his habits, his friends, his favorite hangouts. With a little luck, we'll find the bastard by dinnertime."

CHAPTER FOUR

Jessie was glad she'd had a light breakfast.

Everything had been fine for the first ten minutes of the drive from their downtown station to the Booth Estate in the Hollywood Hills, as Ryan tore north up the 101 freeway through traffic with the siren blaring and beacon flashing.

They even had time to call Jamil and Beth and get some background on Lowden Booth, which they hoped would prove useful when they arrived at the mansion. But once they got off the freeway and began taking switchback twists and turns through the hills, first briefly on Cahuenga Boulevard, then Mulholland Drive, followed by Nicholls Canyon Road, and finally Astral Drive to where it ended at the massive property owned by Booth, Jessie's stomach engaged in an endless series of somersaults that didn't stop even after they arrived at the giant metal gates of the estate with the large "B" and were waved through by the grim-faced security guard in the navy uniform.

"Are you okay?" Ryan asked when she open her door and leaned out. "Are you having head issues again?"

He was referring to the concussion she'd suffered when Andy Robinson had released a grenade in the mine after her escape attempt. For months after that, Jessie had dealt with headaches, memory loss, confusion, and nausea. But that wasn't what was making her ill now.

"No," she said, trying not to gag. "That drive was a little much, Ryan. I feel like I just spent that ten minutes inside a washing machine. I'm a bit queasy. I just don't want to throw up in your car."

"Do you want me to pull over?" he asked.

"I don't want to draw extra attention to us," she muttered. "As long as you drive slowly the rest of the way, we should be okay."

"All right," he said, his voice laced with concern. "You're not just saying that about the drive, are you? You're head really isn't bothering you?"

"It's not that," she assured him. "I haven't had a migraine in three weeks. You've been to all my appointments with Dr. Varma. Every test in the last month has shown improvement. I just don't love taking multiple hairpin turns near the edge of 200-foot canyons first thing in the morning. Call me crazy."

"Well, I hope you get over it soon, because this private road to the mansion may be a quarter mile long, but we're coming to the end of it, and I see our Hollywood Station liaison coming out to meet us."

Jessie closed the passenger door and sat up. Her eyes were slightly watery from the queasiness, so she blinked several times to clear them. Sure enough, a tall, bald, square-jawed officer in his early thirties was walking crisply towards them. But her attention was quickly diverted by what she saw behind him.

Dwarfing the officer was a gigantic manor that extended at least the length of a football field across and rose three stories high. It had a desert sandstone color set off by black balcony railings and white shutters. Jessie could make out part of a tennis court behind the house in the distance and what appeared to be a guest house on a hill about another quarter mile farther up the road. An ambulance was parked near a side entrance to the house, as were three squad cars.

Ryan parked as the officer reached their car. As they got out, Jessie took several long, slow, deep breaths in the hope that she could blow the nausea out of her system and into the ether. It only partially worked.

"Captain Hernandez and Ms. Hunt," the man said briskly. "I'm Officer Creed Bailey with Hollywood Station. I was assigned to secure the scene until HSS took over."

"How long have you been here, Officer Bailey?" Ryan asked him as they all started walking toward the front door.

"I got the call at 7:38 a.m.," he said, looking at his watch. "The first unit was here within five minutes, and I arrived from the station just after eight. It's 8:18 now, so about fifteen minutes."

"All right," Ryan said as the officer pulled open the huge wooden doors for them, "I realize you haven't had much time to process the situation but what can you tell us so far?"

"Yes sir," Bailey said as he led them through a grand foyer filled with sculptures encased in glass that appeared at first glance to date to classical antiquity. "Neither the medical examiner nor the crime scene unit have arrived yet due to the challenges of navigating the sharp turns required to get here. My understanding is that both will be on scene in the next five minutes."

He moved quickly down a long marble-floored hallway with art lining the walls as far as the eye could see. Jessie caught quick glimpses of various rooms as they passed by them: a music room with a grand piano and a harp, a banquet hall, a small library, a second dining room, a tea room, a complete bar.

"EMTs got here a few minutes before you and are currently treating Mrs. Booth," Bailey said as they reached a stairwell that extended to a second floor then doubled back to a third. "They moved her to a guest room so they could work on her away from all the hubbub of the main bedroom suite. Would you like to see her first or visit the scene?"

Ryan looked over at Jessie as they ascended the stairs.

"Thoughts?" he asked.

She turned to Bailey.

"What kind of condition is she in?" she asked.

"The last time I saw her, a few minutes ago, she was pretty out of it. I believe that she suffered some kind of head injury."

"Then let's start at the scene, get what we can there, then talk to her once her head has cleared a little. Just don't let the EMTs take her anywhere before we get a chance to speak with her, okay?"

Bailey nodded and spoke into his radio. Jessie and Ryan stayed quiet the rest of the way as they tried to get to the third floor without visibly huffing. Ryan was almost fully recovered from a stabbing nearly a year ago that had left him in a coma for several weeks. But even though he was back to his well-muscled torso and fit, fighting weight, flights of stairs were still one of his few remaining forms of kryptonite, leaving him winded despite his best efforts.

For her part, one would never know that only thirteen weeks ago, Jessie had been in a mineshaft collapse that left her with a fractured wrist, cracked ribs, a badly bruised ankle, and at least one concussion. Nor would anyone have guessed that a mere two weeks ago, a serial killer who used drones to target his victims had tried to strangle her to death.

She was already back to running five miles a day and had re-introduced Krav Maga into her workout routine. But after the near-vomit-inducing drive up here, two flights of stairs had her struggling too.

They let Bailey lead them down the hall to the bedroom so they could take giant gasps of air without him seeing them. As they walked, Jessie looked out the enormous window that extended up from the first floor all the way to the third, offering a magnificent view of downtown Los Angeles, of Hollywood, and she suspected, on a clear day, of the Pacific Ocean.

In the window's reflection, she also caught a clear view of herself as she walked between Officer Bailey and Ryan. She was pleased to see that she wasn't visibly gasping for air. She was also glad that she'd chosen casual work attire today, with loose-fitting black pants and a thin, long-sleeved olive shirt that Ryan had given her for Christmas, which was a nice contrast to her shoulder-length brown hair, currently tied back in a ponytail.

She noted that her athletic, five-foot-ten frame, once described by Dr. Lemmon as borderline Amazonian, was no big deal compared to the cops in front and behind her. Officer Bailey was easily six-foot-two and thick everywhere. And Ryan, at six feet tall and a rock-solid 200 pounds, was equally impressive. She made sure to push her shoulder blades back as she strode forward.

They passed the guest room where two technicians were tending to a patient on a bed that she couldn't see but was sure was Mrs. Booth, and reached the open door of the main bedroom, where an officer stood guard. Another officer was sitting on the bed in that room with a solid-looking man in his forties, in a suit sporting a gray crewcut.

Bailey led them past him into an immense bathroom and then into a closet. At first, Jessie wasn't sure what she was looking at. The closet, while impressive, didn't seem all that different than those belonging to other uber-rich victims and suspects she'd encountered over the years.

But then she noticed the shard of light coming from what initially seemed to be the back wall of the closet but was actually a door that must lead to the panic room Chief Decker mentioned earlier. She moved toward it.

"Can you turn on the light in here?" she asked Bailey.

He did and she moved closer to get a better look. The design was impressive. Even with the door ajar, she could tell how seamlessly it would fit in with the rest of the closet wall when closed. It had a full rack of long jackets that could mask any imperfections in the faux wall, but there were none to hide.

The wall was solid and well-made, about four inches thick and composed of some kind of metal with a layer of paint on top. It just also happened to be a door that opened outward into the closet. She wondered where the button was to open the door but would have to save that question for another time.

She stepped through the opening to see what was beyond. Ryan followed her in. An officer stood silently in the back of the room, stone-faced. She saw Lowden Booth's body out of the corner of her eye but deliberately chose not to look at it just yet. She would focus on that last. First, she took in the details of the panic room, which were as impressive as the hidden entrance that got her there.

The room was about 12 x 16, the size of Ryan's office at the station, which was more than reasonable for a bedroom and quite large for a panic room. Most of the ones Jessie had encountered were no bigger than a small walk-in closet. The floor was made of cement. There was a panel along the back wall with both digital and analog controls and multiple display screens. There was also an old-fashioned corded phone connected to the wall.

Along one side wall was a metal toilet and sink, both built into the wall, with a curtain attached to the ceiling that could be drawn across for some modicum of privacy. On the other side wall was a large, narrow cabinet. When she opened it, she found two folding chairs inside, along with two cots, which were also folded. There were also a pair of blankets and pillows. On the top shelf was a combination-operated lockbox, which she suspected held a gun inside, one that Booth never got close to using.

Oddly, the room was much more spartan than might have been expected for a billionaire with unlimited resources. She wondered why he hadn't splurged a little more in order to make the space a bit homier. Unfortunately, that was a question she'd never get to ask him.

"What do you think?" Ryan asked her.

She appreciated that he'd let her take in the scene for a while before broaching the question. Ryan may not have been in the field for a few months now, but he'd partnered with her on dozens of cases in the last two years and knew how her profiling process worked: she liked to immerse herself in the scene before discussing it.

"They must not have had much warning at all before the intruder got in," she noted. "Booth never got to the cabinet with the lockbox. Hell, the door didn't even close before the killer got in."

"Agreed," Ryan said. "Frankly, I don't think Booth got very far at all. Let me know when you're ready to talk about the body."

Jessie nodded and turned to look at Lowden Booth. The man was lying on his side, his head resting next to a medium-sized safe not far from the door. The top left corner of the safe had a bloody smudge that appeared to correspond to the large gouge on the left side of his forehead, where blood had seeped out and created a large pool on the floor that now surrounded his entire head and upper torso, as well as the underside of a section of the safe.

Jessie focused her attention on Booth. She already knew his biographical particulars from their call with Jamil and Beth on the drive up here. Lowden Booth, the co-founder of BoothCo Biomeds, was sixty-four years old, and a billionaire a dozen times over. That last detail, even in his current condition, was not hard to discern.

Initially he looked just like any other man in his sixties who'd been woken unexpectedly from sleep. The man was wearing boxers and a white t-shirt. His clearly dyed brown hair was sleep-disheveled, even before the left half became matted by blood. His light blue eyes were wide open, frozen forever, perhaps in horrified anticipation of the imminent collision with the safe. But upon closer inspection, she noticed signs that he'd had multiple plastic surgeries over the years, not just on his face and his tummy, but possibly on his arms, and maybe even his backside.

"I don't think the safe was opened," she said.

"No?"

"I guess the intruder could have come in, forced him to open it, gotten the contents out, closed it, then slammed his head into the corner of the thing," Jessie posited, "but that doesn't feel right to me. I can't explain why. This all seems much more bang-bang. Maybe Booth tripped or maybe he was slammed into the safe right away. We'll find out when we get it opened."

"What makes you think the safe wasn't opened after he was killed?"

"His head is blocking the door," Jessie noted. "There would be blood smears on the cement when it was moved out of the way, but there's nothing like that. I don't think he was touched after he died."

"I just got word that CSU and the medical examiner have pulled up," Officer Bailey called out from outside the door.

"Perfect timing," Ryan said.

"Why do you say that?" Jessie asked.

"I think it's time we get some insights from people who are still alive, don't you?"

CHAPTER FIVE

Jessie was on board with the plan.

They started with Grover Nix, the man in the suit with the crewcut who'd been sitting on the Booths' bed talking to the officer when they walked in. It turned out that he was Mr. Booth's valet and the person who'd discovered the couple in the panic room.

"He's been very helpful," Bailey said before they returned to the bedroom. "He directed one of our officers to the control room where they log video of movements on the estate and he gave us a comprehensive run-down of what happened from the moment he first heard the alarm go off."

"Thanks," Ryan said, as they both reviewed the initial details of Nix's statement, which had already been logged into the digital police report. Once he was done, he looked over at Jessie and asked, "Are you ready?"

She nodded that she was and followed him out.

"You take the lead," she muttered as they approached the valet, whose head was in his hands.

It was Ryan's turn to nod as he approached the valet, who seemed to sense them coming and suddenly sat up straight.

"Hello, Mr. Nix," he said. "I'm Captain Hernandez and this is Jessie Hunt. We're handling the case. We've looked over your initial statement and were hoping to follow up. Are you able to talk with us?"

"Of course," Nix said in a British accent. "I'll help however I can."

"The timeline we have here says you were in the kitchen when you heard the alarm go off at 7:26 this morning, but didn't recognize it as the standard one for the mansion, that you immediately ran to the Booths' bedroom, arrived there between 7:28 and 7:29, discovered the panic room with Mr. Booth dead and Mrs. Booth unconscious, disabled the alarm, and called us at 7:31. Is all that correct?"

Jessie had been watching Nix closely as he listened to Ryan and noted that he was paying complete attention. He wasn't dazed or distracted like most witnesses who had recently discovered a dead body would typically be, especially of someone they knew well.

"Principally yes," he said, "although to be clear, when I disabled the alarm, I thought that Mrs. Booth was dead too. I regret not having checked her vitals initially."

"How did you discover that she was alive?" Ryan asked.

"She moaned," he answered. "It was barely audible. I realized that the intruder must have knocked her out somehow, after tying her hands behind her back. Maybe they thought she was dead too. I suppose that's your job to discern, yes?"

"May I ask you a question, Mr. Nix?" Jessie wondered, speaking to the man directly for the first time.

"Yes ma'am," he said.

"Why did you immediately run to the Booths' bedroom when you heard the unfamiliar alarm?"

Nix looked briefly flummoxed.

"I was concerned for their welfare, ma'am," he finally said.

"But you'd never heard this alarm before, right?" she said. "It could have been tripped accidentally. It could have been an incursion at the outer fence of the property. Why go to their bedroom? Is it because you're not just their valet, Mr. Nix, and you felt an obligation to check on them immediately?"

He smiled reluctantly.

"How did you know?"

"Well, we could start with your precision memory of exactly where you were at any given moment. Then there's your ability to, after finding your employer dead in a panic room, turn off the alarm on a complicated control panel, and have the wherewithal to immediately call the police. Plus, you guided our officers to the security control room and knew about the camera setup. You also managed to get from the kitchen, up two flights of stairs, and to the third-floor bedroom in under three minutes. And unlike most witnesses we talk to, you don't seem undone by the fact that, less than an hour ago, you discovered the murdered body of someone you know lying in a pool of blood. Also, your suit jacket is undone and while you removed your gun and shoulder strap, there is still a visible mark on your dress shirt where you sweated through it during the incident."

"Pretty impressive," Nix said, his eyebrows arched nearly to his hairline.

"It sure is," Ryan said, with an expression that toggled between admiration and arousal.

"Why didn't you just tell us straight out?" Jessie asked Nix, pretending not to notice her husband's eyes lasering into her.

"Because I keep my promises to my clients, even after their deaths," he said, "and Mr. Booth made me promise not to reveal to outsiders what my real role here was."

"What do you mean?" Ryan asked.

Nix stood up, buttoned his suit jacket, and brushed it off.

"I suppose the cat's out of the bag now," he said.

"It is," Jessie confirmed, "so please, be as forthcoming as you can."

"You have to understand," Nix said, extending his chin outward as if he was a knight describing his king, "Mr. Booth had legitimate concerns about his safety. While many feel that the drugs he has developed have improved the lives of millions of people, there are others who oppose the methods he used to bring them to market. Conspiracy theorists accuse him of implanting trackers in patients. Study participants have filed lawsuits against him. Competitors resent him. Government investigators repeatedly scrutinize him. Even former business partners take issue with him."

"Are you saying that none of that is merited?" Jessie asked.

"I'm not commenting on the validity of any of those claims," Nix sidestepped. "That's not my area of expertise. What I'm saying is that all of it puts a target on his back. He had traditional bodyguards, but he wasn't satisfied with them. So someone put him in touch with me."

"Why you?" Ryan asked.

"I guess I came with a good reputation," Nix said. "I'm former SAS, for over a decade before transitioning into private security. When he reached out to me, I was ready to make a change, so the timing was fortuitous."

"How so?" Jessie pressed.

"I was getting older," Nix admitted, "and my body was starting to balk at the physical stressors that come with the grind of daily security work, so we came up with a plan that worked well for both of us; at least I thought it did."

"Do tell," Jessie asked, intrigued.

"We determined that he would get a new security team, one I chose. They would be Mr. Booth's public-facing bodyguards, close to him, visible at all events. I selected them specifically for that purpose and they were excellent at it. They did the heavy lifting. They dealt with the aggressive fans or protesters. But I was ultimately in charge of that team, as well as a smaller, elite unit that would also attend functions and work here at the estate."

"How does that work?" Ryan asked.

"Quite well, for three years actually, until today," Nix said, with a whiff of defensiveness in his voice. "Since we would serve as security *and* real valets, we were able to stay close to both Mr. and Mrs. Booth to offer protection without anyone taking notice of us. Anyone wishing him harm would focus on the huge guys with shaved heads. The quiet fellows off to the side carrying suitcases, holding purses, taking empty glasses, handing over little notes—we were just wallpaper. It made it much easier to do our jobs."

"And here at the mansion?" Jessie wondered.

"We have a separate company called Hatch Secure that handles exterior security," Nix explained. "They work the guard house and patrol the grounds. Unless specifically instructed otherwise, they don't enter the mansion. That's the purview of my people. Exterior security is an eighteen-person contingent, broken up into three six-person units that work eight-hour shifts. Shift changes are at 6 a.m., 2 p.m. and 10 p.m."

"Are they armed?" Ryan asked.

"Patrol officers have stun guns. Shift commanders have handguns," Nix said.

"No offense, Mr. Nix," Jessie said, about to give offense, "but that's a pretty comprehensive security arrangement. How did someone possibly get past it all, into the house, all the way to the Booths' bedroom, to attack them in their panic room?"

"That is a question that is going to haunt me for some time, Ms. Hunt," Nix conceded, straightening his jacket unconsciously. "When you look at the video footage, which I've already reviewed, I suspect you'll be as baffled as I am. I still don't know how the perpetrator got onto the estate or into the house. Frankly, there are a lot of other things I don't know as well."

"Like what?" Jessie pressed.

Nix sighed heavily.

"For example," he said. "I had never heard that alarm before and I'm the head of security for this place. You can imagine how disconcerting that was for me. And when I got up here, I was stunned to discover that there even *was* a panic room. Mr. Booth had never mentioned having one. I don't know if he didn't trust me or if he wanted to have one place that was secure even from his own security. That's not a crazy idea. But I was taken aback."

Officer Bailey poked his head into the room and gave a gentle wave.

"You wanted me to let you know when the EMTs were planning to take Mrs. Booth to the hospital," he said. "They're just about there."

"Thanks," Ryan told him. "Don't let them leave yet. We'll be right there."

"We obviously have to head next door," Jessie said to Nix, "but before we go, tell us this. You've been in charge of security here for three years. You said yourself that as a valet you recede into the background and go unnoticed. With your experience and proximity to the situation, there's probably no one better equipped to give us an opinion: what do you think happened here?"

Grover Nix stared at her and his eyes, dark and penetrating, seemed to size her up, deciding whether she could handle what he had to say. Whatever conclusion he came to in his head, his response was matter of fact.

"I'll preface this by saying that I'm no investigator. I often used to have kill people as part of my job. Now I make my living by trying to make sure people don't get killed. Having said that, despite the mask being worn, the footage I saw of the perpetrator running from the scene suggests a male. You'll have experts who can better determine that, I'm sure. Regardless, he knew the best place to run to avoid being caught by the guards, where there would be gaps in our security perimeter at that time of the morning. Once he scaled the fence, it's only a few hundred yards to Cactus Canyon Trail and then a short jaunt into Runyon Canyon Park. It'd be easy to get lost among the early morning hikers, joggers, and dog walkers in there.

"Beyond that, whoever did this knew where in the house the Booths' bedroom was. This is a giant mansion with over forty rooms, including nine bedrooms. This person knew where to go, how to get there, and just as importantly, how to get out fast. According to the footage, he wore gloves. He was prepared. He knew what he was doing. He had intimate knowledge of the terrain. That suggests someone who knows this place well or who is at least familiar with another person who does."

"An inside job?" Ryan asked. "I thought you vetted everyone."

Nix shook his head.

“I vetted everyone on my security team and everyone who was on the exterior security company workforce,” he corrected, “along with any mansion employee who joined after I took over. But that’s just the last three years. Mr. Booth has lived here for eight years, and he brought some of his staff from his prior home. There are employees here who have been with him for over two decades. I did security checks on all of them. But unless I found something earth-shattering, Mr. Booth wasn’t inclined to do anything. In my time here, he only let me fire one employee, and that was a member of the waitstaff who repeatedly made lewd comments to one of the housekeepers.”

“So you can’t vouch for the personal integrity of staff who were grandfathered in,” Jessie replied, “or say, much younger wives that he married before you came along?”

Nix didn’t bite.

“Mrs. Booth was here before I came on the scene,” he said. “They’d been married for two years before I was hired. And it’s true that I didn’t do anything other than a cursory background check on her to make sure she didn’t have criminal record. Going beyond that would have been a good way to get *myself* fired.”

“Mr. Nix,” Jessie said with mock disappointment, “that doesn’t sound like going the extra mile for your client.”

“I can assure you, Ms. Hunt, Mr. Booth’s lawyers did a thorough workup on her long before I came along,” Nix countered. “In my experience, they leave no stone unturned. But for what it’s worth, I liked her. They already seemed like an old married couple by the time I got here. They were so comfortable together that I was actually surprised when I found out that she was his second wife. You should definitely do your due diligence. She *is* the wife of a billionaire after all. I suppose that inherently equals ‘suspect.’ But I’ll admit to this, when she started moaning and I realized she wasn’t dead, it gave me a little spark of hope. I won’t ever be able to pretend that I didn’t fail this family. But at least someone survived, even if it wasn’t because of me. I’ll hold on to that.”

Grover Nix looked genuinely torn up. Jessie had half a notion to try to buck him up. But a return visit from an anxious-looking Officer Bailey told her that they’d run out of time.

“I think it’s time we visited the Missus,” she said, heading for the bedroom door with Ryan right behind her, leaving Nix to battle his guilt and his demons alone.

CHAPTER SIX

Jessie readied herself to talk to the miracle woman of the Booth Estate.

Before entering the guest room she took a beat to rein in her skepticism about the poor young wife who was lucky to have survived this ordeal. Just because Devon Booth was a perfect suspect didn't mean she was guilty of anything. Assumptions and preconceptions often led to errors, sometimes fatal ones. She took a deep breath to clear her head and stepped through the door.

Almost immediately, she was surprised by the energy in the guest room. She had expected Devon Booth to be frothing at the mouth to leave and the EMTs to be standing in a corner, cowed by the powerful woman, but it was nearly the opposite. Booth was sitting quietly, if a little dazed, on the side of the bed, with her hands resting on the mattress as if for both moral and physical support. It was the emergency medical technicians, or at least one of them, who were agitated.

One, a tall, straw-haired guy in his mid-twenties, was crouched next to Booth, a concerned look on his face, his hand on her forearm to offer her support. The other, a short woman in her late twenties with dark hair in a ponytail, was standing by the bed with her hands on her hips and a huffy look on her face. Her eyes were blazing.

"These are the folks from Homicide Special Sect—" Officer Bailey started to say.

"It's about damn time," the female EMT interrupted harshly. "We've got a concussed patient here who needs to be admitted and we're being slow-walked because you two can't be bothered to amble over and conduct your interview."

Jessie looked over at Ryan, wondering whether he shared her mix of admiration and distaste for the woman. She appreciated the commitment to patient care and resentment about being impeded, but this was a murder investigation, and their patient was a witness at the very least, if not a suspect. Ryan didn't look at all amused, though he was clearly trying to suppress his annoyance.

"Your perspective is noted," he said with impressive calm, "but we're here now and we need to speak to Mrs. Booth for a few minutes. I'm sure that your medical interventions can be postponed for that brief period."

Jessie started to turn her attention back to Devon Booth, hoping to get a better sense of her, when the female EMT started up again.

"I'm not so sure," she shot back. "Concussions are complicated. She could have some bleeding in the brain. Every second is important, and your delays have cost valuable time."

Jessie saw Ryan's whole body tense up. He'd been captain of Central Station for a few months now and his ability to handle the relentless avalanche of frustrating bureaucratic minutiae had improved significantly of late. But this was like having a wasp stinging you during an avalanche and she could tell it was about to send him over the edge.

"Connie," she said warmly, noting the name on the woman's badge, "we appreciate your concern so much. Personally, as a recent victim of a concussion myself, I value how seriously you take this threat. Your commitment deserves to recognized, just like that of your partner…?"

"Lyle," the young man offered weakly.

"Right," Jessie said. "You and Lyle are doing good work here. You've got Mrs. Booth sitting upright. She looks thoughtful and coherent. That's because of you two. I see that she's following our conversation. Her pupils appear normal. And I know that in light of what's happened this morning, she's going to want to do her part to help us before she leaves. Because she was here when a murder occurred, Connie. And what she has to tell us could be crucial to solving that murder. And I know that's as important to you as it is to us. So, since we're all on the same team here, let's get these questions answered and then let Mrs. Booth be on her way so you can continue to give her best care possible. Everyone good with that? Great."

She didn't wait for Connie's answer, though she could see from the woman's expression over the course of her monologue that the fury had faded and the realization that she might be on the precipice of interfering with an investigation had set in.

Jessie focused on Booth, who looked less dazed than she had a minute earlier. Maybe it was the extra time. Maybe it was the intense back and forth she'd just observed. But her eyes were more focused, and her jaw was less slack than when they'd walked in the room.

Whether fully alert or not, Devon Booth was a beautiful woman. And while she was significantly younger than her husband, she wasn't some teenage ingenue. Jessie recalled that during the furious drive up here, Beth had told them that she was thirty-nine, but somehow that hadn't stuck in her brain. Now though, sitting on the edge of that bed, Devon Booth certainly came across like a full-fledged adult teetering on the edge of forty, rather than the child bride Jessie had foolishly imagined.

She had long, wavy brown hair that stopped just above her elbows. Her eyes—big, brown, and warm—reminded Jessie of Ryan's. She had a pert, little nose and full lips that she seemed to come by naturally.

Even though she was seated and wearing a loose-fitting robe, Jessie could see what was underneath. Booth was wearing a night dress that revealed a full figure and long legs. Everything was well-tanned. Whatever combination of exercise, nutrition, genetics, and medical enhancements that had conspired to make Devon Booth look how she did, Jessie hoped she'd be so lucky in eight years.

Of course, some of that beauty was marred by the bruise on her right cheekbone, her badly split lower lip, and the golf-ball sized lump on the left side of her head. She seemed unaware of the first two, although she touched the side of her head absent-mindedly before wincing and retracting it quickly.

It was only then that Jessie noticed the bandage on her wrist. She recalled that Grover Nix mentioned finding her with her hands bound behind her back and she glanced over at her other wrist. It too was bandaged, though some blood was seeping through that one.

"Mrs. Booth," Ryan said, taking a step toward her and kneeling down as the male EMT had done, "I'm Ryan Hernandez with the LAPD. This is Jessie Hunt. First of all, we're sorry for your loss. We're here looking into what happened this morning. We'd like to ask you a few questions about it before these folks take you to the hospital. It's really important that we get your perspective while it's still fresh in your mind. Is that alright?"

"That makes sense," Booth said feebly, before adding to Jessie, "I know who you are. You're the one who catches serial killers. You were kidnapped by the crazy lady a while back."

"That's right, Mrs. Booth," Jessie said, not loving that her new claim to fame was being "kidnapped by the crazy lady" but choosing to move past it. "We know it's hard but we need to talk to you about this morning. Shall we start?"

"Sure. You can call me Devon, by the way."

The affable way she said it made Jessie feel pretty sure that the woman was still in shock, but she had questions to ask. Connie and Lyle could deal with that medical issue when she was done.

"All right, Devon," she began, "try to recall what happened when you first woke up this morning."

"Okay," Devon said, scrunching up her little nose in concentration. "I remember that I woke up earlier than usual because I heard a sound at the door, like a scraping. I checked and it wasn't 7:30 yet, which is when Grover usually knocks on the door to wake us up and let us know that breakfast is ready. I shook Lowden awake and he thought it was weird too. He called out for Grover, but no one answered, and the scraping stopped for a second, but then it started up again and Lowden said he thought someone was trying to pick the lock to the door."

She stopped for a moment, and looked a little unsteady, like she might lose her balance and tip sideways on the bed. But Lyle reached out and put his hand on her shoulder to steady her.

"Are you okay?" he asked.

"Yes, sorry," she said with an embarrassed smile. "Just thinking about this is very intense."

"Can you continue please?" Ryan asked gently.

"Right," she said, returning her attention to him, "so I said we should call Grover, but Lowden told me there wasn't time. We rushed into the bathroom, and he locked that door. We could hear the intruder get into the bedroom and search around. Lowden led me into his closet. We moved to the very back and he did something I couldn't see with one of the hangers. All of a sudden, the wall opened up and this loud alarm started to go off. Lowden said to go inside, that it was a panic room. I had no idea that we even had one of those. So we went in. But it was too late."

"What do you mean?" Jessie asked.

"The intruder had smashed in the bathroom door by then. He was too close behind us and got into the panic room before Lowden could close the door. The man—I'm sure it was a man even though he wore a mask because of the voice and his size—had a gun and ordered Lowden into the corner. Then he tied me up really quickly. He ordered Lowden to open the safe that was on the floor. Lowden refused so the man punched me, twice. I fell to the floor and my vision got blurry. I was stunned but I heard him threaten to do worse if Lowden didn't open the safe. That time, Lowden agreed. He moved over to the safe but then he leapt at the guy, knocking his gun away, and yelled at me to run. It was kind of hard because my hands were tied behind my back, but I got up and started to leave but the guy was much stronger than Lowden and just shoved him away. Then he pushed me hard as I ran by him, and I stumbled. The last thing I remember was my head slamming into the wall. When I woke up, Grover was there. I saw Lowden on the ground with all the blood around him. I don't know if he hit his head when the intruder pushed him away or if the man slammed his head intentionally later on, but I knew he was dead without Grover having to tell me. There was too much blood for him to just be hurt and Grover wasn't rushing to do CPR or anything. Everything since then has been a blur."

Jessie gave the woman a moment to regroup before asking her next question. But sensing that Connie, the EMT, might use the pause as an opportunity to push to leave, she kept the respite brief.

"You did well to identify that the intruder was male by noting his size and voice," she praised. "What else can you recall about him? Tall? Short? Skinny? Heavyset? Did the voice sound familiar? Did you recognize the eyes through his mask? What color were they? Did he have any unusual mannerisms? Use any phrases repeatedly?"

Devon had started shaking her head halfway through the questions and by the end she looked overtly agitated.

"I realize I should know that stuff," she said, her voice starting to crack slightly, "but I was petrified. I had just woken up. Then I was in a panic room with a gun pointed at me. I was tied up and punched in the face. My life was threatened. Now my husband is dead. I'm surprised I remember anything at all to be honest. I wish I could tell you more, but I just can't."

By the end, she had started to cry. Not loud sobs, but quiet, half-stifled gasps that she couldn't quite swallow.

"Can I please go now?" she managed to choke out.

Jessie could sense Connie about to assert herself again, but it wasn't necessary. Though she still had her doubts about Devon, she couldn't help but feel some sympathy for the woman. Besides, they weren't going to get anything useful at this point. She looked over at Ryan, who nodded quickly that he was done.

"Of course," she said. "We may have more questions for you later but you're free to leave for now. We hope you feel better soon."

Devon Booth nodded her thanks as Lyle and Connie guided her out of the guest room. Once she was gone, Jessie turned to Ryan.

"What do you think?" she asked. "You buying the helpless wife routine?"

Ryan tried to stifle a surprised laugh.

"That feels a little harsh," he replied. "I definitely think we should check to see what she stands to gain, but if her story holds up when we check the mansion's interior video, I might be willing to view her as credible. I mean, she *was* tied up."

"How do we know she's not in cahoots with this intruder and didn't have him tie her up so that she'd have an alibi?"

"Fair question," Ryan said. "Why don't we go find out."

***

Much to her displeasure, Jessie had to back down.

As Simon, the man who ran the control room for Grover's security team, walked them through the footage from that morning, it became increasingly clear that Devon's version of events seemed to line up with what they saw.

There were no cameras in the Booths' bedroom, much less the closet or the panic room, but there was one showing the hallway just outside the bedroom. Just as Devon had described, it showed a masked man picking the lock to the bedroom. Then it showed him leaving four minutes later, holding a gun but no money, jewels, or other contraband, and running down the hall in the opposite direction from the main stairs just before Grover came into view approaching the bedroom.

"So if he was in the bedroom area for four minutes, he was only in the panic room for how much of that time?" Ryan asked.

"We know the alarm went off at 7:26," said Grover, who was leaning over Simon's shoulder, "and I arrived at the bedroom three minutes later, just barely missing him. That means he was probably in there for just over two minutes."

Ryan looked over at Jessie with a dubious expression.

"I don't know," he said. "If Devon was in on it, this doesn't seem to fit. Why didn't she leave the bedroom door unlocked for the guy? Or the bathroom door? Why would she have the intruder tie her up to have an alibi when it doesn't seem that anything was stolen? If this was some elaborate plan, it seems like a pretty piss-poor one. Plus her supposed accomplice came within half a minute of getting nailed by Grover, who was going to be up there really soon with breakfast anyway. It feels like she would have tried to avoid that."

Jessie had to admit that those were all good points. But she had one of her own.

"I don't disagree," she conceded, "but there also wasn't a ton of time for everything she described to have happened, like for this guy to tie her up *and* the altercations that followed. It doesn't really add up, to me."

"I don't know," Ryan challenged. "It sounded like it was all happening pretty quickly."

Jessie tried not to get irked by the fact that he was poking holes in everything she said with Grover, Simon, and Officer Bailey all standing around. In theory, he was just doing his job.

"Maybe," she muttered. "And what about audio? Is there none to go with the video footage?"

"No," Grover said. "Mr. Booth thought it would be a violation of personal privacy to have audio recorded in the mansion, so he prohibited it, not just for his protection, but for his employees as well."

"I get it," she said, "but it would be nice to verify the snippets of conversation that Devon referenced, maybe catch bits of any fighting or screaming that could support her version of events."

"I'm sorry," Grover said. "It just doesn't exist."

She looked over at Ryan, who seemed perplexed by her focus on Devon Booth. She knew he wasn't dismissing the woman as a suspect, but he clearly thought that, at least for now, they should move on to other potential options. He was probably right. Until they had something more definitive that pointed to her, it was time to explore alternatives.

Jessie wondered why she was pushing back so hard. Did she really think that the second Mrs. Booth was a murderous gold digger who had ensnared some co-conspirator in her plan to kill her husband, get beat up, and *not* steal his money? Or was she just taking her frustrations with Ryan out on the victim's wife, perhaps unfairly?

Was her animosity towards Ryan for not being forthright about the repeated threats Zoe made toward him, Hannah, and Kat interfering with her ability to give Devon Booth a fair shake? Was she casting doubt on this woman's story just because her own husband had given her reason to doubt his words? She honestly didn't know anymore. And right now, that wasn't her priority.

"Let's have everything sent to the station, all the video, along with the medical examiner and CSU reports," she finally said.

"Let's not forget the safe," Ryan added. "We should find out if anything was actually taken from it, and if so, what?"

"Good idea," Jessie agreed. "In the meantime, we should dig into Lowden Booth's life and see who else might want him dead."

"I'm sure you'll do your own research," Grover told her. "But I have a list I can provide to you. I don't think Mr. Booth would mind at this point."

Jessie tried not to sound snarky when she replied.

"Neither do I."

CHAPTER SEVEN

Mark Haddonfield couldn't believe his good luck.

As he sat on the bench on the trail overlooking the city, he wiped the sweat from his brow and did his best to act like every other hiker out for some mid-morning exercise.

What were the chances that he and Jessie Hunt would cross paths like this? He couldn't have planned this, even if he'd tried.

After all, he'd known for over a week now that his next victim would live in the Hollywood Hills. And just by coincidence, it turned out that Jessie was working a completely unrelated murder case of her own less than two miles from where he would implement the next phase in the project he lovingly referred to as "The Strategy."

Even better, she seemed to be re-teaming with Ryan Hernandez, her husband and boss, with whom she hadn't worked a case since they got married three months ago. Mark knew that detail for the same reason he knew so many details about Jessie's life. In order to destroy her, he had to know her better than she knew herself. And he did.

As he stood up and stretched all of his six-foot-four wiry frame, extending his long arms to the sky before tousling his curly blonde hair and adjusting his wire-rimmed glasses, he chuckled over the irony: this wasn't how he thought it would go. Back when he first transferred from Stanford to UCLA for his junior year nine months ago, it was with the dream of taking Jessie's brand new criminal profiling seminar, impressing her with his knowledge, and eventually becoming her protégé.

But almost from the start it had all gone wrong. Because of overwhelming demand, the university would only permit seniors to take the class. Mark would have to wait an entire year to get in, and even then, admission was through a lottery system.

He'd tried to reach out through the department but was shut down. He even tried to build rapport by approaching her on campus to get an autograph, only to have her and her friend, Kat Gentry, pull guns on him. She claimed she was jumpy because of some prior threats against her. At every turn, he was stymied.

And then, without warning, Jessie announced that she was taking a sabbatical from the university to return to work with the LAPD full-time. She hadn't even taught an entire year and already she was leaving! He had uprooted his life specifically to come here, to learn from her and work with her, and now that was over.

He pumped his legs hard as he pushed to reach the crest of the hill where he would have a better look at the house down below and noted how much more strength and endurance he had now that he'd committed to his new workout routine. He needed both for what was to come. He needed both to show Jessie.

It was like she was rubbing his nose in it, intentionally trying to make him look like an idiot. His mother already thought he was ridiculous for changing schools on a whim. If he had friends, they would have surely said the same thing. His grades in his other classes had begun to suffer. So had his sleep. Jessie Hunt, once his personal hero, had turned into the reason his life was falling apart. And she was oblivious to it.

Then he saw all the stories on the news about her bravery after being kidnapped—on her wedding day, no less! —and it was like salt being poured into a wound. No matter what he did, he couldn't get away from the constant media coverage of the woman who was making his life a living hell.

The final straw was when she was credited with breaking up the so-called Operation Z, a plan by one of Andrea Robinson's zealots to poison the popcorn of thousands of people at a movie theater complex in downtown Los Angeles. No one seemed to care that over two dozen people still died. No, the press had nothing but praise for the Angel of the City of Angels. He decided that enough was enough. It had to stop. Someone had to call her on her hypocrisy. Someone had to reveal the truth about how Jessie Hunt—unintentionally or not—brought more chaos to this city than she prevented. That's when he devised The Strategy.

Mark had followed Jessie's career religiously. He knew most of her cases. But now he did deep dives into all of them, getting copies of the files for each one, learning everything he could about the killers, their methods, the locations, the detectives involved, the victims, and the survivors. He became the world's foremost expert on Jessie Hunt. The Strategy required it.

That was because The Strategy involved destroying Jessie from the inside out. He decided that he would find cases in which Jessie had saved people from being the next victim of a killer, then locate those people, and kill them himself.

The impact would be swift and brutal. Once the pattern was revealed, all of Jessie Hunt's grateful survivors, who owed their lives to her, would realize that they were now potential victims. They would know that their association with her put them at risk. News stories would still refer to her as an angel, but now she would be the angel of death.

And Jessie would be helpless to prevent it. As a profiler, she'd want to solve the crimes. As a human being who knew these people, she'd want to keep them safe. But how could she stop murders that resulted from no motive other than to punish her?

Now who was the one in the dark and who was the one pulling the strings? She was used to being up at the lectern, to being the lecturer, teaching a seminar to hundreds of adoring students, though never to him. She was used to asking them probing questions and then crushing them when they failed to provide adequate responses. How would she feel now that the tables had turned, and *he* was the one posing the questions that she couldn't answer? Now that *he* was the professor, and she would be the clueless student?

He clenched his fists tight, and his face formed a contorted grin at the thought of it. She couldn't predict who the next victim would be or when or why. She could only wait for the next victim to be cut down. And because she had saved so many people, there were so many to choose from. It was perfect.

Well, almost perfect. There was still the small problem of actually killing the people. Until recently Mark had never killed anyone. He had always thought he'd be the one *saving* lives, not taking them. In his most vivid recurring dream, he pictured himself wrestling a knife from the hands of a serial killer, knocking him out, and slapping cuffs on him. He never imagined that *he* would be the serial killer.

That's why he'd been very particular when choosing his first victim. Woody Garnett was a scumbag who not only cheated on his wife but quite literally dumped her in the middle of a therapy session after thirty-two years of marriage. In the mind of their psychiatrist's receptionist, a young woman named Harper Gray, Woody and several other terrible spouses deserved to be punished for their wrongs. She meted out punishments to some of them and had nearly finished off Woody with a knife to the abdomen when Jessie arrived to save him.

So Mark picked Woody as his first "survivor to surrender." He had to psych himself up to sneak onto the man's boat, come up behind him while he drunkenly watched an old western on TV, and shove a knife deep in his gut. But once it was done, he was surprised how satisfied, even giddy, he felt.

He had rid the world of a lowlife. He had committed the kill without a hiccup. And he had finally stopped twiddling his thumbs with all The Strategy planning and actually started living his truth. The next step was to just sit back and wait to see how Jessie responded as he prepared for his next outing.

But now, two weeks later, he'd read the final report on Garnett's murder, and it was clear that she wasn't going to respond at all. She hadn't even taken the case. It was handled by the Sheriff's Department, which had authority over the marina.

Homicide Special Section never made a request to take it over. He saw that they did ask for a copy of the final report once it was closed but nothing beyond that. Apparently they were satisfied with how the case was handled. Mark wasn't sure if Jessie even saw the report. Things would be different this time around.

Mark finally reached the crest of the hill and looked down over Cardwell Place and the home of his second victim. It was hot and he was really sweating now. He pulled out his water bottle and took several glugs from it as he surveyed the property.

He had been up here before, but this was his final scouting session before he did the deed, and he wanted to make sure nothing had changed. He still couldn't believe that after what had happened to her, Janet Goodsen hadn't insisted on more security at her home.

After all, it was only six months ago that she had nearly been killed. A vengeful event photographer named Sloane Baker had been murdering people by throwing acid on them and had chosen Goodsen as her latest victim. The woman was only alive because Jessie had discovered Baker's identity and hurried to Goodsen's tenth anniversary party in time to stop her.

But in the time since, Janet and Nicholas Goodsen had done little to upgrade the security around their home. Yes, there was a metal gate at the driveway near the front of the home and the back of the property was surrounded by a thin, wooden, latticed fence. But it was easily scaled and from where he was, on the hill behind it, all one had to do was hop down into the yard.

That was exactly what he intended to do. The rest of the task would be equally straightforward. The Goodsens had a security system but didn't use it consistently, nor did they always lock their doors. It was disgraceful really, considering that they had two young children.

That was ultimately what would make this kill so hard. Janet Goodsen wasn't a complete waste of humanity like Woody Garnett had been. Yes, she was narcissistic and arrogant and viewed her wealth as a free pass to be bitchy. But she wasn't irredeemable.

She was raising two young children who seemed sweet enough. She was on the board of some foundation that did cancer research. She wasn't *evil* or anything. But she wasn't a very nice person either. And when it came to picking victims, that made her the next best option. She didn't deserve to die, but she was going to.

This was an important next step for Mark. When the time came, it was going to be difficult for him to kill her, especially since it was essential that he do it the same way the original killer had planned: with acid. That was a horrible way to die, one he didn't wish on anyone, much less the mother of young children who might hear her anguished screams and remember them in their nightmares forever. But what choice did he have?

None, really. It had to be done, because that was the only way to make sure that Jessie knew that this murder was connected to the original, event photographer murders. Then she would have to take notice. Then she would have to reevaluate the Woody Garnett death as well. She would realize that she had a serial killer on her hands, one unlike any she'd ever dealt with before. But for that to happen, Mark had to use acid on the mom. He had to.

Mark set that thought aside for a moment as he turned and looked off in the distance. From here he could just make out the Booth Estate, sitting proudly on a hill that it didn't have to share with any other home. He didn't know what case Jessie was working on over there yet, just that it involved multiple squad cars, a medical examiner, and a crime scene unit. He wondered if she would quit in the middle of it once she learned about Janet Goodsen or if it was so big and important that she'd have to see it through first.

As with Jessie's other cases, he'd find out soon enough. Eventually, all of her cases made the news. After all, she was the Angel of the City of Angels, and the media would fall over itself to keep up with her every move. They couldn't know that, very soon, anyone she saved would be terrified to be associated with her. Very soon he'd get his wish and she'd be known as the angel of death.

It was time to get back to work.

CHAPTER EIGHT

Only years of experience and trust in her coworkers prevented Jessie from panicking.

On the drive back to the station from the Booth Estate, she and Ryan had asked Jamil and Beth to compile a list of potential enemies from Lowden Booth's personal and professional life. By the time they arrived back at Central Station and walked into the research office, it was waiting, and it was long—extremely long.

Beth, usually so sunny and full of positive vibes, had a hopeless look on her face. Jamil didn't seem much more optimistic, though he always seemed more taciturn, even before his recent emotional struggles. Pretty quickly, it became clear why. It didn't take much time to see that, over the years. Lowden Booth had left a lengthy trail of crushed dreams and broken people in his wake.

"He's been sued dozens of times, both individually and through BoothCo Biomeds," Beth said, shaking her head in amazement. "Multiple trespassers have entered his headquarters to confront him over the years, sometimes armed. Protesters have pelted him with everything from eggs to paint bombs to dead animal carcasses."

"And that's just the performative stuff," Jamil noted. "He's had home intruders twice before, both prior to Grover Nix taking over security. One of them carried a hatchet."

Luckily, once Jessie handed over Grover Nix's list of what he called "human risk factors," and they cross-referenced it with the research team, the process became more manageable. The number of potential threats was still large, but no longer astronomical.

Grover's team had already done the laborious work of background research on many of the people that Jamil and Beth had flagged, sifting through them to determine who was a credible threat and who was just bluster. Though Jessie wasn't going to trust the views of a private security operative alone, the fact that his job depended on getting these evaluations right gave the list at least some credibility. Apparently, she wasn't the only one who had mixed feelings.

"Listen," Ryan said, staring at names, "this list is a solid place to start, and I got a good vibe from Nix, but we can't base any of our investigation on his research unless we have confidence in him and his team. So I need you to run backgrounds on all of them to make sure there isn't anything fishy about them. Same with all the people who were on Hatch Secure, the exterior security company. Looks for anyone with red flags."

"Will do," Beth assured him.

"Maybe you could also hunt down the people who designed that panic room," Jessie suggested. "It's possible that when it was opened, that activated some kind of recording system that we're unaware of. It's a long shot but it can't hurt to check."

"On it," Jamil said.

"I'm sorry to do this but I have to run to my office for a few to do some captain stuff," Ryan told them all. "I'll be back when I can. If anything breaks, let me know and I'll be right over. And don't forget to check family too. See if there are unresolved issues that might have escalated. Good luck!"

Once he left, the remaining three of them went through all of the people that Nix's team had dismissed and who they also agreed were pretenders, removed them, then looked at where they stood.

The original list, which had over 141 names on it, had been reduced to 38. That was still far too many, and it didn't account for people with axes to grind who had never expressed any kind of public displeasure with Booth. But it was good starting point, which is exactly what the research team needed. Jessie watched Jamil and Beth dive into the process without hesitation and, as usual, admired their odd-couple working chemistry.

They were the same age—twenty-four—but they couldn't be more different. Jamil, the head of the department, was an unquestioned genius, who had joined HSS specifically to work with Jessie and Ryan. He was capable of filtering through massive databases, sorting surveillance video into manageable buckets, and making complex financial records understandable, all seemingly in the blink of an eye.

But his giant computer brain was contrasted by diminutive size. And despite beginning an intense workout regimen in recent months, he remained incredibly skinny. That, coupled with his thick glasses and total lack of fashion sense, made him the poster boy for nerd culture.

Beth Ryerson, on the other hand, was a walking, talking ad for cool. An unfussy attractive former college volleyball star at UC-Santa Barbara who at over six feet tall, dwarfed Jessie, she never wore makeup and oozed perpetual chill. But her casual demeanor had hidden advantages. First, it masked an especially sharp mind, which people tended to underestimate. Secondly, her relaxed vibe helped center her more jittery boss, keeping him focused and positive.

Right now it seemed to be working. Jamil had already created a database including possible suspects who had done one or more of the following: filed a lawsuit against Booth or were being sued by him, threatened him personally or professionally in either physical or metaphorical terms, assaulted him in some way, or made allegations against him or the company in the media.

Then they matched those names with people whose lawsuits were still active, who had criminal records, a verifiable record of mental health history that involved hospitalization, or who had deep enough pockets to come after Booth publicly. If anyone met more than one of those criteria, they got a special checkmark, meaning a file was created for someone to do additional research on them. In addition, the three of them worked to determine if they could eliminate anyone from the list by seeing who might currently be incarcerated, hospitalized, or financially harmed by Lowden Booth's death.

Jessie had been going at it for a half-hour when she glanced up from the file she'd been studying for a brief moment to give her brain a break. Almost immediately, she felt guilty at the sight of Jamil and Beth, who were grinding away with their heads down.

She tried to return her attention to the file in front of her but found that she couldn't stop fixating on another name with several checkmarks beside it. Every time she tried to return to the file she was tasked with, she kept coming back to it. Eventually, she decided to stop fighting the recurring itch and just scratch it.

"I'm going to take a two-minute break," she said, standing up and stretching. "Be right back."

She left the research office and walked into the interior courtyard of the station, where some staff went to smoke. She liked it because it was the only green space available without leaving the confines of the station, a little oasis where she could get away to think. Much to her surprise, Karen Bray was sitting on a bench underneath the large tree in the middle of the courtyard, munching on a sandwich.

Karen, who had transferred to HSS from Hollywood Station after hitting it off while working a case with Jessie a year ago, was a veteran detective. Approaching forty, she was older than most of the rest of the unit and the only team member with a child, unless someone counted Hannah, which no one did.

Petite and self-effacing, she normally dressed casually and wore her dirty blonde hair in a ponytail. But today she wore a business suit, and her hair was styled, likely concessions to her witness testimony. Jessie walked over to join her.

"I thought you had court today," she said, sitting down beside her.

"I do," she said. "We're in recess until 2 p.m., so I figured that rather than wait around the courthouse I'd come back here and catch up on casework. Plus, my son made me this rockin' peanut butter and jelly sandwich, so I'm enjoying my lunch break."

"I'm jealous," Jessie replied, only half-kidding. She realized it was midday and she was getting hungry.

"I'd offer you a bite, but he's got a sixth sense about these things," Karen said. "He'd know and he'd disapprove. Also, I'm starving."

"Understood."

"How's it going?" Karen asked, her mouth full. "I hear you've got a whopper of a case right now and that Ryan's working it with you."

"Both are true," Jessie told her. "We'll see how the partnering goes. It's our first time together since tying the knot and his promotion to captain, so it's a process. As to the case, I'm just trying to decide whether I should go with my gut on something, even though all the facts aren't in yet."

Karen took another big bite of her sandwich before replying.

"In my experience working cases with you, your gut's always been pretty solid, but if you want to bounce an idea off me, go for it."

"Okay," Jessie said, eager to get a fresh perspective. "Jamil and Beth are culling through a database of potential suspects in the murder of this pharmaceutical billionaire, Lowden Booth. And one guy keeps sticking in my head."

"Who's that?" Karen asked.

"His name is Anson Greco," Jessie explained. "You know him?"

"I've heard of him," Karen replied. "He used to be Booth's partner for a while. Now he does health supplements or something, right?"

"That's right," Jessie confirmed. "The name BoothCo Biomeds doesn't actually mean Booth Company. It was a mashup of Booth and Greco when they first got the idea for the pharmaceutical firm as pre-med students."

"Seems like Greco wasn't really thinking ahead on that one," Karen noted drily.

"A point that he has regretted ever since," Jessie said. "In fact, once he got frozen out of the company, that was part of his first lawsuit against Booth. This was *after* a fistfight they got into, during which Greco threatened to kill him."

"But that had to be years ago, didn't it?" Karen asked.

"Decades now," Jessie said. "But the animosity doesn't seem to have faded. Greco went on to have his own successes but never to the level of his former partner. And there are multiple instances of him threatening to destroy Booth in public and private in the years since—so many in fact that ignoring them would be irresponsible."

"Then what are you still doing here?"

"I guess I was waiting to see if Jamil and Beth came up with a stronger suspect," Jessie conceded. "I didn't want to just jump at the chance to go at the sexy choice when more likely ones might pop up soon."

"But this guy seems as strong a suspect as anyone else," Karen said. "Why can't you question him and if the research team gets a better hit in the interim then switch it up? I think you just feel guilty because you'd be leaving all the grunt work to Jamil and Beth, but you shouldn't. They're researchers. That's what they do. You're a criminal profiler. Apply your skills where they're most effective, Jessie."

Jessie stood up, not only convinced by the detective who currently had strawberry jam on her cheek but filled with anticipation to tackle the interview. Karen was right. She didn't need to apologize for wanting to follow her instinct. That's what she was here for.

"Thanks Karen," she said. "I'm going to see if I can tear Ryan away from his captaining. And you should probably wipe that jam off your face before you go back to court. It might undermine your authority as a law enforcement professional."

Karen smiled, apparently not overly concerned, as Jessie darted out of the courtyard to find her husband and get back in the game.

CHAPTER NINE

Had the circumstances not been so serious, Jessie would have laughed out loud.

If Lowden Booth wanted to give off an air of American royalty, Anson Greco seemed to be all about projecting a punk rock vibe.

Earlier this morning, Jessie and Ryan had visited a gorgeously maintained property on a secluded pieced piece of land, high in the Hollywood Hills, attended to by staff in traditional servants' wear. Now they were in the heart of Hollywood, exiting an elevator on the twentieth floor of a high-rise on the corner of Sunset Boulevard and Vine Street, which led to the offices of Greco Health Solutions.

The moment the door opened they were pummeled by the song "Self Esteem," from the 1990s punk band The Offspring, playing at a volume that seemed inappropriately loud for any office environment, especially one that specialized in health & nutrition products. They stepped out into an open space that looked modeled on a cross between a coffeehouse and a skate park, with small ramps in one section and beanbag chairs clustered around low coffee tables in another. There was stylized graffiti on all the walls.

A dozen people milled about, most of them eating, but one actually lazily zooming his skateboard up one ramp and down another. Everyone was dressed like they were headed to the Coachella Festival after work. No one looked to be over thirty.

"Are you the detectives who called?" asked someone from behind them.

Jessie and Ryan turned around to see a diminutive young man wearing pressed, acid-washed jeans and a black t-shirt with the words "The Revolution Will Be Streamed" written on it, walking toward them. His black hair swept down over the right side of his forehead and into his eyes, but he made no effort to move it.

"I'm Captain Hernandez with LAPD," Ryan announced loudly, struggling to be heard over the music and the skateboard. "This is Jessie Hunt. We made the appointment to speak with Mr. Greco."

"Right," the young man said, "that was me who made the appointment. I'm Stokely. I coordinate Anson's schedule. He's in the back pod right now if you're ready to workshop with him."

Jessie again stifled a laugh.

"Sure, we'd love to workshop with him," she said.

Stokely smiled and motioned for them to follow him just as "All Signs Point to Lauderdale" by A Day To Remember kicked in. Their guide bopped his head nonchalantly to the beat and his hair flopped casually about.

"I don't get it," Ryan muttered to her as they kept a few paces behind him. "What kind of health supplement company plays this kind of noise?"

"Hey," Jessie objected, "I like this noise. I remember listening to it in college. It helped me work through a lot of undirected anger. I just didn't expect it to be blasting out of the speakers of a place like this. Maybe I'm being unfair, but I feel like it kind of cheapens it."

Once they rounded the next corner, she realized that she wasn't being unfair at all. They had reached the back pod, which was really just another way of describing Anson Greco's giant office. It was a glassed-in workspace with exposed brick interior meant to make it look like a SoHo loft. The furniture inside was edgy and worn in an overly deliberate way. Posters on the walls hyped sixties new wave films and seventies bands like New York Dolls and the Stooges. Everything about the place felt like it was grasping desperately to be cool and youthful, nothing more so than Greco himself.

He was at an upright desk, staring at his laptop, simultaneously talking to someone via his AirPods and doing lunges while holding twenty pound dumbbells. He was wearing navy leggings and a body-hugging white t-shirt. Though he was in his mid-sixties, he was in great shape—muscular, without a hint of fat.

His hair, completely gray, was lustrous and thick, and Jessie wondered whether he had let nature take its course or found a hairpiece that cleverly recreated it. He was tan, in a borderline questionable way, but not so bronzed as to be obviously artificial.

Despite all his efforts, Anson Greco was not an especially good looking man. His eyes were pinched and angry-looking, and his jaw seemed to just go slack. Everything about the man suggested that he was overcompensating for something.

"Anson," Stokely, said after gently rapping on the glass door, "I've got the LAPD here. Are you available now?"

Greco held up one finger as he finished a lunge.

"We're gonna have to table this," he said to whoever was on the line. "I've got a priority meeting. But let's circle back once the next round of results are in. Early next week enough time? Good. Later."

He looked up and waved them in with a smile. Stokely opened the door.

"Captain Hernandez and Ms. Hunt, this is Anson Greco, CEO and Founder of Greco Health Solutions."

"Come on in, guys," Greco said, putting down the dumbbells and wiping his face with a towel. "Can Stokely get you anything? Vitamin water? Kombucha? Aqua kefir? Pressed juice?"

"I'm good," Jessie said, taking a seat in one of the less oddly shaped chairs in the room.

"Me too," Ryan agreed, doing the same.

"Okay then, you can go Stokely. I'll buzz you if I need you to call my lawyer." He laughed loudly as his assistant left, before adding, "That is, unless you guys really think I should call him in here. His pod is just down the hall."

"That's totally up to you, Mr. Greco," Ryan said. "We're just in information gathering mode right now but if you're more comfortable talking to us with legal counsel here, that's certainly your prerogative."

"Well, considering I don't even know what this is about," Greco said, "I wouldn't have the first clue what I need."

He took a large sip of his own vitamin water and swallowed lustily, As he did, Jessie saw his eyes dart back and forth between her and Ryan anxiously. Somehow, she knew he was lying and decided to call him on it.

"We all know that's not true, don't we, Mr. Greco," she said. "You know exactly why we're here. And if you were really concerned that you couldn't handle speaking with us, your attorney would already have been here when we arrived. So shall we just cut to the chase?'

Ryan glanced over at her with a mix of surprise and annoyance. Clearly he'd have liked to have been clued in on her unexpectedly aggressive play, but considering that she didn't know she was going this route until just now, there was no way to warn him.

"What do you mean?" Greco asked, still acting the innocent.

"You either know what happened because you're so obsessed with your old nemesis that you have someone on the inside feeding you info or you know because you're somehow involved," Jessie pressed. "Which is it?"

"I resent the insinuation that I'm somehow involved in…anything that may have happened to Lowden Booth!" Greco huffed, his back straightening defensively.

"At least now you're acknowledging that you know," Jessie retorted. "Now that we've got that out of the way, can we be straight with each other?"

Greco sighed heavily and sat down in the elevated chair in front of his desk.

"Of course I know," he conceded. "You don't think I got to where I am in business and in life without keeping tabs on my biggest competitor? I probably knew about his death before you did, no offense."

"Then you can understand why we're here," Ryan said, bouncing back admirably from his earlier shock, giving Greco no indication that he hadn't been privy to Jessie's suspicions about him until this point. "You and Lowden Booth have had your…conflicts over the years and we wouldn't be doing our due diligence if we didn't talk to you."

"Of course," Greco said. "I'd be insulted if I didn't get a visit. But the truth is, other than healthy professional competition, Lowden doesn't really play a significant role in my life anymore."

"Anson," Jessie said disapprovingly, knowing it was a risk to use his first name but doing it anyway. "You were finally being a straight shooter and now this retreat to public relations pablum? This guy has been in your head for over forty years. Even when you were partners, he screwed you out of the company name. When he cut you out of the business, you got in an actual brawl with each other. You broke his cheekbone. You threatened to kill him."

"That was a youthful indiscretion," Greco countered. "It was over twenty-five years ago."

"Yes, it was a while ago," Jessie conceded, "but I'd hardly call it a youthful indiscretion. You were almost forty at the time. And it's not like you've let things go in the meantime. Should I remind you of other incidents since then?"

"You wouldn't be the first to offer a rundown of my greatest hits," Greco said sounding purposefully amused. "Go right ahead."

"Okay," Jessie replied, "in addition to that death threat, you've also promised to destroy him both personally and professionally on multiple occasions, in public and in private. You hired a private eye to pay a prostitute to try get him in a compromising situation. There were even allegations that people were paid to taint the supply line of one of BoothCo's drugs."

"That allegation was never proven," Greco interjected.

Jessie moved on, undeterred.

"At one of the protests against him, you were arrested for tossing a dead rat carcass at him."

"Nailed him too," Greco shot back happily. "Pretty good aim, if you ask me."

"You hired a pilot to fly a plane over a shareholders meeting with a banner that read that *BoothCo Biomedics tests their drugs on chimpanzees*."

"I had been misinformed," Greco conceded, "and later issued an apology."

"He sued you and won damages," Jessie noted. "In addition to these myriad instances of animosity, your recent history suggests that you might be losing your better judgment. You've been in three physical altercations with strangers in the last four years, including two barfights. And excuse me for being so blunt, but while we find no official record of hospitalization, we know that you've gone to rehab twice in the last three years. All of this suggests someone who might be spiraling out of control and willing to make rash decisions."

Greco smiled.

"If I'm such a mess, how could I look this good? I'm a senior citizen for God's sake!"

"That's the other thing, Anson," Jessie said. "Our research shows that you're a big time health and fitness enthusiast. We saw you working out when we arrived. We know that you're into parkour and boxing as well. And while those are very impressive endeavors for anyone, much less someone of your age, they also suggest that you might have been able to physically access the Booth Estate and get to your old adversary without too much difficulty. Barring that, you'd certainly have the resources to hire someone to do such a thing. Can you really tell me that this theory is completely absurd?"

"Ms. Hunt," Greco replied, his tone dripping with condescension, "I know that you're supposedly this brilliant profiler, but are you actually suggesting that I snuck onto Lowden's estate and did him in? Do you think I'm capable of that? Do you think I even care that much?"

Jessie shrugged.

"Capable? I'm not so sure," she conceded. "But do I think you care that much? Here's how I look at it. You claim that you had a 'healthy professional competition' with Lowden and yes, you have certainly had success since he cut you loose from BoothCo all those years ago. But let's be honest, since then you've never reached his heights or been as respected. Until this morning, he ran one of biggest pharmaceutical companies in the world. You operate a reasonably successful nutritional supplement company that airs infomercials in the middle of the night. It's not quite the same, is it? That must eat at you."

Jessie knew that she was baiting the man, but she needed to do something to shake him out of his comfortably arrogant vitamin water-drinking, dumbbell-lunging private pod universe. She needed to know who she was really dealing with.

She could tell that it had worked.

CHAPTER TEN

The condescending expression on Greco's face had disappeared, replaced by one of barely contained fury. The man suddenly leaned forward in his chair and Jessie noticed Ryan do the same in his, ready in case Greco made a particularly foolish decision.

But then the CEO seemed to catch himself and leaned back again. For a moment, his expression turned contemplative, and Jessie thought he might be about to confess to something. Instead he broke into a hearty, seemingly genuine laugh.

"I have to admit that I have really gotten into the parkour thing lately," he said. "Lots of new bumps and bruises. And I've always loved the sweet science. So the idea of using those skills on Lowden sounds pretty damn appealing. I wouldn't have minded getting him into a boxing ring or a dark alley and laying a real ass kicking on him. I mean, let's be real, the guy wasn't about to enter any triathlons any time soon. I would have wiped the floor with him. And who knows, maybe I could have gotten onto his property. I'd like to think I could swing it. But then again, perhaps not. Even if I couldn't, you're right—I'm sure I could have hired someone with the ability to do it."

"You're not exactly making the case for your innocence here," Ryan noted.

"Maybe this will," Greco replied. "Once I—or my proxy—got on the property, where would I go after that? I've never been to Lowden's mansion. I'm not exactly on the permanent guest list."

"You said you have an insider on his payroll," Jessie reminded him.

"That's true," Greco admitted, "And I guess now is as good a time as any to reveal who that is. Her name is Alejandra Rojas and she works as a server, food prep assistant, and dishwasher at the Estate. She gives me tips on Lowden's comings and goings and sometimes catches snippets of his mealtime conversations, which she'll pass along if they seem pertinent. But from what I hear, Lowden was killed in his bedroom and to the best of my knowledge, she never leaves the kitchen and dining area. So giving me a secret route to his private quarters isn't really her area of expertise. But you're welcome to question her to see if she's really some kind of home design mastermind."

"You could have purchased the plans for the house," Ryan said, "gotten the layout that way."

"I suppose," Greco conceded, "but that brings me back to something that Ms. Hunt said before. As long as I'm laying my soul bare, you were right about something else too."

"What was that?"

"I wasn't ducking your point earlier," he said. "Lowden and my paths diverged after he excised me from BoothCo. It's true that I'm not as successful as he is. He's a titan of industry and I've carved out a respectable niche for myself. I'm sure if I saw a therapist, she'd tell me that's why I live the crazy lifestyle that I do, partying all the time, taking drugs I shouldn't, getting into fights with men less than half my age. She'd probably say it's why virtually my entire office staff is under thirty; why I blast loud music all day long and I have a frickin' skate ramp in my office. Do you know many times I've been told that thing is a liability? Our legal counsel is worried someone is going to smash through a window and fall twenty stories onto Sunset Boulevard. This hypothetical therapist would probably say my obsession with Lowden is why I freak out if my body fat exceeds ten percent and why I haven't had a meaningful relationship or even a date with a woman with wrinkles in the quarter century since he kicked me to the curb."

"That's what your imaginary therapist would say?" Jessie asked, choosing to focus on the absurdity of that statement because everything else he'd said was too raw to respond to.

"Sure, completely imaginary," he said with a self-effacing shrug. "And her imaginary office is in a Beverly Hills building on Doheny Drive. Here's the heart of it: while I resent what he did to me and our places in the pecking order, I'm also clear-eyed about it. I know how I'm perceived, which means that the second I heard he was murdered, I knew I'd be the prime suspect. How could I not be?"

"It's a good question," Jessie noted.

"With the litany of my offenses that you listed, it's a no-brainer," Greco agreed. "That's why I immediately began compiling a tick-tock of my whereabouts for the entire morning. Alejandra told me the mansion's security people have footage of an intruder leaving around 7:30, so I used that as my guidepost. The real reason the company's lawyer isn't here with us is because he's been scrambling all morning, working with my personal attorney to get you full access to all the GPS data for my phones and cars—I have several—as well as all my bank records."

Jessie barely managed to keep her jaw from falling. Ryan impressed her by acting as if he'd expected this response all along.

"Personal and business records?" he pressed.

"All personal and most business," Greco replied. "I used my personal funds for Alejandra's payments, but I realize you may want to do a forensic analysis to see if I could have paid some assassin through a secret corporate dummy account or something. The company's legal counsel objected to handing over details on *every* account because it might reveal trade secrets but he and my private attorney compromised on any account for which I personally had authority to transfer funds. It shouldn't be an issue though. If you discover any that seem suspicious down the line, we'd be open to allowing them to be viewed without a court order if there's reasonable cause."

While Jessie had managed to visibly hide her shock, she couldn't help but ask the obvious question.

"Why are you opening everything up like this when you know it might still not be enough to exonerate you? After all, you could have some secret Swiss bank account somewhere that you used as your assassin fund."

"Fair point," Greco acknowledged, standing up and bending down to touch his toes with impressive ease. "Here's why: I'm hoping you'll see that I have nothing to gain from Lowden's death."

He stood up again. His face was red. At first Jessie thought it was from blood rushing to his head during his stretch, but she realized he was blushing. When he continued, she understood why.

"When you see the financials—both the company's and my personal ones—you'll discover a little surprise. The nutritional supplement industry has been booming in recent years, but Greco Health Solutions hasn't gotten in on the fun. We're viewed as too old-school. People used to respond to the infomercials but now they consider them a joke. We recently did a marketing survey and one person used a word to describe the company that stuck with me: musty. We've lost millions in the last half-decade."

Greco sighed heavily and Jessie wondered if he was even going to go on, but eventually he did.

"So about nine months ago, both the company and I personally started secretly investing in BoothCo Biomeds You'll see the details when you look at the financials, but the gist is, if BoothCo loses money, then Greco Health Solutions loses money and I lose money.

And I have a feeling that their CEO being murdered is going to cause their stock to tumble big time, don't you?"

He didn't wait for a response before continuing.

"Listen, I can't say it publicly because it's bad for my brand, but financially, Lowden's death is terrible for me, like 'risk of bankruptcy,' terrible. I know this is cold considering that I've known him for forty-five years and should be thinking about the man and his family's loss, but from a practical perspective, I needed Lowden alive. I shouldn't be your prime suspect. If I was there this morning, I would have tried to save him myself."

"That does sound pretty cold," Ryan told him.

Greco looked at him like he wanted to argue but he didn't seem to have much fight in him.

"You want to know why I'm being so honest with you?"

Jessie and Ryan nodded at the same time.

"I'm hoping that you'll investigate all of this quietly, and that ultimately, you won't arrest me," he said. "Not just for me, although obviously that would be nice. But think about what's likely to happen in the next few hours. The news comes out about the CEO of BoothCo Biomeds being murdered, leading to a huge loss in the company's value and as a result, the value of Greco Health Solutions. Then, possibly, more news comes out that Greco's CEO has been arrested in connection with the murder of BoothCo's CEO. That twin hit would be too much for this company to survive. There are eighty-one people in this office who would lose their jobs and another 337 in our production and distribution facility in the Moreno Valley who would lose theirs too. I'm a cold, shallow, narcissistic asshole, but even I can't walk around with that on my conscience."

Greco slumped back in his chair and for the first time since they'd arrived, he looked all of his sixty-four years. Jessie knew they'd have to follow up on all of it—the finances, the phone and vehicle records, everything—but based on what she knew so far, she felt confident that Anson Greco was telling the truth. If he was willing to open all his accounts and potentially expose any number of other secrets, it was a strong sign that he was confident the move would prove his innocence.

"It was my mistake," Greco muttered under his breath, more to himself than to them.

"What was?" Ryan asked.

"I should have followed my own advice," he said, "the advice I gave to everyone else who asked about getting involved with Lowden:

if you don't want to get burned, keep clear of the flames. But after so many years, I forgot my own advice, and now I'm paying the price for it. Only this time, Lowden didn't even do it to me on purpose."

"Who else didn't follow your advice?" Jessie asked. "Who else didn't keep clear of the flames? Who else got burned bad enough that they might want to kill Lowden Booth?"

Greco laughed bitterly.

"I can't count that high."

CHAPTER ELEVEN

Despite Anson Greco's proclamation, they didn't have an obvious second choice.

As she sat in the passenger seat of Ryan's unmoving car, Jessie could hear the frustration in Jamil's voice as he tried to explain why he and Beth hadn't made more progress on the list of potential suspects while she and Ryan had been questioning Greco.

"We've managed to eliminate a lot of people who've made threats," he said, his dour tone at odds with the positive news he was sharing. "A surprising number are in psychiatric facilities. A few are incarcerated. Others have left the Southern California area. Some seem to have lost interest in opposing Booth altogether. One competitor who railed against him for years just sold his company to BoothCo Biomeds a few months ago. We had 38 credible possible suspects when you left. We're down to 26 now. Unfortunately, out of those 26, we haven't been able to elevate any of them to the point where we think they pose a risk beyond the others or justify a formal interview."

"That's okay," Jessie said quickly, not wanting Jamil to think they were disappointed in his efforts even if the results weren't what they had hoped for. "Just keep plugging away. Something is bound to pop at some point."

It occurred to her that while she'd done as Dr. Lemmon had requested this morning and forwarded him the information about the survivor's guilt support group meeting, she hadn't checked her email since then to see if he'd responded. At this moment, hearing the dejected tone of his voice, she wished she had. Of course there was no way to broach the subject now while on a call with Beth and Ryan, but she made a mental note to check in with him later.

"What about Booth's family?" Ryan asked, interrupting her thoughts. "Weren't you going to pursue that too?"

"We've continued to hit a brick wall on that front," Beth said. "Lowden Booth's coterie of attorneys did an excellent job of keeping almost everything related to them under wraps. Not just the terms of any prenup with Devon, but the specifics of his divorce from his first wife, Gwendolyn too. We can't get any information on the will or possible inheritance. Even getting basic details on the status of their two children has been challenging. We know a little about their son Ethan because he's over eighteen now, but it was hard to even uncover that their underage daughter's name is Louisa. We're still plugging away but it might take a while."

"I think I might know where we can get some folks to be more forthcoming without having to pull teeth," Jessie said, the idea only just now coming to her.

"Where's that?" Ryan asked.

"Let's go back to the Booth Estate. We know that Anson Greco's mole, Alejandra, will be willing to spill what she knows. And remember, Grover Nix said some of those people have been with Lowden for decades. Surely some of them will want to help put his killer behind bars."

Ryan had already started the car and pulled into traffic before she finished the sentence.

***

Because he didn't take the turns as fast this time around on the way up to the Booth Estate, Jessie never came close to throwing up, though she did get borderline dizzy on one occasion, which she kept to herself.

Jessie hadn't had a migraine or a spell of confusion in weeks, but she knew that even a passing mention of a potentially concussion-related issue would get Ryan's nerves jangling. And considering the already heightened tension between them today, she didn't see any reason to increase his anxiety, or her frustration with it.

This time, when they arrived at the outer gates of the estate, they had to weave through a maze of television vans that had assembled on the grass on either side of the road. Jessie grabbed a baseball cap, pulled it low over her eyes, and ducked down in the passenger seat, though she knew she was probably too late. Some of the cameras had already caught them pulling up and more were rushing over as the car stopped for the security guard to let them pass. She was sure to be recognized.

This was already going to be a huge case with major media attention, simply because it involved the murder of a well-known, controversial billionaire. But now that local stations would be able to splash video of her at the scene on their next newscast, the press attention was only going to get crazier.

They would likely throw up chyrons on viewers' screens with more ridiculous titles for her like "Angel of the City of Angels." As if in active response to her concerns, a news helicopter shot across the sky just as the guard opened the gate to let them pass through.

Once they got to the house, they saw that there were still two squad cars on the property. As they approached the front door, a youngish blonde-haired officer they didn't recognize from earlier opened it and welcomed them in.

"I'm Officer Cleland," he said. "Officer Bailey told me to give you anything you needed."

"Thanks," Ryan replied. "Right now, we just want to talk to some of the staff. Is Grover Nix able to coordinate that for us?"

"He's not," Cleland said, "but his deputy security chief is around, some guy named Rufus."

"Some guy named Rufus at your service," said a young man with black buzzcut hair, who had just rounded the corner.

Jessie recognized him from the control room earlier that morning, where he'd been present but never spoke. He was dressed in a tailored suit, just like Grover. But he didn't have a British accent and he was younger than his boss by about fifteen years, and thicker too. Like Nix, he didn't have the stereotypical bodyguard build. Both men presented more like retired gymnasts than bodybuilders. Rufus just looked more recently retired than his superior.

"Where's Grover?" Ryan asked.

"At the hospital," Rufus explained. "Mrs. Booth is being kept there overnight for observation after her head injury and she started to get a little…apprehensive that she might not be safe."

"She thinks this intruder might be after her?" Jessie pressed.

"It crossed her mind," Rufus said. "She's worried that maybe this guy thinks she could identify him even though she swears that she can't or that perhaps he meant to kill both of them all along and intends to return to finish the job. Needless to say, she feels very exposed and insisted that Grover stay at the hospital tonight."

"Hard to blame her," Jessie muttered under her breath.

While the demand may have sounded overblown and self-involved at first blush, one had to concede that it wasn't entirely ridiculous. Until the killer's motives were established, Devon Booth's fears couldn't be completely dismissed.

"Yeah, well, I don't know what happens after that," Rufus said. "She says she doesn't feel safe here anymore and that she doesn't see how she can return to the mansion where her husband was killed. She's talking about going to stay with her sister, Tricia, for a while. Her sister lives in an ungated 2500-square-foot ranch style house in Ladera Heights. I don't see how that's safer."

"What about tonight?" Ryan asked. "Is it just Grover at the hospital—no other security?"

"It's not just him," Rufus said. "We'll also be using a three-person team from our exterior security crew here for the hospital floor. And Grover will have our interior team rotating shifts. I'll be on duty from 4 p.m. to 10 p.m. But he'll stay with her now and again overnight."

"Sounds like you've got a full day ahead of you," Jessie said. "We hate to complicate matters, but we were hoping to speak to some staff members about Lowden and the family. We think they might be able to offer some insights that could help with the case."

"Of course," Rufus obliged. "Who would you like to talk to?"

"We'd like to start with Alejandra Rojas," Jessie told him.

"Certainly," Rufus said, leading them down the long hall, "she's in the kitchen."

"While we're doing that, maybe you could put together a list of his longest-serving staff, the ones he liked the best and who liked him the most—the true loyalists," Jessie suggested.

"Not a problem," Rufus assured her as they arrived at the kitchen, and he waved past the other staffers to a petite woman in her mid-thirties with curly, strawberry-blonde hair tied up in a bun who was sorting silverware.

"Alejandra," he called out, "these folks would like a word."

The woman looked over, and when she saw them, her whole body slumped. She nodded passively.

"Why don't we step outside?" Ryan recommended quietly once they walked over, pointing at a side door.

When the three of them were alone on the covered patio just outside the kitchen, Ryan took the lead.

"I'm Captain Ryan Hernandez with the LAPD. This is Jessie Hunt. She works with us. Do you know why we're here?"

She nodded slowly.

"Because of Mr. Greco?"

"Did he warn you that we'd be coming?" Ryan asked.

"He said the police might come to ask me questions."

"Did he tell you what to say?" Jessie wanted to know.

She shook her adamantly.

"He just said that I should tell the truth, that he had already revealed everything, and that there was no point in lying. He said that compared to what was going on with Mr. Booth, the things I had done wrong were pretty small and that hopefully the police would see that and show me some mercy. But that if I lied, they probably wouldn't."

"All right, then I'm going to ask you some questions, but first I need to read your rights," Ryan told her.

After he read her the Miranda warning, Alejandra waived her right to silence and to a lawyer. She subsequently confirmed just about everything they'd heard from Anson Greco.

"Why did you agree to do this?" Jessie asked after listening to the details of how Alejandra passed along information to Greco. "Did you have something against Mr. Booth?"

"No, he was nice enough," Alejandra said. "But I was approached with this offer for money. It was hard to turn down. Thousands of dollars just to repeat what I saw and what I heard. It didn't seem like such a big deal. Plus Mr. Greco promised to pay for my son's college. I'm a single mother and I had my boy when I was seventeen. I never got past tenth grade. And my son got into Claremont McKenna College. It's a really good school and I was so proud. But even with scholarships and financial aid, the burden was going to be huge. And this man said he'd pay the tuition off in full every year. That's $60,000."

"Did he pay?" Ryan wondered.

"So far," Alejandra replied. "Noah just finished his sophomore year. I don't know what will happen now."

None of them spoke for a moment. Jessie wanted to offer her words of hope but knew they'd feel false. She had no idea what would happen either. And that couldn't be her priority right now anyway. She focused on what was.

"How long have you worked for Mr. Booth?" she asked.

"Seven years."

"If we asked you to put together a list of his most loyal, trusted, longest-serving staff, could you do that for us?"

"Sure."

"Before you do that," Ryan said, "you said that Mr. Booth was 'nice enough.' Do you know if any staff felt differently?"

Alejandra thought for a moment, then shook her head.

"I know that he had a reputation in the media for being really rough in business and hard with friends, and I definitely heard him get that way on the phone," she said. "He would yell and scream sometimes. But I don't remember him ever being that way with us. Of course, I didn't spend a lot of time with him, mostly just at meals. But even if he didn't like the food or service, he was never cruel or mean. He might say a cross word or two, but that's about it. And I never heard rumors from others."

"What about Mrs. Booth?" Jessie wondered. "What was she like? Did she ever have a cross word for people? For Mr. Booth maybe?"

Alejandra smiled and Jessie thought she might finally be about get some dirt.

"No, she was fun," the woman answered. "Everything livened up once Mr. Booth married her. She made him take himself less seriously. She was a good time waiting to happen."

CHAPTER TWELVE

Alejandra Rojas wasn't the only one who felt that way and it was frustrating the hell out of Jessie to hear it.

After she and Ryan combined Alejandra's list with Rufus's to put together the Booth Estate staff all-stars—the employees who knew Lowden Booth the best—they started questioning them and there seemed to be a consensus about the Booths: Lowden was nicer than the public thought and Devon was a big reason why.

Neither of those facts helped explain why he was dead, but Jessie kept digging in the hopes of finding that one little nugget of information that would. She kept thinking she was about to strike gold. There were multiple staff stories of how Lowden, while gracious to the staff, had become increasingly curt and insular in the years since his first marriage ended.

More than one person talked about him, in the pre-Devon days, obliviously keeping them on call well past midnight simply because he'd lost track of the time while working. Kitchen staff acknowledged that before he remarried, he sometimes had them remake entire dishes because "something just didn't taste quite right." He wasn't a jerk about it. He just instructed that it be done, on a few occasions remaking a dish three times, seemingly unaware that the people making the meal should have clocked out hours earlier.

But when Jessie pressed the staffers on how they felt about these incidents, no one seemed to hold a grudge. She challenged them pretty hard, and no one took offense at the question. They understood that it was weird that he did it and that they gave him a pass for it. But the forgiveness seemed genuine. Jessie got the sense that they pitied more than resented him.

That all changed when Devon came on the scene. The two apparently met while Lowden was in Las Vegas for a pharmaceutical convention. She was his server at dinner one night. They hit it off. A whirlwind romance ensued, and they were married. That was five years ago.

Every staffer they spoke to agreed that Devon was impulsive, liked to drink, had lavish tastes, and was prone to getting excited about things before quickly losing interest. Many thought the marriage wouldn't last a year. But it turned out that she never lost interest in Lowden, doted on him, seemingly adored him.

"She viewed him as a teddy bear when everyone else saw a grizzly," according to Horace Deets, Booth's longtime butler, who, now sixty-two, worked reduced hours because of bad knees. "I've been with the man for two decades now and I never saw him giggle until he met her, not even around his kids."

Horace, the second-longest serving member of the staff, had been understandably somber for most of their conversation, which took place at a poker table in a casino room that also had a blackjack table, a craps table, and a roulette wheel. Jessie was about let him go when his face suddenly brightened.

"What?" she asked.

"I was just remembering the night they met," he said. "You heard it was in Vegas, right?"

"At some fancy restaurant, right?" Jessie replied.

"Nah," Horace corrected, waving dismissively. "That's what these newbies say but none of them were there. I was actually on the trip with him. You want to know the real story?"

"Of course," Jessie said, leaning in closer, as did Ryan. They both knew that sometimes the best intelligence came when a witness was just telling a story casually, unaware of the significance it might have.

"So we went to the fancy restaurant," he began. "Mr. Booth was there with some bigwigs from his company. I was hanging around to assist if needed, seated at a tiny two-top a few feet away. He was already agitated because the convention hasn't gone like he hoped—there was some contentious press conference. A reporter was asking about a study with questionable data or something."

"Do you remember anything about the study?" Jessie interrupted.

"Ms. Hunt," Horace said, clearly irked. "I know you're just doing your job, but you are screwing up the story. I don't know a thing about the study or the press conference. I only know this much because Mr. Booth told me that was what had him in such a dark mood. May I continue?"

"I'm sorry," Jessie said, somehow feeling guilty for trying to do her job. The disapproving look she got from her police captain husband told her that he too, had been sucked into this alternate reality where they felt ashamed for asking a witness a relevant question.

"Anyway," Horace continued with raised eyebrows, "they're at the place for about ten minutes and he sees the main courses brought out at the table next to theirs. He goes off because the dishes are so tiny. He's looking at the prices for what he's seeing on the plates and calling it a scam. So he decides right then and there they should leave. So they do. A half-dozen men in suits, seven if you include me, get up and march out."

"Where did they go?" Ryan asked.

"Now you see, *that's* a good question," Horace said, fixing a disdainful eye on Jessie before continuing. "Mr. Booth sees a casino next door with a flashing sign for a restaurant inside that reads *surf & turf special: $59.99*. So we all go in. We get a big banquette. He has me sit with them this time. We're all squeezed in, and the future Mrs. Booth comes over to take our order. Mr. Booth is in a bad mood and starts giving her a hard time about how the place next door had tiny little servings and saying that he expects a better experience here."

"How was that received?" Jessie asked.

"Not well," Horace said with a wheezing laugh. "She gave as good as she got, better even. She told him that with that kind of attitude he'd be lucky to get anything. I remember she said that maybe he should just sit there in his fancy boy suit, keep his mouth shut, and see what she brought out. Then if he didn't like it, he could complain."

"Did he keep his mouth shut?" Ryan wondered.

"He didn't get a chance to," Horace said. "All his yes men started blustering, saying 'how dare she talk to him like this?' and 'didn't she know who this was?' but she didn't care. She said he looked like an accountant to her. He loved it. They went back and forth like that all night, bantering. It was like tennis match with words. By the way, he loved what she ordered for him. It was chicken fried steak. She quit her job the next day and flew back on the private plane with us."

"And it stayed that way ever since?" Jessie pressed. "No fights?"

"None of any consequence that I saw or heard," he confirmed, "But still a lot of bantering and doting, although the food selections got a lot healthier since that night."

"So no issues with the wife," Jessie said, "and the staff seems fond of him. Anyone else you know who had a grudge against Mr. Booth? Maybe some of those company bigwigs from that dinner got a little jealous? Maybe one of them had it in for him?"

"I can tell you that all the men on that trip were real bootlickers whose success was completely tied to Mr. Booth. And I can give you their names, though I assure you, none of them would harm a hair on his head. But that doesn't really help you very much, does it, Ms. Hunt?"

Why do you say that?" Jessie wondered.

"Because that's not really my area anymore," Horace said. "I know the mansion social dynamics pretty well. But I haven't gone to the office or on trips with him very much in recent years. I'm afraid that I'm out of the loop on all the back-biting these days."

"What about the family prior to Devon?" Ryan asked. "What was their relationship like?"

Jessie knew the question was coming and she knew what the answer would be, even before Horace opened his mouth—the same answer they'd gotten from every other staffer they'd asked today.

"I'm sorry, Captain," the man said. "I'm happy to talk about Mr. Booth or the current Mrs. Booth, but I've signed a nondisclosure agreement about the other members of the family. My understanding is that it's enforceable even after Mr. Booth's death, so I'm not able to speak on them."

"Excuse me for interrupting," Rufus said, poking his head in, "But Vera is awake and willing to talk. In fact she demands to."

Jessie was pleasantly surprised by the news. Vera Przekop was the Estate's senior-most staff member. She'd been Booth's housekeeper for over thirty years, back before he'd married his first wife. In her late seventies, her position was mostly ceremonial now, though she apparently still got dressed in her uniform every day, made a point to clean a couple of rooms, and most importantly, kept a stern eye on the rest of the staff to make sure they weren't slacking off. Described by other employees as shrewish and sharp-tongued, she was not beloved.

She had also taken Booth's death hard. After learning of the news this morning, she had broken down, been given a sedative, and been sleeping ever since. Jessie hadn't thought they'd get to speak with her. But apparently Vera was making it a priority.

"Well then, let's do it," Jessie said, standing up.

"Be careful," Horace warned. "That woman's a witch."

CHAPTER THIRTEEN

By the time Rufus left them in Vera's room, Jessie half-believed there might be a bubbling cauldron in the middle of the floor.

Of course, other than a small rug, there was nothing on the floor at all. The space was immaculate, if worryingly dark. She couldn't even see Vera clearly, just a shadowy figure hunched over on the side of the bed. Then the figure turned on a lamp and Jessie got a look at who they were working with.

Sitting in front of them was a wizened woman of Eastern European heritage with gray hair tied back in a tight bun. Her eyes were slits hidden behind wrinkled skin made even more pronounced by a prominent scowl. She wore a housekeeping uniform covered by a black housecoat.

Jessie didn't know exactly what Vera Przekop wanted to tell them, but she got the distinct impression that this was a woman who would shoot straight. She hoped her impression bore out and would allow them to get the dirt they needed.

"Thanks for meeting with us, Ms. Przekop," she said, stepping into the room. "We're sorry for your loss."

She looked around but there was nowhere to sit. The one chair in the room had been placed upside down on the tiny desk in the corner as if to say, "this is not for you." So she simply stood on the rug awkwardly. Ryan joined her there.

"First of all," the woman replied in a gruff but unexpectedly strong voice, "I won't say a word about the family. I hear you two keep asking about the first wife and the kids, trying to get someone to air dirty laundry. They didn't and I won't. We clear?"

"Yes ma'am," Ryan said, unconsciously slipping into the compliant, respectful youngster mode he often adopted in the presence of authoritarian female elder types. It was something that Jessie had pointed out to him on numerous occasions but he couldn't seem to shake the habit.

"Normally I wouldn't allow this kind of informality with strangers, but since you're law enforcement types, I suppose you may call me

Vera," the woman grumbled reluctantly, as if she was performing a great act of charity.

"We don't want to waste your time, Vera," Jessie said, deciding to take charge before the older woman completely rolled them, "and I'm sure you don't want that either, so let's get right to the point: who do you think might have wanted to kill Mr. Booth?"

The housekeeper sat up straight on her twin bed and thought about the question, her face wrinkling up even more than Jessie would have thought possible. When she answered, she spoke slowly, as if she was choosing each word carefully.

"I don't know about his business enemies," she said. "I hear there were a lot of them. I did keep tabs on the folks who threatened him personally, the real crazies. A wild man got on the estate a few years ago with a hatchet before being dragged down on the lawn. He died of a drug overdose last year, so I know he didn't do this."

She reached into the cabinet of her bedside table, pulled out a manila folder, flipped to a sheet of paper, and handed it over. It was a coroner's cause of death top sheet verifying what she had just said. As Jessie reviewed it, the woman handed over a second sheet of paper from the department of corrections.

"Another crazy person promised to boil Mr. Booth's children," she said. "This was a decade ago, but I kept track of him because the threat stood out for one reason: he knew the kids' names, which were not publicly available. That was very troubling to me and showed that this person was willing to go the extra step. Eventually, the man turned his fixation to someone else, a pop singer. He was arrested for breaking into her house and waiting for her in her bedroom, along with a duffle bag full of manacles, electric tape, and a cattle prod. Luckily, the singer was out that evening. He's been in prison for the last six years so he's not the intruder."

"Wow," Ryan marveled, "you've been doing your homework."

Jessie agreed, though she was equal parts impressed and disturbed by the fact that this second intruder sounded so much like the man that she and Nettles had just busted yesterday at a TV actress's pool house. It seemed like duct tape and cattle prods were standard supplies for psycho stalkers, no matter what decade it was.

"There have been others," Przekop said, "and as I told you, I don't know about the adversaries from his business. I don't know much about his business at all, really, though I've heard it said by some that his company has done more harm than good. Others say that he was a bad person. That seems strong, though I know he alienated a great many people and that he was a hard man to like. He definitely enjoyed pissing folks off."

Jessie fought hard not to let her eyebrows rise at hearing such salty language from a near octogenarian. The woman was on a roll, and she didn't want to interrupt her.

"He tended to sabotage himself," Vera continued. "He viewed everything as a competition, and almost everyone as an enemy."

"*Almost* everyone?" Ryan pressed.

"Not people like me," Vera clarified, "the help, the staff. He wasn't in competition with us. He didn't view us as threats, so he was good to us. He was good to me."

"What do you think of Devon?" Jessie asked point blank.

"I hated her," the housekeeper said flatly.

Finally, someone is going to be real. All this time it took a crotchety, medicated, housekeeper emeritus to spill the beans.

"She was too bubbly, too fake. Always excited about this or that, always spending Mr. Booth's money. Yes, he was a billionaire, so he wasn't going broke any time soon, but she spent a *lot* of it. She was too young for him, taking advantage of him, always getting him to do this or that, almost like she wanted him so busy all the time, so that he'd drop dead of a heart attack so she would get everything he owned. The worst was that no matter how hostile I was to her—and I was very hostile—she was still nice to me. It was like she was friendly out of spite. She was just terrible. But…"

Jessie's heart sank at the word.

"But what?" she asked hesitantly.

"But then something happened about three and half years ago," Vera said, almost as if she couldn't believe what she was saying herself. "It was late. Most of the staff had retired for the evening. Mr. and Mrs. Booth were getting set to watch a film in the screening room. I was done for the night but decided to see if they needed any popcorn or other snacks. I was just coming into the room when I saw Mr. Booth fixing drinks at the mini bar off to the side of the room. Suddenly he collapsed."

"Heart attack?" Ryan guessed.

"Yes," the housekeeper said in a hushed whisper. "That wife of his hopped up out of her seat, ran over to him, and leapt into action. She asked him questions—was he okay? But he couldn't talk. She got on the house phone and called security right away—ordered them to call

911 and bring those paddles people use to shock the heart—called an AED, I think. Then she started giving him CPR right there on the floor. She was pumping his chest and doing mouth-to-mouth like something right out of TV."

The woman paused for a second to catch her breath. As she did, she clutched her fist to her chest, as if the memory of the event still overwhelmed her. After a moment, she went on.

"I'm ashamed to say I stood there in frozen shock for much longer than I should have—probably a good fifteen or twenty seconds—before I snapped out of it and came over to help. But there wasn't much I could do. I couldn't pound his chest. I can't even get on my knees like that anymore. So I just stood there and prayed. A short time later, half a minute maybe, the security guys came in with the paddle thing and took over. They shocked him and he came back. He returned from death's door."

"Why didn't we ever hear about this?" Jessie asked.

Vera Przekop gave her a patronizing smile.

"You should know better than to ask that by now dear," she said. "Mr. Booth would never want to show weakness to the world. He had them cancel the call to 911 and say it was a false alarm. His personal doctor came over to check him out. Then he secretly went to the hospital for a battery of tests. The doctors said that without Mrs. Booth's quick action, it could have gone quite differently. That's when I started to see her in a new light."

"What do you mean?" Ryan asked.

"I mean, she had no idea I was around, that I had seen what happened," Vera pointed out. "As far as she knew, she could have just left him there on the floor and no one would have known the truth. She could have said the movie was on and she didn't hear him fall over the noise. He'd have died and she would have gotten all his money, or at least a lot of it I bet. Surely that must have gone through her head if she had malice in her heart. But she didn't hesitate for second. She was at his side quicker than I could blink. Then I started to think about other things."

"Like what?" Jessie asked, though she wasn't sure she wanted to know.

"Like how she always tried to make him eat healthy," Vera answered. "I thought she was being a nag but then I reconsidered. What if she actually loved the man and just wanted him to stick around longer? And then there were all the expensive things she bought with his money. It hit me that they weren't things for her."

"What do you mean?" Ryan pressed.

"They were things for him," Vera explained, "like a sailboat, which she said was so he could get away from his phone and de-stress where no one could reach him. Plus, she bought an entire mini-amusement park in Garden Grove, which she said he should use to spend time with his daughter. She told him they could close it to the public and just ride the rides together or that his girl could invite her friends for the day whenever she wanted. I thought Mrs. Booth was just trying to curry favor with him but if I gave her benefit of the doubt, it made sense. He was having trouble connecting with the young lady. What if this was simply an attempt to help him find a way to bridge that gap with his little girl?"

Jessie and Ryan were quiet, not sure what to make of this surly woman turning into a character witness for what had once been a halfway decent suspect.

"Anyway," Vera muttered, slouching again, "She sanded the edges off a pretty prickly man, so I guess she's not so bad. But sanded down or not, that doesn't mean that there aren't still a lot of people out there who would have liked to see him suffer. I just don't know who they are."

Vera put her hands in her lap and sighed heavily. Then, with a finality that suggested there would be no debating the matter, she added, "Now I think you need to go because all this talking, on top of everything else, has wiped me out."

Jessie and Ryan, though startled by the abrupt end to the conversation, nodded and started to head out as the woman took off her housecoat and began to get into bed. They were just leaving the room when she called after them.

"And I don't want to hear anything about me having violated my non-disclosure agreement with that amusement park story," she insisted. "That was just for context. I'll deny it if you try to get me to repeat that in court, got it? I'm an old woman and I don't need anyone suing me. Now get!"

They left the room and walked down the corridor, making turn after turn, until they reached the main hall that eventually led to the central foyer.

"What do you think?" Ryan asked.

"About her or the case?" Jessie countered.

"Let's stick to the case," he replied. "We can save our discussion of Vera Przekop for some other time when you want to go back to teaching your profiling seminar at UCLA. She might take up a whole semester on her own."

"Okay then, here's what I think," Jessie said, unable to keep her frustration from bubbling to the surface despite his quip. "We've got a wife who apparently was more interested in saving Booth than killing him, and a house staff that genuinely liked him, even when he had them work long hours and re-cook meals multiple times. The longtime housekeeper just eliminated two suspects for us. No one around here has a clue about anyone from Booth's business life who might be suspicious. And other than heartwarming amusement park stories, we can't get any information on the man's first wife or kids. I'd say we're no closer to catching Lowden Booth's killer than we were when we walked out the front door of this mansion this morning, and that was almost five hours ago."

"At least we get to take in this nice view again," Ryan offered with a wry smile as he opened the front door for her, nodding at the sight of the gleaming city laid out in front of them.

Jessie wasn't amused.

"Right now all I can see is red."

CHAPTER FOURTEEN

Kat was starting to wonder if she was a terrible private eye.

It was already mid-afternoon. Maybe she shouldn't have expected to have found Hank Keene by now, but she figured that she'd be close, at least.

That's what she'd told Violet Sheridan to expect this morning after the scared woman had given her a list of every old haunt she could think of that her common law husband typically frequented. And it's what Kat had reiterated to her a second time before sending her off with Mitch.

It was just dumb luck that Kat's long-distance boyfriend, Riverside County Sheriff's Deputy Mitch Connor, had been in town staying with her the last few days. As a result, he and Reed Coolidge, another deputy friend who'd driven into the city with him, were available to take Violet back to their stomping grounds in the small San Bernardino County mountain town of Lake Arrowhead, just two hours northeast of L.A.

There, Mitch would let her crash in the guest room of his cabin until Kat gave the all-clear. Violet had seemed temporarily comforted by the idea of being escorted to an out-of-the-way spot by two large, armed, law enforcement officers.

But now, half a day later, Kat had no news to share with her. It wasn't for a lack of trying. Within minutes of Violet's departure, Kat headed out too, pursuing possible leads. She left Hannah in the office, explaining that the places she was visiting were potentially dangerous and the people she'd be talking to were dodgy at best. To her surprise, her young intern didn't object. She got that it wasn't safe.

"Besides," Hannah had said sarcastically, "someone's got to stay here to run down the leads the old-fashioned way, on the computer."

So while Hannah checked databases for possible tips on Keene's whereabouts, Kat visited every potential Hank hangout or hideout that Violet had given them. She tried two apartments that were listed as residences of guys he used to run with when he was robbing jewelry and electronic stores, but in both cases the former associates had moved out.

She tried legitimate jobs he'd worked to see if he'd returned in search of a potential paycheck. Her first stop was at a construction company, where the owner said emphatically, "I told that guy never to come back. He kept stealing equipment from job sites."

Next she went to a meat packing plant where the manager informed her that Keene wasn't welcome anymore. "One day he rented a U-Haul trailer, packed it with ice, and walked out of here with four beef carcasses. That cost us thousands of dollars. It was easier to write it off as a loss than hunt him down, but he's not allowed anywhere near here again."

Realizing that she might not have much success pursuing the man through his business endeavors, Kat decided to try the social route and made stops at three different bars that Violet had listed as favorites of Keene's. Since they were all pretty rough and she got the impression that asking around about the man might be looked on with suspicion, she walked in wearing her most casual work clothes—jeans, plaid shirt, leather jacket—and mostly kept a low profile, hoping she might get lucky and catch sight of him. But he never showed.

Only at the third bar, when she was starting to get desperate and felt the afternoon starting to slip away, did she try another tactic. The place, just off Western Avenue in a dingy section of Koreatown, was called Cutter's. The place was a hole. Dilapidated, with chairs that looked like they might break at any minute, thick dust on the tables made visible by the occasional shards of sunlight that peeked through the broken blinds on the windows, and a generally moldy stench, the joint had a total of seven patrons.

After sitting at a small table by the restroom for five minutes and peering through the dim, smoky light to establish that Keene wasn't among them, Kat approached the bartender, a man who easily weighed 350 pounds and had sweat trickling off the ends of his long, thick beard.

"What can I get you?" he asked.

"How about a Bud?" she said.

"Five bucks."

She laid down a twenty as he poured her a glass and plopped it in front of her.

"Keep the change," she muttered.

When he saw the bill, his eyebrows rose slightly.

"I was also hoping you could help me out," she added quietly. "A girlfriend of mine is looking for her old man but can't get hold of him.

She said he comes in here sometimes but she's not feeling great today and asked me to check up on him for her."

"Who is it?" he asked unenthusiastically, as he took the bill.

"Violet Sheridan," she said. "She's looking for Hank—Hank Keene. I guess he just finished serving a few months and stopped by to see her late last week. But now he's not returning her calls."

The man shrugged noncommittally.

"Maybe he's not calling back because she's a pain in his ass," he wheezed.

"Is that what he said?"

"Does that sound like something Hank would say?" he challenged.

Kat leaned in conspiratorially. She had to be careful here but hoped to mask her caution under the cover of familiarity.

"Truthfully, man, I don't know. I've never met the guy. I'm just trying to do a solid for a work friend who's feeling under the weather. But I'm guessing he's not the flowers and chocolates type."

The big guy laughed heartily, sending his beard sweat flying everywhere, including into Kat's beer, which she delicately pushed to the side.

"He's not that," he agreed. "but here's the thing: I don't know what Hank's deal is. I haven't seen that bastard since before he got locked up. Last time he was in here, he threw a guy into the jukebox and broke the damn thing. He promised to pay to fix it. Of course he didn't. Owner said he wasn't allowed through those doors again until he paid up or bought a new one, and even then, I'm not sure that'd be enough. So I don't have the first clue why he's not getting back to Violet. Probably just being his usual mean cuss self."

And with that dried-up lead, Kat returned to the office, where Hannah was having the same level of success. She'd called up every former employer, group home administrator, apartment complex manager, and probation officer she could reach, but none had seen or heard from him.

"I even called up a few of his former associates on the pretense of wanting to reach him for a new job and they didn't know anything," she said.

"Hold on," Kat pressed. "By 'associates,' do you mean fellow former criminals, and by 'job,' do you mean you implied that you were looking to interest him in illegal activity?"

"Yes and yes," Hannah answered with straightforward enthusiasm. "Don't worry, I blocked my number and used a voice modulator. I sounded like a forty-something dude with throat cancer, and no one could trace the calls to me. The point is, of the guys who would actually talk to me, none had a clue where he was or how to reach him. One actually used the phrase 'gone to ground,' which got me thinking."

"You know how nervous I get when you start thinking," Kat teased. In truth, some of their biggest successes in recent weeks had come from her intern's out of the box mindset, although she did sometimes push the envelope in terms of what might be considered acceptable investigative methods. "Go ahead."

"As I've gone through Keene's history," Hannah said, "I've noticed that there are weird gaps."

"What do you mean?" Kat asked, walking over to the computer screen, and looking over her shoulder.

"Look here," Hannah said, "when I started to pick up on it, I put together a spreadsheet. There are long gaps in his employment history, which aren't that odd. I mean, he's a multiple count felon. But the gaps don't always match with when he's in prison. And there are also holes in his housing record, and they don't necessarily match up with his time inside either. Then I checked his military record, and there were strange gaps there too."

"He was in the military?" Kat asked, as a little tingle went up her spine. Something about that seemed relevant.

"Yeah, he was a Marine until he was court-martialed for wrongful distribution of a controlled substance. He spent three years locked up at Fort Leavenworth. I don't understand all the acronyms but before he got busted he was part of something called MARSOC and he was in MSOT, whatever that is. I was just about to look those up."

"You don't need to," Kat said. "MARSOC is Marine Forces Special Operations Command and MSOT is a unit within that command called a Marine Special Operations Team. It's an elite unit that takes on very specific tasks. What was his listed element in the unit?"

"It says that he was a Critical Skills Operator," Hannah said as she scanned the document. "What is that? It sounds bad."

"It sounds bad because it is," Kat said. "It was bad for the people they targeted. It's bad for Violet, and it's bad for us. The casual name for a Critical Skill Operators is Raider. He was a Raider. But that's not what I'm really worried about."

"That's not bad enough?" Hannah asked, looking back at her. "What then?"

"You said there were gaps in his record as a Raider. That makes me wonder what he was doing during the missing time."

"What do *you* think he was doing?"

"We're about to find out," Kat said, pulling out her phone and calling the burner phone that she'd given Violet. The woman picked up before the end of the first ring.

"Kat?"

"Yes," she said. "You're still at the cabin?"

"Yes. Is everything okay? You sound concerned."

"Do you feel secure?" Kat asked, wanting to start positive before pressuring a woman who'd already been through so much. "Everything going okay up there?"

"Yeah," Violet said. "Mitch has been great, other than going on too much about his new fancy new pickup truck the whole drive here. He set up the bedroom for me, showed me where everything is in the kitchen, even gave me his Netflix password. I have his cell and Deputy Coolidge's too, as well as the main and emergency lines for the local sheriff's station. He said to call if I have any concerns, no matter how silly they might seem. But he said I should stick to the house, not go on any walks or anything, just as a precaution."

"That all sounds good," Kat said. "I'm glad you're settling in, Violet. Now I need to ask you a tough question, okay?"

"Okay," the woman said, her voice getting quiet. "Are you mad at me, Kat?"

"No, of course not," she promised. "I just need some information. Do you remember how we took your phone and dumped it, destroyed the SIM card too, just to be safe in case Hank tried to track you?"

"Yeah," Violet said. "That's why you gave me the one I have now. It makes a lot of sense."

"It does," Kat agreed, "especially now that I'm learning about Hank's military history in special forces with the Marines. Were you aware of his time with them, Violet?"

The other end of the line was quiet for several seconds before she finally heard a whispered "uh-huh."

"Why didn't you mention it?" Kat asked, making sure to keep her voice calm and non-accusatory. "I only ask because, with his background, he almost certainly knows how to track GPS signals and if we hadn't destroyed your phone, he might have been able to follow you up to the mountains."

"I guess I wasn't thinking clearly," Violet admitted, her voice shaking slightly. "I'm really sorry."

"That's okay, but that's why it's important that you be honest with me now," Kat told her. "Our research shows that Hank was separated from his unit for several stretches while on active duty. That's pretty unusual. Do you know why that was?"

Again, the other end of the line was quiet.

"I need you to be straight with me, Violet."

The woman sighed heavily.

"I think I do know why but I'm scared to say."

"Why?" Kat asked.

"Because I knew this earlier and I didn't tell you. I was worried that you wouldn't take the case if you knew and now I'm worried you'll be angry and drop me as a client."

"I'm not going to do that," Kat promised, "but I have an eighteen-year-old kid working for me here, Violet. I need to know what I'm dealing with."

"Okay," she said, "one time a few years ago, Hank got really drunk and he told about how he got pulled from his unit and trained for this special assignment. I think he called it wet work. He said they told him he had a 'unique aptitude' for it. Then they would remove him from the team from time to time to do special jobs. He didn't come right out and say it, but he implied that those jobs were secret murders assigned to him by the government."

Hannah looked up with horror in her eyes. Kat held her finger to her lips to keep her quiet. Violet kept going.

"Anyway, he told me that if he ever wanted to, he could kill me and never get caught, that he would just disappear afterwards. He asked me, almost like a joke, if I could even be sure that Hank Keene was his real name. Then he passed out. The next morning, he seemed to have forgotten that he'd said any of it and he never mentioned it again. I definitely didn't say a word about it. But I couldn't forget. And now I can't help but wonder if he's going to do what he talked about that night."

Now it was Kat and Hannah's turn to stay silent.

"Are you still there?" Violet asked.

"Yeah, of course," Kat said, snapping out of it. "Thank you for telling me. This is good. Better to know what we're up against. It doesn't change anything. We'll still find out where he is, see if we can get him arrested, or at the very least get you a head start out of the state.

Just stay out of sight, watch some movies, and we'll be in touch, okay?"

"Okay," Violet said, "and sorry again for not coming clean right away. This is why I was hoping to get the fake ID, because I was worried he'd track me down."

"We can't do that for you," Kat said, "and to be honest, even if we could, I doubt we'd be able to secure anything good enough to outsmart him. But we'll find some other way to get you to safety. Trust me."

"I *do* trust you, Kat," Violet said. "I'm just scared of what he might do, you know?"

"I know, but try not to worry about it," Kat told her with a tone of optimism she didn't feel. "You're in good hands."

After they hung up, Hannah called her on it.

"It's way worse than you let on, isn't it?"

Kat nodded.

"If what Hank told her wasn't just drunken grandstanding, then yes. If he was doing wet work, that means he was engaging in covert assassinations, maybe of foreign government officials, probably at the behest of intelligence agencies. That's high level stuff. Even if he's been reduced to popping in and out of prison for low level jewelry heists, that skillset likely hasn't completely atrophied. And if it's paired with a thirst for vengeance toward a woman he feels strongly about, it could be a dangerous combination."

"Are you sure you're not giving him too much credit?" Hannah asked.

"Maybe," Kat conceded. "It's possible the guy is passed out drunk on some dirty mattress in an hourly motel somewhere, completely oblivious to what Violet's doing, but the question is: do we want to operate based on that assumption?"

"That's a hard no," Hannah told her.

"Agreed. So, until the case is resolved, I don't trust that this place is safe," Kat said. "Keene might have tracked Violet's phone here. He might even be watching this building. We need to leave now."

"But won't he just follow us wherever we go?" Hannah wondered.

"Hopefully not," Kat said. "Those GPS signals aren't that specific. Typically they only show the building where the phone is, sometimes just the city block, so he wouldn't know which office she went into. And I'm guessing he doesn't have access to her call log either."

"What makes you say that?" Hannah asked.

"Because if he did have it, he'd know that she called Gentry Investigations," Kat said. "Then he'd know who I was, and based on what we now know about him and his military background, he'd have grabbed me up some time earlier today to torture me into saying where she was. All the same, we're taking my secret, emergency exit out of here."

"We have one of those?" Hannah asked, impressed despite the situation. "That's so cool."

"Stay focused, kiddo. It'll be a hell of a lot cooler when we're talking about it in the past tense."

CHAPTER FIFTEEN

"I can tell that you have good news." Jessie said.

"How?" Jamil asked, startled.

She wondered if she should give away her trade secrets. But that would mean telling him that she'd noticed that he wasn't as hunched over as usual when she and Ryan walked into the research office, or that he had actually spun around in his chair to face them rather than keep his back to them, or that he had the slightest hint of a smile at the corners of his mouth.

"Proprietary profiler secrets," she told him. "What's the word?"

"First the bad news," Jamil said.

"I wouldn't expect anything less," Jessie said. Whether Jamil was struggling emotionally or in a good place, one thing she knew she could always count on from him was that he never sugar-coated anything.

"We still haven't been able to access possible prenup terms with the current wife," he said. "As far as the original family goes, we haven't uncovered much of anything useful at all. No divorce terms with the first wife, Gwendolyn, and very little on the children. Like I told you before, the lawyers that set up the legal agreements between Lowden and Gwendolyn were paid big bucks for a reason. It's like they created a black hole of documents. But I haven't exhausted all my options yet. I'll keep you posted."

"Thanks for keeping our expectations in check," Ryan said, mildly amused despite his disappointment. "So what's the good news?"

"You go first," Jamil said to Beth.

The junior researcher smiled, stood up, and walked over to a reversible whiteboard in the corner with a series of calculations on it that Jessie couldn't begin to understand.

"This morning we managed to reduce our list of credible suspects from 141 to 38 and from there down to 26. I'm proud to say that after following up on the statuses of those 26 suspects, we've been able to definitively eliminate another…drumroll please!"

To Jessie's amazement, Jamil actually did a drumroll on his thighs with his palms. Beth flipped the whiteboard over.

"Seven suspects!" she announced. "We're down to 19."

“That’s fantastic,” Ryan said, matching their buoyant mood, no doubt in part to make up for Jessie’s, which had been sour since they left the Booth Estate. She wanted to be excited by this development as well, but deep down she feared that pursuing everyone on the list would be as much of an exercise in frustration as their visit to the mansion had been.

“Thanks,” Beth replied, “we’ve got contact information on most of them but didn’t want to reach out directly without your approval.”

“We’ll dive in now,” Ryan told them, “but first, did you have any luck with Grover Nix and his security crew, the exterior security service, or the designer of the panic room?”

“That was actually the second piece of good news,” Jamil said. “We have results on all those fronts. Grover Nix and his entire team came back clean as a whistle. He had actually submitted full background checks on himself and his people to me before I even started to look into them. I still did my own independent check, but everything was tip top. As to the Hatch Secure crew, the company had a few people with misdemeanors on their records, but Nix appears to have red flagged them himself so that they were never assigned to the Booth Estate. He also had personal psych evaluations conducted for everyone on his team and Hatch Secure before bringing them on. All of those were submitted to us as well and nothing popped.”

“That’s good news,” Ryan said.

Technically Jessie agreed, as it meant they could have confidence in the research they’d been using all day, although it also meant they had to eliminate 19 other suspects.

“Here’s some other news,” Beth offered, “although I don’t know if it’s good or bad. We got the warrant for Booth’s safe. The report says there was no attempt to open it forcibly. When the locksmith opened it, everything listed in the insurance record was still inside, primarily jewelry and cash. Apparently nothing was taken.”

“So no actual robbery,” Ryan noted. You’re right. In terms of advancing the case, I don’t know if that’s good news or bad news either.”

“What about the panic room itself?” Jessie asked. “Any luck contacting the designer?”

“Some,” Jamil said. “His name is Buckley Taverner. I spoke to his assistant here in L.A. Apparently he’s been out of the country, helping set up a security system for a client in Fiji. He’s currently on his way back via his private plane and will be available to talk tomorrow. Hopefully that's soon enough?"

"I guess it'll have to be," she replied. "Good work, both of you."

"Agreed," Ryan said. "I know there's a lot left to do, including calling on those remaining 19 suspects you whittled the list down to. I hope to help with that as soon as I can. But first, I have to do a spot check. I've been largely neglecting my duties as station captain for hours now. I have to check in on the case Valentine and Goodwin are working, see how Bray's court testimony went, update Chief Decker on this case, and attend to a bunch of other boring stuff. It might be a while."

"Enough with your excuses," Jessie said, waving him off, "we know you just want to avoid the tough stuff. You're not fooling anyone."

Ryan flashed her a smile that most bosses wouldn't give their employee before he ducked out of the room. Jessie was about to take a seat and start making calls when she reconsidered.

"Hey, Jamil, do you have moment?" she asked, motioning for him to join her in the hall.

He nodded and got up tentatively, giving Beth a hesitant glance before following her out.

"What's up?" he asked once they were out of eavesdropping distance.

"I've been so crazed all day," she said quietly. "I didn't know if you got a chance to check out that email Dr. Lemmon had me send to you about the survivor's guilt group counseling session she recommended that you, Hannah, and I join."

"I did," he said, his tone and expression indecipherable, in part because he was staring intently at the floor.

"Any thoughts?" she asked.

He looked up at her and she was surprised to see that he was almost smiling.

"I've decided that I'm going to go," he said. "I think it might really help me get out of my head to hear other people's stories, to know that I'm not the only who gets torn up like this. Are you going to go? Is Hannah?"

There was a plaintive color to his query that caused a tiny, unexpected fissure in Jessie's heart.

"I haven't had a chance to talk to Hannah about it yet," she said, deflecting his question about herself, "but I plan to tonight. I'll let you know. But I'm really proud of you for being willing to open yourself up like this, Jamil. It's a big step."

"Thank you," he said, his eyes back on the ground again.

"Shall we end this awkward moment and get back to work?" she asked.

"Yes, please," he said quickly.

"Okay then, lead the way."

He hurried back into the research office, and she followed close behind. Jessie didn't mention to him her own doubts that she'd hear any stories like her own, unless there happened to be someone else in the survivor's group who'd also used a person's teenage assault as a way to get the emotional upper hand over them.

She knew intellectually that what Dr. Lemmon had told her repeatedly was true: that the person she'd manipulated wasn't a fourteen-year-old girl who'd been raped by her uncle. It was Andrea Robinson, the adult woman that girl became, who kidnapped Jessie and threatened her life, the lives of her loved ones, and thousands of other innocent Angelenos.

Jessie had used whatever tools were at her disposal to survive the situation, including trickery and emotional manipulation. But that didn't make her feel any less ashamed when she closed her eyes and thought about who Andy had been before she gave in to the darkness.

Jessie blinked hard and ordered herself to set those thoughts aside and focus on the task at hand. Within minutes she had completed her first call, crossing one of the remaining 19 suspects off the list. She moved on to the next, with an equal lack of success. Out of the first four names on the list, three had alibis that could be verified while she was on the phone with them, and one required simply checking some security camera footage to confirm his claim that he was at Disneyland and had been since 7:00 a.m. that morning.

When Beth tapped her on the shoulder to say that she and Jamil were heading out to get a bite, she looked at the clock on the wall and couldn't believe how much time had passed. It was after 6:00 p.m. She'd been at this for close to three hours. Among the three of them, they'd eliminated eight more suspects, bring the possible options down to eleven total. But in her estimation they hadn't come close finding one that she thought she could elevate to "interview in person" worthy.

"Captain Hernandez must have had a lot of boring stuff to attend to," she noted to the researchers, "because unless I missed it, he never came back to help us."

Neither Jamil nor Beth was willing to respond to that, nor could she blame them.

"I'm going to find him, update him, and call it a night, guys," she said. "I suggest you do the same. Make that bite a full-on dinner. You guys deserve it."

She left them to decide how to proceed as she walked down the hall toward Ryan's office. As she passed through the bullpen, she noticed that she'd missed a voicemail from Kat that had come in about 20 minutes ago when she was on the phone with one of the leads that ended up being a dead end.

She played it back as she moved through the maze of bullpen desks, divided by waist high partitions that gave the barest illusion of privacy. As she listened, she picked up the pace. By the time the message was complete, she had broken into a run.

Ryan's door was closed, but she didn't even bother to knock before she barreled in.

CHAPTER SIXTEEN

"So let me see if I've got this right—" Jessie said, doing her best to keep level-headed.

"I thought we explained it pretty clearly," Hannah interrupted, apparently unable to hide her irritation.

Jessie looked at her younger sister across the breakfast table in the house they shared with Ryan, who was seated next to her. Kat was in the other chair. That's where she and Hannah had been waiting when Jessie and Ryan got home from work.

"Forgive me if I'm having a little trouble processing all this," Jessie said, trying to keep the acidity out of her voice. "But you've known for a couple of hours that you might have inadvertently taken on a case involving a former special forces assassin. I've only been dealing with it for a few minutes."

"It's a lot, Hannah," Kat said, playing the voice of reason. "I'm still wrapping my head around it. Give them some time."

"Did you notice anything when you were leaving the building or coming back here?" Ryan asked flatly.

Jessie had been nursing a simmering resentment toward her husband all day because he'd kept Zoe Bradway's threats from her for so long. But right now she appreciated how efficiently he defused the sisterly tension by simply redirecting the conversation to the essentials of the situation: status and safety.

"No," Kat said. "We took a hidden exit out of the building. I paid a TaskRabbit to drive my car out of the garage and we trailed him in a rideshare to the Dodger Stadium parking lot, which was open for a swap meet. As far as I could tell, no one followed him. I checked the car for trackers, then drove around the stadium multiple times and through nearby neighborhoods and didn't notice a tail. We took an hour getting back here, using all manner of double backs. I went the wrong way down one-way roads. I got on and off the freeway suddenly. I'm fairly positive that he didn't follow us here."

"How do you know he didn't already have the address?" Jessie asked, pointing at Hannah. "Through her."

“She’s not listed as an employee of the detective agency,” Kat said. “There’s no formal record of her working for me, per your extremely specific instructions before agreeing to let her intern. And she never left the office today, so Keene wouldn’t have known she had any affiliation with me. He might know that I know you, but why would he come here instead of sitting on my place?”

“Maybe he figured you’d come here to enlist our help once you found out what you were up against?” Jessie suggested.

“Possible,” Kat conceded, “but in that case, I’ll make the same point I did with Hannah earlier. Let’s assume the worst: that Hank Keene was serious about killing Violet if she wasn’t more compliant the next time he came looking for her. So he comes looking and sees that she’s bailed from her place in a hurry. Now he’s really pissed and ready to do it. Plus, he still has the skills he’s been taught and tracks her phone before we destroy it, so he knows she’s come to my building. All that seems conceivable, right?”

“Very,” Ryan said.

“But let’s up the ante,” Kat continued. “He manages to access her phone data and sees that she called me, so he knows we’ve been in touch, and he knows that her phone went dead soon thereafter, which he can assume means she hired me and I’m helping hide her. Now what do you think a guy like this does next?”

She didn’t wait for suggestions.

“He’s forty-four years old and he’s been sent to prison four different times, five if you count Leavenworth, for a total of eleven years, once for selling drugs, twice for robbery, and twice for assault. Is he the kind of guy who would wait patiently for me to lead him to the woman who ‘wronged’ him? Or is he the kind of guy who would snag me while I was walking into one of those three bars today, throw me in a trunk, take me to some warehouse, and use the techniques he’d learned to find out where she was? I think we all know the answer. If he knew who I was, if he was following us, I wouldn’t be here right now, talking to you.”

“So where do you think he is?” Jessie asked. She had to concede that she was nowhere near the expert that Kat was in matters like this. And yet, she didn’t share her friend’s confidence that the guy wasn’t parked across the street right now.

“Three options: one, he’s still sitting outside that building, waiting for Violet to come out. Two, we got lucky and destroyed the phone before he figured out where she went and he’s doing what I did today, beating the bushes around her old haunts, trying to get some intel on where she went. Or three, we're way overestimating him and he's out partying with his boys somewhere, completely unaware that Violet is even gone yet."

"Okay," Jessie said, "two and three I can live with, but what do we do if it's number one?"

"I was going to suggest we work from here tomorrow," Hannah interjected.

"What?" Jessie and Kat asked at the same time.

"We obviously can't just drop the case," Hannah explained. "Whether it's right now or in a week, Hank Keene is going to come for Violet, so we need to find out where he is so we can get her to safety. Plus we have $30,000 of her money. That means we keep looking for him. If we can't do that at Kat's office, then what better place than right here? Jessie, with all the security you've put into it, this house is a fortress. Not even a Marine Raider could get in here, especially if we're prepared for him, and definitely not if one of us used to be a badass Army Ranger."

The rest of them considered the idea for a moment. Ryan was the first to respond.

"It's not a bad suggestion," he said. "We could keep a roving patrol in the neighborhood going throughout the night and into tomorrow. I could also order a BOLO for Keene centered in the area around your building, Kat. If he's loitering nearby, we'll pick him up. What do you think?"

"Works for me," Kat said.

Jessie couldn't think of a reason to object. She could try to insist that Hannah drop the case on safety grounds, but her sister was an adult and could—and probably would—say no. Besides, there didn't seem to be any point to such a request anyway. And frankly, the idea of having Hannah in this house, with all its security, with Kat right here next to her and cops circling the neighborhood, was about the best she could hope for.

"I guess so," she said, though she still felt unsettled, as if everyone was in constant danger.

***

It was only later that night when she figured out where the unsettled feeling came from.

She forgot about it for a little while, when she was busy setting up Kat in the guest room, and later when she told Hannah about the survivor's guilt group session. Her sister was more circumspect than Jamil had been but agreed to think about going, which was more than she'd expected.

It was after all those boxes had been checked, when it was just her and Ryan in the bedroom, that it clicked for her. She tried to let it lie, knowing that nothing productive could come from bringing it up just before bed, after the day they'd had. She sat on the chair in the corner of the bedroom, rubbing her temples, trying to soothe herself, but in the end she couldn't stop herself. She was about to speak but Ryan, lying in bed, beat her to it.

"Do you have a headache?" he asked.

"What?"

"You're rubbing your temples," he noted, concern in his voice. "I just wondered if you felt a migraine coming on."

"I haven't had a migraine in weeks. Just because I touch my head doesn't mean it's concussion-related," she said sharply. "This helps me de-stress. Please don't jump to conclusions."

"I'm sorry," he said, clearly hurt. "Can't I worry about you?"

"Can't I just have a rough day without it being a medical emergency?"

He didn't respond to that. He didn't need to. She went on anyway.

"You know the sort of danger Hannah and Kat potentially faced today is exactly the kind of threat all three of you might be dealing with because of Zoe."

"What?" he said, confused.

"I haven't forgotten this morning, Ryan," she chided, her voice somewhere between a whisper and a yell. "You kept Zoe Bradway's threat to kill the three of you from me for *months* because you were worried about how I might react and because you didn't think she could deliver on it. But guess what? She doesn't have to do the deed herself. Turns out there are assassins out there, like Hank Keene. What if Zoe hires one of them who is less of a screw-up than he is? What's to stop her from doing that? She's got access to Andy Robinson's money. Hell, maybe she already did it and that killer's out there right now plotting how to take you out, or Kat, or Hannah, Maybe all three of you."

"I get that you're upset with me, and you have every right to be but—"

She cut him off.

"If you had told me when she made the very first threat back in that movie theater two months ago, maybe we could have placed an informant or an undercover officer in Zoe's wing of the psychiatric detention center. By now, they could have won her trust and we'd have some intel on how she plans to put the other half of Operation Z into effect. But even if we start that process tomorrow, it'll take weeks or months to get close to her. And based on the call I got from Zoe, whatever she's planning is much more imminent."

Ryan sighed.

"Look, I'm sorry," he said. "I guess I just didn't take her seriously. I'm still not a hundred percent sure that she's not just trying to mess with your head. But we've taken precautions. We started tracking all her visitors after she called you. Other than lawyers and psychiatrists, she's had none, by the way. We put alerts on her bank accounts and every one of Andy's that we're aware of, even those that were closed, looking for unusual activity. There hasn't been any. We're working on getting authorization to listen to her phone calls. That's been slow going because Western Regional Women's PDC has raised objections, as they always do, but we should have a warrant no later than next week, maybe even later this week. We're doing things."

Jessie shook her head in frustration.

"Too little, and much too late," she said.

"Jessie, we have to find a way to get past this," he pleaded.

She looked at him and felt sympathy for his plight, but not enough to get over her anger at his deception. There was nothing he could say that was going to make this better right now.

"Yes, we have to get past this," she agreed, "but it's not happening tonight."

CHAPTER SEVENTEEN

Zoe Bradway was starting to get nervous.

Visitor calls weren't allowed at Western Regional Women's Psychiatric Detention Center after 10:00 p.m. and it was already 9:49. This was cutting it very close.

She sat on the couch in the "social room," pretending to watch the television mounted to the wall. But her brown eyes, hidden behind her short dark hair, were actually fixed on the clock on the wall next to the TV. She was hoping to hear her name announced, ready to pop up the moment it was.

At just a shade over five feet tall and barely a wisp over a hundred pounds, she hardly took up any space next to the other patient inmates on the couch beside her, especially in her current position, curled up in a tight ball, hugging herself. She silently reminded herself not to get too agitated, not to pick at her hangnails and make them bleed or do anything else that would draw unwanted attention from the staff or a fellow inmate.

Then, finally, at 9:52, an orderly called out, "Bradway, you've got a call. Better make it quick."

She was up and hurrying to the phone room before he'd even finished the sentence. She knew this was likely the last chance she'd be able to talk freely. After her call to Jessie two weeks ago, the authorities would have begun the process of trying to get a warrant to listen to her calls.

Western Regional PDC would have fought it, as they invariably did. Sometimes they won. Even when they lost they could usually delay the process by a month. But they'd never failed to make the government jump through all the legal hoops, which meant two weeks minimum. That would be tomorrow. So tonight, she could talk without fear of being recorded, though she'd still be careful just in case.

"This is Zoe," she said after picking up the phone.

"We're a go," replied the emotionless voice on the other end of the line. "It should happen tomorrow."

"Are you sure?" Zoe asked. "No hiccups?"

“I can’t make any guarantees obviously,” the caller replied, “but they’re clueless. They have no idea that I know exactly where the bait is, dangling, unaware of its fate. Frankly, I could have gotten the job done today if I wanted to, but I know that’s not how you want this to play out. So I let my trigger finger itch.”

“Good,” Zoe hissed into the phone, “remember, this has to be done the right way if you want full payment. Portion two only comes after I see video evidence on the news, Ash.”

“Don’t call me by that name,” Ash hissed in return. “And don’t question my ability to get the job done. Underestimating me is a mistake that I’m all too used to by now. Why do you think I cultivate this perception? It’s so that I seem like I’m not a real threat, but that misperception makes it easier for me to strike. You hired me for a reason. Remember, I facilitated coups while in the military. I performed covert assassinations for the CIA. I did similar work as a private contractor. I come with impeccable references. I’m the best. I just hide it under ‘normie’ camouflage so that no one would ever think that someone with my personal reputation could also be a contract killer. I’m like Clark Kent.”

“I’d hardly compare you to Clark Kent,” Zoe said.

“You get the point,” Ash said. “Anyway, I’ve got to go. I don’t want to make the same mistake other people do and underestimate *your* friends. There’s always a chance they could do some extra digging and figure out what’s really going on, so I need to play it cool and keep a low profile. After all, you never know when law enforcement might sneak up on you unexpectedly.”

“When will I know if it’s done?” Zoe asked.

“Keep an eye on tomorrow’s local evening news,” Ash said. “I have a feeling it won’t be boring.”

CHAPTER EIGHTEEN

They didn't talk about how they'd left things the night before as they got ready the next morning.

Jessie was still quietly seething about Ryan's decision to prioritize her "mental well-being" over full disclosure of the risks facing her loved ones. Seeing all of the people who had been threatened by Zoe sitting around the breakfast table together didn't help her move past the issue.

But she said nothing. There was no point in rehashing the topic again when they couldn't do anything to resolve it at the moment. Plus, they had a major case to solve and sniping at each other all day wasn't going to be conducive to the process. That was especially true after seeing the morning news, where Lowden Booth's death was splashed everywhere, not just locally but on the national newscasts as well.

"Anson Greco was right," Ryan said after they finished watching one report. "The stock has already started tanking for the day. This could open up a whole new collection of suspects—people who were just as interested in harming the company as the man."

"I don't know," Jessie countered. "The way his head was smashed against the side of that safe sure made it seem like there was a personal component to the killing. If this was a plan to tank the company's stock, it's an awfully convoluted one."

"How long before the feds start to butt in?" Kat asked. "With the kind of questions that you're asking, is this still an HSS case for much longer or is the FBI going to try to take it over?"

"That's a good question," Ryan noted.

"And a good reason for us to get moving. We should head out to the station," Jessie said, before turning to Hannah and Kat. "Are you guys good here?"

"We're all set," Kat assured her. "I talked to Mitch this morning. Violet had a good night's sleep at the cabin. She seems to be in decent spirits this morning. He and Reed Coolidge are going to alternate checking on her throughout the day. Meanwhile, Hannah has been reacquainting me with some of the security measures you have in the house. I remembered that you guys had your own panic room, but I'd forgotten about the bulletproof doors and windows and the sleeping gas feature you can activate from the alarm panel."

"That's not the half of it," Hannah noted.

"We can review the rest later," Kat said. "Anyway, with all that and the boys in blue patrolling outside, we should be good. And don't forget that there's also me, the human security system."

***

They were halfway to the office when Jessie finally managed to shake off her apprehension that Hannah and Kat were going to play show and tell with the weapons locker. Just as she was getting comfortable, they got the call from Jamil.

"Can you tell if I have good news or bad news?" he asked.

Even though Jessie couldn't see his body language, the very fact that he was willing to be playful enough to ask that question gave him away.

"Well, Jamil," she said, "I'm pretty sure it's good news, but since you're constitutionally incapable of sharing purely good news without a dose of cold hard reality, I'm going to guess—both."

"Damn, she's good!" Beth said on speaker in the background.

"That's right," Jamil told them, sounding mildly disappointed. "Unfortunately, I'm still waiting to hear back from Buckley Taverner, the panic room designer. His assistant won't give me any more updates on his arrival time or when he'll call, which I guess is on brand for a security consultant type, but it is frustrating."

"Now tell them the good news," Beth whispered.

"Right," Jamil said, the enthusiasm returning to his voice. "We got a break on the Booth family front. I've been beating my head against the wall trying to find ways to outsmart Lowden Booth's lawyers without success. But then I had a thought. His son, Ethan Booth, is legally an adult now. He's actually twenty-two years old. What if he wasn't always as careful about how he handles his business as his father? Turns out he wasn't."

"Maybe you should ask them where they are, Jamil," Beth suggested.

"Why?" he said, confused.

"Because after you give them the next bit of info, they're probably not going to want to come here."

"Um, guys," Ryan said, "sorry to interrupt, but should I pull over? We're on our way to the station at the moment but if we should plug in a new destination, maybe let us know."

"Sorry, yes, pull over," Jamil said excitedly. "I'm texting you an address in West Hollywood right now. As it turns out, Ethan founded a music label called Eeyore vs. Tigger Records. His lawyers tried to keep his name out of the legal papers and mostly did, except on one document signing a lease for rental space under the company name EVTR. Upon further examination, I found that last year, EVTR sued a company called Notterb 143, whose business address is in the same building as the headquarters of BoothCo Biomeds. Notterb 143 just happens to be 341 Bretton spelled backwards. Lowden Booth grew up on 341 Bretton Street. When I investigated, I found that Notterb 143 looks like it's one of his shell companies."

"Wow," Jessie marveled. "That's incredible, Jamil."

"Here's the key thing," he replied, ignoring the compliment. "The lawsuit is actually quite technical, but once you dig into it, one thing becomes pretty clear in between all the legal mumbo-jumbo: Ethan did *not* like his father very much."

"Really?" Ryan said. "Can you tell how long that's been going on?"

"Not really," Jamil admitted.

"Actually," Beth piped in, "based on the multiple passing references in the suit to the 'chicken fried steak lady,' I'd say it was from right about the time that Lowden met Devon."

Jessie turned to Ryan.

"I think it's time that we pay Ethan a visit and see if we can't pick at that scab a little."

CHAPTER NINETEEN

"This is a waste of time," Hannah said, unable to hide her frustration.

"You've got to be kidding," Kat replied, sounding mildly amused. "We've been at it for less than an hour."

Hannah knew she sounded like an eighteen-year-old kid who was restless and bored, but she couldn't help it. Even after this short a time at the breakfast room table, the writing was already on the wall.

"Yeah, but we're just going over the same old leads as before," she said. "You checked out every place Violet gave you yesterday, suggesting where we should look for Hank. We've reviewed all the other prior addresses, jobs, and known associates that we could find on our own and came up empty. Most of those were so outdated that it feels like it was pointless to even try."

"It's never pointless to try," Kat reminded her.

"What if I have a different idea, something out of the box?"

"I'm not sure I like the sound of that," Kat said carefully.

"What happened to 'it's never pointless to try?'"

Kat reluctantly smiled at her.

"Lay it on me."

"Okay," Hannah said, turning her laptop so they both could see it, "something about these gaps in Keene's military record feels off to me."

"How so?"

"The fact that we can access it at all," Hannah said. "I mean, I knew my way around a database even before hooking up with you, and between what you've taught me and a few tricks I learned from Mr. Jamil Genius in HSS research, I know how to search in nooks and crannies, but should we really be able to access the fact that Keene had gaps in his service record at all? Isn't that the sort of thing the military and CIA powers that be would want kept hidden?"

"What are you suggesting," Kat asked, "that someone *wanted* us to access his file, with the service gaps unredacted?"

Hannah shrugged.

"It occurred to me. But if so, who? I'm thinking…could it actually be Keene himself?"

"It's possible," Kat said. "If he really is still in the game, then he'd surely know about my military history. He'd know I'd be able to understand what the gaps meant. The glass half-full interpretation is that this might be his way of letting us know what he's capable of, warning us off."

"You think Hank Keene is the kind of guy who would go to these lengths to warn us off getting further involved?" Hannah asked dubiously.

"No, I don't," Kat said. "It's just as possible that it's a challenge, a way of telling me that I have no chance and taunting me, getting me to make a mistake that will lead to revealing where Violet is. That's the glass half-empty interpretation."

"Or maybe he just wants to scare the hell out of us," Hannah offered. "Because if that's his plan, it's working, which is where my idea comes in."

"I'm listening."

"You were an Army Ranger," she said. "I'm sure you still have contacts of your own with high level security access. Can you call one of them and ask them to look at Keene's file? If he's somehow manipulated what we're able to see in a publicly accessible database, don't you want to get a look at the complete record? Maybe that'll help get us some answers."

Kat looked to be considering the idea when her cell phone rang. Hannah jumped involuntarily before turning red in embarrassment.

"It's just Mitch," Kat said. "It's his second call this morning. I guess distance really does make the heart grow fonder."

"Gross," Hannah muttered.

"Hey babe," Kat said giddily after picking up, "I already got your early morning report. To what do I owe the pleasure of a second call before noon? Just wanted to hear my voice?"

The call wasn't on speaker, but Hannah could hear Mitch's words clearly.

"Kat—Violet is missing. Reed is dead. You should get up here now."

CHAPTER TWENTY

Jessie knew they were taking a calculated risk.

They could have gone to the offices of Ethan Booth's music label, Eeyore vs. Tigger Records, but she doubted he'd be there. Whether he loved or hated his father, he was unlikely to spend the day after the man's death working out those emotions in an office surrounded by people who would be pretending to offer support but probably secretly taking video of him to send to TMZ.

No, he'd want to be home. And for Ethan, home was a secluded, highly secure West Hollywood high-rise condo complex overlooking the Sunset Strip. They were met by the doorman, went through the metal detector, and signed in at the reception desk where they were greeted by an armed security guard.

"We need to speak with Mr. Booth," Ryan explained to him, "and we need our visit to be unannounced."

After the guard complied, they took the elevator up, along with a couple that had clearly just come from the gym. Both were in their late twenties. The guy, deeply tanned with long, golden locks, was wearing a turquoise tank top and bike shorts. He was about five-foot-five and looked like he was in training for the Mr. Universe competition, with muscles bulging everywhere. He was sweating profusely.

His hand rested on the hip of his girlfriend, who made six-foot-tall former volleyball star Beth Ryerson look short. She was even blonder than her boyfriend, but had pale skin, and icy blue eyes that matched her yoga outfit. She wasn't sweating at all and seemed not to love that any part of her guy's perspiring body was touching her own.

When they got off the elevator, Jessie and Ryan managed to wait until the doors closed before breaking into a shared giggling fit.

"I can forgive you for a lot of things," Jessie told him, "but if you ever come home wearing a tank top like that, I'm filing for divorce."

"So the hair's okay then?" he asked, unable to stop laughing. "You're cool if I dye my hair blonde, grow it long, and get a perm?"

"Oh yeah, that was totally sexy. It was just the shirt that bothered me."

"Noted," he said as the doors opened.

They took a moment to gather themselves as they stepped into the hall. It felt good not to be mad at Ryan, even if only for a few minutes. Watching him try to shove down his adorable smile and plaster on a professional expression reminded her that no matter how frustrated she got with him, he was almost always acting from a place of love. They would always find their way back to each other. She just wasn't sure how.

They reached Ethan Booth's door and Ryan rang the bell as he held out his badge in front of the peephole for the young man to see. A voice on the intercom system beside the door responded, "not interested."

Jessie looked up and noticed a small camera embedded in the ceiling above the door and indicated that Ryan should point his badge there. Then she replied.

"Mr. Booth, if you could direct your attention to whichever of your screens shows you the hallway, you'll see that we're not solicitors, reporters, or employees pretending to care. We're with the LAPD and we need to speak with you, whether you're interested or not. Please open the door."

It took half a minute, but the door eventually buzzed open. They stepped inside and saw that Ethan Booth had opened it remotely because he was sprawled out on a sofa fifty feet away, across the expansive living room. Ryan closed the door as Jessie took in the place.

The condo was massive but stunningly sterile. Painted all white, with exclusively black and gray furniture, it looked like something out of a futuristic film in which color had been outlawed from society. Floor to ceiling windows in the living room behind Booth's sofa offered an expansive view of the entire city. The terrace appeared to have a hot tub and a fire pit.

They walked over to Booth, who was wearing sweatpants and a t-shirt for his record label under a ratty, olive-green bathrobe. His brown hair was shooting in all directions, and he hadn't shaved. He was bleary-eyed as if he hadn't slept much, but his eyes weren't puffy or red, suggesting that he hadn't done much crying recently.

He looked shockingly like the file photos Jessie had seen of Lowden back when he and Anson Greco had first been developing their ideas in college. Jessie couldn't help but notice that he also generally matched the height and build of the intruder in the video from the Booth Estate.

"How did you even find me?" Booth asked in a languorous tone that immediately told her that he was high. "This place was supposed to be, like, off the grid. My name's not connected to it. Not even my staff knows where I live."

"Well, we're not your staff, Ethan," she told him, using his first name to establish that they wouldn't be letting his wealth or family connections determine how this interview went. "We're the Homicide Special Section of the Los Angeles Police Department. We have resources. We used them to locate you and we intend to use them to determine what happened to your father. We'd like your assistance with that."

Ethan shifted position on the sofa to get slightly more upright.

"If you're so good," he said caustically, despite the supposedly mellow drug in his system, "then you should know that me and my dad haven't talked in months. Hell, I haven't seen him in person in like, two years, so I'm not exactly the best person to give you special insight into what was going on in his life."

"Yeah," Ryan said, stepping into the young man's personal space, "we understand that you and your dad had a real falling out after he started getting close with the—what was she called, Jessie?"

"The chicken fried steak lady," Jessie offered.

"That was it," Ryan agreed.

Ethan scrambled to his feet angrily, though in his robe he was a bit clumsy as he tried to avoid tripping over the glass coffee table in front of him. Once he was upright and face-to-face with Ryan, he put his finger on the police captain's chest.

"You don't know, man," he said. "You make cracks, but it's not as simple as him marrying some shiny, happy bimbo. Don't pretend to know my life."

"Can you please stop poking your finger in my chest, Ethan?" Ryan said softly. "Technically, I could take you downtown for assault just for that, but we only want to have a conversation. So maybe you could sit back down and answer our questions in a calm and thoughtful manner."

Ethan left his finger where it was for a second, then thought better of it, and put his hand at his side. In that moment, Jessie's phone rang, and she quietly cursed herself for not putting it on silent. She did so now.

"Here's what I'm gonna do," Ethan said, sidestepping Ryan and walking toward the kitchen. "I'm gonna make myself a sandwich because I'm hungry. Then I'm going to take a nap. You can submit your questions in writing to my attorney. And if I'm interested, maybe I'll answer them."

Jessie saw Ryan's nostrils start to flare and put her hand on his forearm to calm him. She gave him her best silent "let me try" look. He nodded.

"I'm not sure that plan works so great for us, Ethan," she said soothingly as she began to follow him. "Maybe we can find a compromise—."

"I'm not interested in any compromises!" he shouted, spinning around unexpectedly. As he turned, his shoulder clipped Jessie, slamming her backward.

She lost her balance and tumbled in reverse. She saw Ryan reach out for her, but her arm slipped through his grasp. She felt her back smash into the glass coffee table and she threw her elbows out to break her fall as she stretched her neck forward so that her head wouldn't take the brunt of any imminent collision.

Luckily, when she landed, the back of her head and her shoulders hit the cushion of the sofa that Ethan had just been sitting on before gravity sucked her to the floor. Her head still connected with the cushion hard enough to hurt, but at least there was some give to it. She sat on the floor, mildly stunned, unmoving. The two men were still as well.

"Jessie?" Ryan finally said.

"I think I'm okay," she said slowly. "I don't feel any sharp pain in my back, so I don't think any glass penetrated me. Just give me a second to regroup and we can check."

"You hit your head," he noted. "I saw it snap back."

"Yeah," she conceded. "But it was on a sofa cushion. It doesn't hurt…in that way."

"I'm sorry," Ethan said, standing there forlornly, his olive green robe hanging open. "I didn't see you."

Jessie watched Ryan's nostrils flare again and knew that this time there was nothing she could do to stop him. She didn't even bother trying.

"Ethan Booth," he said, stepping toward the man and twisting his right arm behind his back violently before snapping on the first handcuff, "you are under arrest for assault. And that may just be the tip of the iceberg."

He snapped the other cuff on Booth's left wrist. He was shaking with such fury that Jessie was impressed that he didn't break any of the guy's bones.

***

"We just don't have many details yet," Kat said unsatisfyingly.

Jessie was pretty confident that the confusion she felt wasn't coming from a couch-based-concussion but from a litany of shocking events occurring in quick succession.

First, their interview subject had inadvertently struck her, which was why he was currently in the back seat of their car on the way to Central Station. Other than a dull headache, sore neck, and a few small cuts, she seemed to have escaped largely unscathed.

But once they got in the car and she checked her voicemails, she got a stunner from Kat and immediately called back to learn more.

"All I got from your message was that Violet is gone, taken by Hank Keene, and that Reed Coolidge is dead."

"Actually, I have learned more than that," Kat replied, "but before I get into it, I wanted to make sure you're okay with Hannah coming with me to Lake Arrowhead. We're in the car on the way up there right now."

"Hi, sis," Hannah said over the line.

Jessie was starting to worry that maybe she really was concussed. She looked over at Ryan, who looked equally perplexed.

"Kat, why in the hell would I be okay with you taking my sister to the place where a potential former CIA hitman killed a sheriff's deputy and abducted his former wife? That seems like the last place she should be."

"Maybe I should have led with the other stuff I learned then," Kat said. "Sorry, I'm juggling a lot of balls here. Mitch had video cameras set up at the house. They show Keene abducting Violet and the vehicle he left in. Mitch was able to use other county cameras posted on local highways to track that vehicle and it showed that Keene took California 18 to California 330 before dumping the vehicle right next to the 10 freeway. He's clearly not going back to the cabin so there's no reason to worry about taking Hannah up there. And since that's where I'm going, I figured the safest place for her was with me."

"But if he's not going there, then why are you?" Ryan asked.

"I'm hoping that maybe he left behind something we can track that might tell us where he's headed," Kat said.

"Or maybe Violet was able to leave us a clue before he got to her," Hannah suggested. "Something that Mitch and the Sheriff's Department guys might miss that Kat and I would notice."

"I don't know," Jessie said, "Maybe it's time to call in the FBI on this one."

"Mitch is already doing that," Kat said. "A team from Palm Springs is going to be there this afternoon. But they'll be starting from scratch. We can give them valuable intel to help get them up to speed."

Jessie sighed.

"Where are you now?" she asked.

"Diamond Bar," Hannah said. "At this rate, we should be there in an hour."

"What were you going to do if I said no?"

"I'd drop her off at the next exit and she'd get a rideshare back," Kat said. "But I had faith in you, and I knew you'd have faith in me."

"Keep us updated regularly," Jessie reluctantly relented, "and keep her safe, Kat."

"Always."

CHAPTER TWENTY ONE

Jessie wondered what was taking so long.

She sat in the Central police station observation room, staring through the one-way mirror at Ethan Booth, who sat forlornly in interrogation room three, handcuffed to a metal table, just wearing his t-shirt and sweatpants now that his robe had been removed. He'd been waiting that way for ten minutes as Ryan attended to some cryptic business in his office. She was just about to go light a fire under him when he walked in.

Even before he spoke, she knew the news wasn't going to be good. His shoulders were hunched, and his chin was pressed against his chest, as if he was preparing himself to deal with her inevitable reaction once he revealed what he'd learned. Instead of asking what the problem was, she waited for him to share it on his timetable. He didn't need extra pressure from her.

"I just talked to Chief Decker," he said, when he finally raised his head and made eye contact, "and he gave me an update. It's not great. He said that there's no official word yet, but he's getting informal pressure from the feds to take over the case. Because of the stock market implications for BoothCo Biomeds, they're close to bumping this up from a straight murder case to something that falls under their jurisdiction."

"How long do we have?" Jessie asked.

"They don't want to do anything while the markets are open on the East Coast," Ryan said. "He said they'd probably make an announcement after the end of the business day out here so any time after 5:00 p.m. our time."

"That's only six hours away," Jessie said. "If we don't solve this before then, that's a failure for HSS. With new leadership at the helm—"

"You mean me?" he pointed out.

"And several new detectives," she continued, "we can't afford that."

Ryan looked like he wanted to add something else but stopped himself and nodded.

"We better get in there then," he said, as they left the observation room. "How do you want to play it? You think this guy is capable of killing his own father?"

"I don't know," she replied. "Just because he's high as a kite today doesn't mean he always is. Plus he matches the intruder's build. He knows the mansion. And he resented his dad *and* his dad's wife. I'm not ruling him out."

They entered the interrogation room. Even though it had been a while since they'd done this together, they slipped into their old routine like comfortable shoes. Jessie took the chair opposite Ethan Booth while Ryan stood against the wall behind her, recreating the intense, angry vibe he'd maintained throughout the entire drive from Booth's condo back to the station. The young man stared up at Ryan fearfully before turning his attention to Jessie.

"Listen," he said before being asked anything, "I'm really sorry for banging into you. You have to know that it was an accident. Like I said on the way over here, I had no idea that you were right behind me."

Jessie shrugged.

"I'd like to believe that, Ethan," she said. "Just like I'd like to believe that whatever substances you had in your system when we arrived were legally obtained. And I'd also like for those assault charges against you to be dropped. After all, you're just a young kid starting out in life."

"Right," Ethan agreed emphatically, "I've never been in trouble with the law."

"Then again," Jessie noted. "You are over eighteen and, legally, that means you're an adult and responsible for your actions. Responsibility usually involves prison time. Now I'm not sure how well you'd do in that environment, and I'd like for you to avoid finding out. But for that to happen, I'd need you to prove that you were really and truly remorseful for what you did."

"How?" Ethan pleaded.

"By answering all of our questions honestly and fully, without any attorney mucking up the works. You'll recall that Captain Hernandez read you your rights when he arrested you, but he was too upset by your actions to actually question you. We'd like to do that now. How would you feel about that?"

"I'd be okay with it," Ethan said.

"Let's make it official then," Jessie suggested. "Captain, would you read Ethan his rights again?"

Ryan stepped forward, read them, after which Ethan waived his right to silence and to have his lawyer present.

"Okay," Jessie said, diving in before the guy had a chance to have second thoughts, "we know you've been estranged from your father for a while. Tell us how long and why? Did it start with his marriage to Devon?"

"That didn't help," he said. "But no, it was before her."

"We were told that she tried to smooth things over between him and you kids and your mother," Ryan told him.

"I guess," Ethan conceded. "But it didn't work. Her suggestions were all about buying us off. It actually made things worse. Plus he spent all his time with her, and because she was so plastic, he started acting the same way. It was gross."

"But you said the problems started before then," Jessie reminded him.

"Yeah," Ethan said, sitting up straighter, "the older I got, the more I learned about how he made his money, about BoothCo Biomeds and how corrupt it was. I started to resent the company, how it just mowed down anyone in its way, crushed all opposition: people, other businesses, whole towns. I didn't want to be associated with it, or him. So I just stopped hanging around him very often."

"How did that go over?" Ryan asked.

"Not well," Ethan said with a caustic snort. "He eventually said that if I didn't like him or the company that had provided so much for me, maybe I'd prefer not to have any of the wealth that came with it. He wrote a check to me, handed it over, and said I should deposit it because it was the last money I'd ever get from him. He was cutting me out of the will."

Jessie made sure not to visibly react to his words, hoping not to give the young man any indication that he'd just admitted to a giant motive for murder. But he seemed oblivious to the revelation, continuing on as if what he'd just said was no big deal.

"I wasn't a minor," he told them, "so it wasn't complicated like my sister's trust. He just did it. I had no recourse. He was very matter of fact about it, cold even. I imagine that's what he's like with his competitors. Anyway, I said that was fine. That was the last time we saw each other in person, two years ago."

"So after two years of being cut off," Ryan pressed suddenly, "maybe you decided to get what was yours and went for the safe in your dad's panic room."

"What panic room?" Ethan asked, looking genuinely befuddled.

Instead of answering that question, Jessie hit him with one of her own.

"Where were you yesterday morning at 7:30 a.m.?"

Ethen looked briefly bewildered by talk of safes and panic rooms before being whiplashed into demands for alibis.

"Um, that was Wednesday, right?" he said.

"It was," Jessie confirmed.

"I know!" he said excitedly. "I was at the studio. We pulled an all-nighter. I signed a band this spring called Bunk Bed Billy. We're recording their debut album. The session started Tuesday night at 10:00 p.m. and ran until eight in the morning."

"I assume multiple people can confirm you were there the whole time?" Jessie said.

"Sure," Ethan said, gaining confidence. "The producer, the sound engineer, the whole band, even their manager. What was that about a safe and a panic room?"

"Are you saying you didn't know your father had either of those things?" Ryan asked skeptically.

"I assumed he had multiple safes, but I never saw them," Ethan replied. "I had no idea about any panic room. And as far as breaking in because I was cut off goes, you should probably know, that check my dad gave me was for five million dollars, so it's not like I was living hand to mouth. How do you think I afford that condo?"

Jessie put her head in her hands and rubbed her temples. That giant motive for murder he'd admitted to moments earlier had just shrunk considerably. This kid was giving her a headache.

"Let's step out for a minute," Ryan said to her.

She nodded and they started for the door. They were almost out when Ethan called after them.

"Can I go?"

Ryan looked back at him and sighed.

"Write down the name of everyone who was in that studio with you," he said. "Authorize us to look through your phone and to access any video from the studio security cameras. If they verify what you've said, then you'll be out of here in a few hours."

He closed the door and studied Jessie's face with concern in his eyes.

"What?" she asked.

"Come with me," he said.

"Where?" she demanded.
"To the hospital."

***

"This was a waste of time," Jessie said, trying to control her irritation.

"How can you say that?" Ryan demanded as they walked out the door. "It's your health at stake here."

"Twenty minutes to get here," she replied, picking up the pace as they returned to the car. "Thirty to get evaluated. Thirty to get the results that say I'm fine. And now twenty minutes back to the station. That's nearly two hours that we don't have, lost to this unnecessary visit."

"First of all, Dr. Varma didn't say you're fine," he reminded her. "She just said that the tests don't show anything right now, but that the effects might be delayed. Secondly, you admitted that you had a headache during that interview with Ethan Booth."

"It was a tension headache because we'd hit another dead end in the case—," she objected.

"Third," he continued, undeterred, "I saw the way your head snapped back when it hit that sofa cushion in the condo when you fell. And even though it was a cushion, there was a loud thwack and you looked momentarily stunned to me. The doctor has warned us about the possibility of Second Impact Syndrome and how we need to take it seriously. If you suffer a second concussion before completely recovering from the first and get brain swelling, there's a chance that you could die. Put all that together and I make no apologies for insisting that you get checked out. I don't give a rat's ass about a billionaire's murder or a pharmaceutical company's stock or even Homicide Special Section's future if it means putting you at risk. So you can put that in your pipe and smoke it, lady!"

Jessie turned to face him as they reached the car and tried mightily not to laugh in the face of her husband and boss.

"You can put that in your pipe and smoke it, lady?" she repeated, feeling the snicker rise up in her chest before she could stifle it.

Suddenly it was out, a full-on guffaw that echoed throughout the parking garage. Ryan tried to keep a straight face but eventually he broke too and ended up half-stifling a snorty horse-laugh.

"I like to bust out old-timey phrases when I feel strongly about something," he said, trying to hold on to some measure of dignity.

"And how's that working out for you?" she asked.

"Super well."

"Listen, I appreciate where all this is coming from," she said, grabbing his hand and pulling him toward her, "and the truth is, that cushion did hurt a bit when I fell. But I really do feel fine. I promise to tell you if that changes. Now can we please get back to trying to solve this murder in the little time we have left before it's taken away from us and the reputation of our unit gets damaged because the feds got greedy?"

"Okay," he agreed, "but how? Booth doesn't look like he's going to pan out. We're running out of potential killers here. Maybe we *should* let the feds take over. If some other competitor billionaire hired a hitman to take Booth out, the FBI may have more resources to pursue that."

"First of all, maybe don't talk about hitmen right now," Jessie chided. "I'm already on edge."

"You know what I meant."

"And secondly," she barreled ahead, "are you kidding? They're going to have to pry this case from our cold, dead hands. Let's go back to the station. The answer to solving this thing is in front of us. I'm sure of it. We just have to be willing to see it. And I'm more than willing."

CHAPTER TWENTY TWO

Hannah didn't need to see the body.

When they arrived at Mitch's Lake Arrowhead cabin, Kat had prohibited her from going into the guest bedroom where Deputy Reed Coolidge's body was lying on the floor under a bedsheet, waiting for the San Bernardino Sheriff's Department crime scene unit to arrive and for the FBI team from Palm Springs to follow suit.

But as she listened from the living room, she could still clearly hear the couple's conversation. Either they didn't realize that their voices traveled so easily in the small cabin, or they didn't really care.

"What do you make of it?" Mitch asked.

"Entire throat slit from behind," Kat said. "The blade cut all the way through the trachea, larynx, and the carotid artery at the same time to both prevent making noise and make the victim bleed out fast. It's the sort of maneuver one would expect from a professional trying to secure a position quietly. Maybe he snuck in and did this to Reed so he couldn't warn Violet, then grabbed her when she was unaware. Or maybe he did it right in front of her, to terrify her. No way to know. But it was quick. Reed never had a chance."

They came out of bedroom and Hannah quickly looked out the window, as if she'd been focused on a squirrel sitting on a branch all this time. Mitch, a normally jovial, mountainous, sandy-haired specimen of a man, lumbered sadly over to the couch and sat down.

Hannah looked over at Kat and noticed something she rarely saw. The former Army Ranger was dabbing at her eyes, which were red and rimmed with tears. It hadn't been apparent from listening to her measured tone when describing what had been done to Reed Coolidge, but the deputy's death had clearly made an impact on her.

Hannah briefly considered asking if she was okay, but then thought better of it. Kat wasn't okay. But there wasn't anything she could do to make it better and it wasn't really her place to try. She was bailed out anyway when Mitch motioned for both of them to join him on the couch. They took spots on either side of him as he pulled up a video clip on his phone.

"This is hard to watch," he said, looking at Kat. "Are you sure it's okay for her to see it?"

"No actual murders, right?" Kat checked.

"No, but there's violence."

"She's seen worse," Kat said.

"I have," Hannah assured him.

"Okay," Mitch said with a shrug and hit play. "This is from one of my exterior cameras posted on a tree facing the driveway. It had the best view I could find."

The video showed a Sheriff's Department SUV pull up in front of the cabin and Coolidge get out.

"This was our hourly check-in," Mitch said. "He was first. I was scheduled to do the next one. The camera is motion-activated and runs for thirty seconds after detecting movement."

Coolidge approached the door, knocked, and was greeted by Violet, who was barely visible in the corner of the frame. He clearly said something but there was no audio. Then he stepped inside. A moment later, the screen went dark.

"Did you see that?" Kat asked.

Hannah didn't know what she was talking about.

"What?" Mitch asked. "I was about to show you the next video."

"Can you replay that one again?"

He obliged.

"Watch at the very end," Kat said, pointing at a clump of trees at the top of the phone screen. "After Reed goes inside, I thought I saw movement there."

Sure enough, in the last second of the video, before it cut to black, Hannah saw it too, some flash of movement, like sunlight hitting metal.

"It almost looks like a moving vehicle," Kat mused.

Mitch stared at his girlfriend in amazement.

"I hadn't noticed that moment before, but you're right," he said, switching to a new video.

Emerging from behind that clump of trees, around a bend on a dirt road was a battered pickup truck. It pulled up in front of the cabin, though not as close as Coolidge's SUV, and a man wearing camouflage gear got out and walked stealthily toward the back of the house.

The man was in his mid-forties, of average height and build, with salt and pepper hair, a scruffy beard, and a bit of a beer belly. Hannah recognized him instantly from hours of computer searches. It was Hank

Keene. He disappeared from the frame and, moments later, the screen went black.

"How did he know she'd be here?" she asked. "I thought we took so many precautions."

Kat shook her head and looked over at Mitch.

"Maybe he followed you guys up here yesterday," she said. "Or maybe he put some kind of locator device on her purse or in her shoe the last time he saw her. We didn't dump anything other than her phone when we sent her off with you because we didn't realize what Keene was capable of at the time. That was our mistake."

"But why not attack yesterday?" Mitch wondered. "She was alone for part of the day and my overnight security system isn't exactly state-of-the-art. Why wait until this morning when there was a deputy around?"

"I just don't know," Kat admitted. "Maybe the other videos will help it make sense?"

"There's only one more," Mitch said. "This is the one I was hesitant to show you."

"Go ahead," Kat told him.

He hit play to reveal Hank dragging Violet, barefoot and wearing jeans and a white t-shirt, out of the cabin. She was gagged and her hands were tied in front of her. At one point, she broke free and started to run away but he caught up and shoved her to the ground. This time, when he dragged her to the truck, it was by her hair.

He tossed her in the back seat of the pickup truck, where he looked to be tying her to something to keep her out of sight. Then he pulled out, passing Coolidge's SUV, and heading down the main road. After a few seconds, that video went dark too.

"Like I said, we were able to track the truck using highway cameras," Mitch explained. "It was abandoned in a Home Depot parking lot in Redlands right next to the 10 freeway. We assume he switched to another one at that point, but we don't yet have any reports of stolen vehicles in the area, so we don't even know what we're looking for."

Hannah stared at the blank screen of Mitch's phone, trying to answer the question that was eating at her: why had Hank waited until this morning to make his move? She thought she had an idea.

"I don't know where's he's headed," she said quietly, "but I can guess why he waited to kidnap her."

"Why?" Kat asked.

"If he's really this former military badass covert assassin type, he would have been staking out your cabin, right? He would have known about your cameras. But he waited until Deputy Coolidge was there. Then he drove right up. He killed a law enforcement official when he didn't have to. He dragged Violet out in full view of that camera. He got in a truck he knew you could identify. He wanted us to see all of that. He wanted an audience. He's telling us that we can't stop him, that he's in charge."

Kat and Mitch sat quietly for a moment.

"He may be right about that," the sheriff's deputy finally said, standing up. "Unfortunately, right now, as unpleasant as it is, I have to set aside the investigative side of this. I have a team of devastated deputies waiting for me back at the station for an all-hands meeting in ten minutes. I hate to leave you guys like this, but I have no choice."

"That's okay," Kat said. "It'll give us a chance to look around. Maybe Keene inadvertently left something behind in all the chaos that will give us some hint as to where he's going."

"Or maybe Violet saw him coming and had time to write something down or provide some other clue for us, knowing we'd show up," Hannah said hopefully.

"It's worth a shot," Mitch said unconvincingly. "Obviously, just don't touch anything. The county crime scene unit should be here in the next half-hour. They're a little short-handed because of a murder-suicide in San Bernardino a couple of hours ago. The Palm Springs FBI people should arrive soon after that. Let me know if anything pressing happens in the interim. I'm sorry I can't stick around."

He gave Kat a kiss and headed out. Once he was gone, Kat handed Hannah a pair of gloves and they began meticulously checking the house, looking for any sign of where Keene intended to take Violet, maybe a matchbook from a cheap motel that had fallen out of his pocket or some muddy footprint that CSU could trace to a particular region of Southern California.

Hannah kept her eyes peeled for any scrap of paper that Violet might have scrawled a note on or even a dusty section of a countertop or table where she might have hastily written something with her finger, but there was nothing.

After ten minutes of that, they stepped outside to get some air.

"This can't just be it," Hannah said. "After everything we've done, he's just going to torture and kill her and there's nothing we can do, even though she paid us to prevent exactly that?"

Kat was about to respond when her phone rang. Her eyes went wide. When she showed Hannah the screen it was clear why. The call was coming from the burner phone she'd given Violet. She answered it and put the call on speaker.

"Hello?" she said.

"Is this Kat Gentry?" a male voice asked.

"It is," Kat replied, her own voice impressively even keeled. "Who am I speaking with?"

"I think you know who this is, Kat. I go by many names, but for the sake of simplicity, you can call me Hank."

CHAPTER TWENTY THREE

Hannah gulped so hard that she thought the man would hear it over the phone.

She looked over at Kat, who, to her amazement, displayed no obvious sign that this development surprised her. When the detective responded, she sounded like it was just another day at the office.

"Is Violet okay, Hank?"

"For now, she is," he said, "but that could change. Her well-being depends on you."

"What does that mean exactly?"

"I'm going to keep this real simple for you, Kat," he said. "This may surprise you, But I don't really care about Violet that much, despite our shared history. She can live. She can die. I'm not as obsessed with the outcome as you might think. What I am interested in is that $30,000 I know she gave you. That's really my money, Kat. Most if it came from my hard work. And I'm going to need it to disappear the way I want to."

"You want to disappear?" Kat said skeptically.

"You sound dubious but it's the truth," he answered. "I know my previous line of work for Uncle Sam might suggest that I could do a lot better than that but with my recent string of incarcerations, I'm not exactly a hot commodity these days. In fact, I have a real concern that my former employer might decide it's better to remove me from the equation entirely than risk me saying the wrong thing to the wrong person. But with $30,000, my skillset, and experience, I can drop off the grid for good. All I need is for you to bring me the cash. Then I'll release Violet into your care, and we can go our separate ways. No harm, no foul."

Kat shook her head even though Keene couldn't see her.

"What's to prevent you from taking the money and killing both of us?"

"Nothing I suppose," he admitted, "but that wouldn't really help with my 'drop off the grid' goal. I'm trying to stay low profile. Let me ask you this: are the authorities more or less likely to look for me if I kill a decorated former Army Ranger and well-regarded private detective?"

"But you've already killed a sheriff's deputy," Hannah pointed out. "So it's not like you're off people's radar."

Kat frowned, unhappy that she'd joined the conversation.

"Is that young Hannah Dorsey?" he asked. "I wondered when the little spitfire was going to add her two cents. You're right of course. That won't help my cause. But the ugly truth is that Deputy Coolidge, whatever his virtues may have been, isn't besties with Jessie Hunt. And a multi-count felon like me knows that if I took out Jessie Hunt's best friend, there's probably no place in the world I could hide that she wouldn't find me. I don't need that kind of heat. So I'd rather just make the simple trade: money for the missus. What do you say?"

"Why do I feel like it's not that going to be that simple?" Kat wondered.

"But it is," Keene promised, "as long as you follow these simple rules. You bring the money, or I will kill Violet. You come alone or I will kill Violet. I guess you can bring your little sidekick there, but no one else. If you involve law enforcement, including your charming boyfriend or Captain Hernandez at HSS, Violet dies. And even though she's a civilian, that goes for Jessie too. You tell absolutely no one. Are we clear?"

Hannah shook her head vehemently at Kat, who ignored her.

"Yes," she said.

"Be aware that I won't be taking your word for that, Kat," Hank said, "and if I find that you've broken that word, I will kill Violet by removing her extremities one at a time, letting her bleed out slowly and painfully. Understood?"

"Speaking of Violet, put her on," Kat said. "I need to know she's really okay."

"Proof of life," Hank said, chuckling, "of course. Here she is."

After a moment a new voice came on the line.

"Kat," Violet said, her voice quavering with fear, "you don't have to do this."

"It's going to be okay," Kat told her soothingly. "Don't worry. I'm going to take care of it."

"I'm so sorry that I got you into this," Violet said, clearly trying to fight back tears. "I just wanted to go someplace safe. I never meant for any of this to happen."

"You just hang tough," Kat told her. "I'll be there soon."

"Let's hope you come through for her," Hank said, having re-taken the phone. "Head back down to Redlands and the 10 freeway. I'll call with more detailed directions momentarily. You girls be good."

The line went dead.

"You don't really believe him," Hannah said, "that he's going to just take the money and let both of you go, right?"

"I don't believe it for a second," Kat said as she started back into the cabin.

"Then let's find some backchannel way to reach out to law enforcement and get some help," Hannah said. "Maybe we don't go through the normal lines. I have the number for Jessie's buddy at the FBI, Agent Jack Dolan. I could call him on his personal cell and tell him the situation. Maybe he could set up a helicopter to track us as we go to the meet. It won't be through official channels so Keene won't know."

"First of all," Kat said as she walked to the kitchen sink and tossed water on her face, "as promising as that sounds, can you be sure that Keene didn't think of that? What if he did? Are you willing to risk Violet's life on that chance? Second, there is no 'we go to the meet.' You're staying right here."

"But I'm the one person he said he didn't mind coming with you," Hannah protested. "And you'll need backup."

Kat grabbed a dish towel and dried her face before turning to her.

"No offense, Hannah, because you have proven yourself to be an impressive young woman," she said, 'but you are not *backup*. We are dealing with a former military and CIA assassin, and you are a recent high school graduate. Also, your sister would murder me herself if I let you anywhere near this situation. You know that. So let's be real. You stay here. Wait for CSU. Walk them through what happened. If the FBI shows up, refer them to Mitch. Don't lie to them because that's a crime but don't reveal anything that will put Violet in danger either, okay?"

Hannah nodded reluctantly, before she thought of another objection.

"Wait, how are you going to fake him out if you don't even have the money?"

Kat lifted up her shirt and pulled her jeans away from her stomach to reveal Violet's money belt.

"I brought it with us when we left the office yesterday," she said. "It didn't seem like a great idea to leave it there overnight and with everything going on today, I thought the safest place for it was on my person. Guess that was smart move."

"With this guy, I'm not sure there is a smart move," Hannah muttered.

"Well I can't obsess over that at this point," Kat said. "I can tell you that I'm going to make one smart move and run to the bathroom real quick because I don't know when I'll get another chance. Then I'm out of here."

Hannah watched her walk down the hall and waited for the door to close before she grabbed her mini-backpack and darted back outside. As she hurried over to Kat's car, she fished out the AirTag that she kept hidden in the fold of one of the backpack pockets, opened the passenger door, and tossed it under the seat. Then she closed the door and dashed back over to the porch, where she sat down just as Kat came outside.

"You good?" her boss asked.

"Yeah," Hannah said, "just taking in the majesty of nature."

"I can't tell if you're being sarcastic or not."

Hannah stood up without answering.

"Keene didn't say anything about not calling me, so could you please keep me updated on what's going on while you're driving?" she pleaded. "I'll go crazy just twiddling my thumbs up here in the mountains by myself."

"That I can do," Kat said giving her quick hug, before hurrying over to her car.

"And don't forget," Hannah added, "you have to come through this okay. You're my ride back to L.A."

That at least got a laugh. Kat pulled out of the driveway and headed down the same road that both Keene and Mitch had used earlier this morning. Once the taillights disappeared, Hannah returned to the cabin. She knew she didn't have much time.

While Kat had been drying her face and refusing to let her come with for the meet, Hannah had been eyeing the padlocked cabinet on the wall in the hallway. She figured it was a good first place to check. After doing a cursory hunt for the key to the small padlock and having no success, she went with a more primitive method.

She found a meat mallet in one of the drawers and began whacking. After five solid hits, the cabinet was open, and Hannah was staring at a collection of keys. She found the one for the exterior garage and for the new Ford F-150 Lightning electric truck that Mitch had recently bought and was always bragging about. It was the vehicle he'd used for the trip to and from L.A earlier this week and had apparently even bored Violet by discussing it on the way up here.

She grabbed both the garage and truck keys, wrote Mitch a brief note of apology, then went outside with her mini-backpack and an old parka she'd borrowed from his closet. She had no idea where Hank wanted to meet Kat and she wanted to be prepared for whatever the weather conditions were.

Then, feeling less guilty than she probably should have, she opened the garage, turned the truck on, eased it out of the garage, locked the sad, empty-looking place back up, returned the key to the cabinet, hopped back in the vehicle, and pulled out onto the road.

She wasn't sure exactly what her plan was, but she knew that Kat needed her. Despite her experience and training, the private detective wasn't thinking clearly. She unquestionably felt an obligation to help Violet. She was torn up about Reed's murder. And she was being placed under tight time constraints with no time to think.

Hank Keene was manipulating her. And tough as nails, as she was, she might be susceptible to his machinations right now. She needed backup, and at the moment, the only person who could provide it was a recent high school graduate with some basic training in Krav Maga, an awareness of the situation, and a serious anger management problem. It was Hannah or no one.

She had driven less than a tenth of a mile when she passed the San Bernardino County CSU van headed in the opposite direction. She kept her eyes pointed straight ahead, as if she was just a local resident out on a casual drive and not an eighteen-year-old in a kind-of-stolen truck following a detective who was trying to prevent an assassin from slaughtering his own wife.

CHAPTER TWENTY FOUR

The answer was supposed to be right in front of Jessie, but she couldn't see a thing.

When she and Ryan had returned to the station, she had been optimistic that something would click if she just focused hard enough. But after over two hours of reviewing every lead they had, it felt like they were spinning their wheels. Worse, every lost hour meant they were an hour closer to having the case taken from them.

Ryan had gone off briefly to check on the status of the other HSS case being handled by Susannah Valentine and Sam Goodwin, as well as to confer with Karen Bray, who had been called back for a second day of testimony for the trial in which she'd been the primary detective. Jamil and Beth were hunched over their computer screens, staring at Google docs and comparing them to papers strewn about their desks.

Jessie, seated on the research room couch behind them, stood up and stretched, hoping the extra blood flow would juice her brain a little bit. She need any help she could get. Ethan Booth was still in the interrogation room where they'd left him, but they were just waiting for security video footage from the recording studio on Wednesday morning to corroborate what others had told them and officially alibi him out. He was likely to be free within the hour.

No one else on the suspect list they'd gotten from Grover Nix had panned out. In fact, three more names had been officially eliminated. They were down to eight people to investigate, not that there was enough time to check them all out before 5:00 p.m. today, even if she thought one of them might actually turn out to be a credible suspect.

"What's the status on that Taverner guy who built the panic room?" she asked Jamil. "Have you heard back yet?"

"He handed that off to me because he was getting so frustrated," Beth said. "They've been giving us the run-around. I was supposed to get a call back in the last half hour, but I haven't. I wanted to play hardball, but I don't know if I have that authority. What do you want me to do?"

"What I want is to go over to his office, kick down his door, assuming it's not iron-reinforced, drag him here, and make him panic a little in one of *our* rooms," Jessie admitted, feeling her blood pressure rise and her brow knot up along with it. "But I can't do that without conferring with Captain Hernandez. So why don't you give them another fifteen minutes. If you don't hear back by then, call again. If they blow you off, let me know, and we'll pay them a visit. I'm starting to get a little suspicious here."

Meanwhile, every little brow furrow and twinge in her head made her wonder whether she should be taking the sofa collision earlier today more seriously. Her husband was worried about her, and she was starting to think it was unfair for her to be so cavalier in reaction to his concerns. Maybe he was a little overprotective, but she understood why. She was potentially just one hard blow to the head from irreversible brain damage, or even death. She kept pushing it out of her head, but clearly he couldn't.

She couldn't help but wonder what would happen in a worst case scenario. She'd set up a new will, a living will, and health directive last year when she'd assumed custody of Hannah, as well as a minor's trust for the girl, but she probably needed to update it all now that she was married and Hannah was eighteen.

Hearing those words in her head made something click and she couldn't help but smile—finally a click. They reminded her of something that Ethan Booth had mentioned in passing during their interrogation of him. He'd said that when his father cut him out of the will, it wasn't complicated, not like his sister's trust. His sister had a trust.

From her own experience, putting a trust together was a complicated, frustrating experience. If that was the case for her, she could only imagine what it was like for the divorced, estranged parents of a young daughter.

"I'll be back," Jessie said to Jamil and Beth.

"Where are you going?" Jamil asked.

"I'm going to do a little trust exercise," she said as she headed for the door.

"I don't know what that means," he said.

"It's probably for the best," she sighed. "I'm tired and it was a cheesy line anyway. Wish me luck."

But she was out the door before he could.

***

Jessie waited in the uncomfortable chair in Ryan's office for him to get off the phone. As she did, she felt a buzz in her pocket and peeked at her cell phone. There was a text from Hannah. It read: *How's your case coming?*

Jessie typed back: *No killer caught yet. How about for you guys?*

Hannah's answer came quicky: *Still don't know where he took her. Palm Springs FBI will be on the scene soon to help. Wish us luck. Hope you have some too!*

Thanks. Good luck!

She put her phone up, feeling a little ashamed that she was happy about the feds stepping in with her little sister's case. But if it kept her safe, so be it.

When Ryan hung up, his whole body sagged, and she saw that he'd been holding it together for the call but had nothing left.

"Who was that?" she asked.

"Public relations," he said. "They want a statement on the status of the investigation, something that will brush back the feds for a couple more hours, so we can keep investigating. I got a text from Decker saying they're circling like vultures. At this rate, we may not even have until 5:00 p.m."

Even as she felt the well-deserved karmic gut punch of having her sister's misfortune potentially visited upon her too, Jessie managed to give Ryan her most comforting smile, one that she typically reserved for the living room after a rough day rather than for the office. He seemed like he really needed it.

"What if I told you we might be able to give them some red meat?" she asked.

"I would ask you to go on," he said, sitting up straight.

"I think you should tell them that HSS has a promising lead that could result in an imminent arrest of a suspect unconnected to BoothCo Biomed's corporate interests. That should hold the feds back for a while."

"Is that true?" Ryan asked.

"Possibly," Jessie said. "Shall I explain?"

"I'm all ears," Ryan said, leaning forward over his desk.

"I just came from talking to Ethan Booth," she said. "He didn't know that we were minutes away from releasing him, so he was still willing to be pretty forthcoming. I asked him about trusts."

"Trusts?"

"Yes," Jessie said. "Remember how he mentioned that his dad set one up for his younger sister. I asked him to go into more detail on that. It turns out that before everything fell apart, back when everything was rainbows and lollipops for Lowden and Gwendolyn Booth, they set up a trust for their daughter, Louisa. And despite the divorce, both parents were still co-trustees. Ethan didn't really know all the particulars of the trust language, but he did have the document in an old email from his mom, which he shared with me. Would you like to know what it states?"

"Very much," Ryan said.

"Apparently the ex-Mrs. Booth didn't get much in the divorce—Lowden's lawyers hard at work again--but according to the rules of Louisa's trust, if one trustee dies, the other one becomes the sole trustee, administering funds valued at over $100 million."

"You're kidding!" Ryan exclaimed, actually standing up.

"Hold on," Jessie said, getting up too, but more slowly. "Technically, the remaining trustee cannot use any of the money or property in the trust to benefit him or herself. But since the beneficiary, Louisa, is only fourteen years old, inevitably some of those funds are going to have some overlap, when the mother is caregiver and guardian."

"How did we not know any of this before?" Ryan asked, flabbergasted.

"Because Lowden Booth was so fanatical about his privacy and made sure his army of attorneys protected it," Jessie said. "Only in this instance, it backfired, and may have protected the person responsible for his death. Meanwhile, everyone's fixated on which of his competitors took him out to sink the company. It's the perfect cover. If not for Ethan, we'd never have gotten access to the contents of this trust."

"Well, I think maybe we should pay Gwendolyn a visit," Ryan suggested, "that is, assuming we can figure out her address if it hasn't been completely hidden too."

Jessie smiled.

"You know," she said, "we just might have already gotten lucky on that front too."

CHAPTER TWENTY FIVE

Jessie couldn't hide her surprise.

She knew that Lowden Booth had managed to silo off virtually all his money from Gwendolyn when they got divorced, but she hadn't expected this.

When they pulled up in front of the charming but modest one story bungalow in Westchester, not far from the campus of Loyola Marymount University, she had to double check to make sure they had the right address.

"It's right," Jamil told them over the phone as they parked out front. "The place is actually a rental. Based on the information that Ethan Booth gave us about the alimony she receives, this is what she can afford."

Before she and Ryan left the station, Jessie had told Ethan that he was free to go as long as he answered any remaining questions that the research team had for him.

"What about child support?" Ryan asked as they got out of the car and walked up the path to the house.

"She doesn't get any," Beth said. "Apparently the couple share custody of Louisa but the Booth Estate is her primary residence, that is when she's not attending boarding school on the East Coast, which is where she is now."

"But it's the summer," Jessie noted.

"According to Ethan, she's staying with cousins in New York through the end of the month."

"Does she even know her father is dead?" Jessie pressed.

"Ethan said he wasn't sure," Beth said. "He's left vague texts and voicemails asking her to call him back. He didn't want to say their dad died in a message. Apparently she texted back that she wasn't feeling great and would get back to him later. But she hasn't called yet."

"This is one messed up family," Ryan muttered as they reached the front door. "Thanks, guys, we'll be in touch."

He rang the bell and they waited for a response. Jessie looked at the time on her phone. It was 4:08 p.m. She wondered if the press release that Ryan had helped the public relations department craft before they headed over here was the reason the FBI had held off on taking over the case yet or if they'd be getting an unwelcome call any minute.

After thirty seconds without a response he tried the doorbell again. Thirty seconds later he knocked loudly and announced who they were.

"Stay here," he told her, "I'll try around back."

He was just getting ready to hike himself over the side gate when a window slid open on the house next door and an older woman, probably in her seventies, wearing a wide-brimmed floral, gardening hat, poked her head out.

"I was out back in my yard and couldn't help overhearing you say that you were with the police," she told him. "Could I please see some ID before you go hopping into Gwen's yard?"

"Sure thing, ma'am," he said, stepping close to her and holding it out.

Jessie watched her lift her bifocals off the necklace they were attached to, peer at the ID for a moment, and then stare up at him.

"To be frank with you, Captain Hernandez," she said, "I wouldn't know if that was real or if you got it in a party store. But you have a respectable look to you, and I recognize the lady with you from the news as the Angel of the City of Angels so I'm going to give you the benefit of the doubt."

"I appreciate that," he said. "Do you know Gwen well?"

The woman made a "tsk tsk" sound, as if she felt a mix of pity and disapproval toward her neighbor.

"Not really," she said. "She tends to keep to herself. Although, she does get a little chattier when she's had two or six glasses of Rosés. Then she'll go on about what a jerk her ex is. But don't expect her to share any of that with you."

"Why not?" Ryan asked.

"Because she's not home," the woman said. "She left a couple of hours ago."

"Did she say where she was going?" Jessie asked.

"No, but she was carrying two big suitcases and she seemed very happy. I think she might have already had a few glasses today."

"Thanks very much, ma'am," Ryan said, already starting back toward the car.

Jessie turned to follow him when the woman called after her.

"Wait," she yelled, "I wanted to tell you something."

"I'm sorry ma'am," Jessie said, "but we're in a bit of a rush."

"I'll be quick," the woman said. "I just wanted to thank you for everything you do for this city. We all know that you've put yourself in grave danger many times to save people you don't even know."

"Thank you but I'm not the only one who does that, ma'am," Jessie insisted. "There are thousands of good people who do the same thing every day in this city."

"I have no doubt," the woman said, wagging her finger, "but they don't all have targets on their backs. They don't all have serial killers out to get them. You may not have wings, but you *are* an angel."

"We've got to go," called out Ryan, who was already at the car and had missed this back and forth.

"Thanks," Jessie said. "You've made my day."

"My pleasure," the lady replied, "now go catch whatever bastard you're after!"

***

"No pressure but we're almost there, Jamil," Jessie said as they pulled into the departure lane of the Los Angeles International Airport.

She knew they were taking a calculated risk, but it felt like a smart one. Gwendolyn Booth's bungalow in Westchester was less than a ten minute drive from LAX. It was the most logical choice for her to be going with her two suitcases, though the L.A. area had multiple other airports, not to mention a major port with several cruise lines, as well as giant train and bus stations.

"I've got it," Jamil said. "She's leaving on Aeromexico flight 350 to Mazatlán out of gate 24. That's Terminal 3. The flight leaves at 4:30."

Jessie looked at her phone.

"That's less than ten minutes from now," she said. "Can you call airport police and get them to stop her before she boards or just delay the flight?"

"I can try," he said.

"Good," Ryan said, "because we're pulling up to the terminal now."

They hung up and came to a stop right next to an airport police car and an officer who did not look amused.

"You go ahead," Ryan told her. "I'll explain the situation to our friend here, then catch up."

Jessie nodded and darted toward the automatic doors, ignoring the shouts from the officer, who she hoped wasn't pulling a weapon on her.

She looked around for the passenger screening area, saw a long line of people waiting to go up an escalator, and headed in that direction. She skipped the escalator entirely and took the adjoining stairs, waving off the TSA agent, who called out even more angrily than the cop outside had.

When she reached the second floor, she approached a TSA officer who looked to be in a supervisory capacity—a heavyset, bald man in his forties with an impressive comb-over—and pulled out her badge.

"My name is Jessie Hunt," she said between gasps of air. "I'm a criminal profiler who works with the LAPD."

"I know who you are," he said, looking at her like she was a movie star. Sometimes the local notoriety paid off.

"Great," she said. "Then you probably know that when I show up like this, it means there's a situation. There's a passenger who's either already on or preparing to get on a plane about to leave this terminal. She's a murder suspect and I need to get to her ASAP. Can you get me through security and help stop that plane from taking off?"

"The first part for sure I can," he said, already motioning for her to follow him. "The second part, I have to make some calls. But tell me the airline and flight number and I'll do my best."

"Aeromexico flight 350," she said as they passed along the side of the security line, completely avoiding the crowd of people.

"Alright," the guy said. "I'll call now. Good luck to you."

"Thanks," she said, starting to head out before turning around. "My partner will be coming up here any second—Captain Ryan Hernandez. Can you hook him up too?"

The agent saluted her like he was a soldier, and she was his general. She gave what she hoped was something close to a salute back and sprinted down the concourse. By the time she reached gate 24 just over a minute later, the jetway doors were closed and her lungs were burning.

She raced over to the gate agent, desperately sucking in air so that she could speak. The woman, a perky blonde in her twenties, didn't wait to hear what she had to say. Instead, she pointed off to the left. Jessie looked over.

Somehow, in her mad dash to get to the gate doors, she had completely missed the woman sitting in an uncomfortable-looking gate chair, surrounded on either side by large airport police officers, one of whom had attached a handcuff to her wrist and another to his own.

Gwendolyn Booth despite her circumstances, still managed to maintain something of a regal bearing. A half-decade younger than her deceased ex-husband, the former Mrs. Booth had clearly taken advantage of his financial assets when they were available to her. She was buoyant and taut in ways that didn't accurately reflect her age. Her auburn hair flowed majestically down her back, and she wore fashionably comfy travel attire that Jessie guessed cost more than her roundtrip airfare did. Having said that, she definitely looked a little tipsy. And more than a little annoyed.

Jessie staggered over to them and allowed herself a few more seconds to catch her breath. As she did, the officer cuffed to Gwendolyn, whose nametag read Lorenzo, spoke.

"I'm assuming you're Jessie Hunt?"

She nodded, bending over, and putting her hands on her knees.

"Someone in your office, a persistent fella name of Winslow, insisted we pull a Gwendolyn Booth off this flight on account of she might have committed a crime of some kind. So we did that. I have to say, she wasn't especially gracious about it, which is why the handcuffs."

"Thanks very much," Jessie said, finally able to form words. "You guys are real lifesavers."

"According to you," Booth said huffily. "I take a very different view. This embarrassing incident has already created a terrible start to my Mexican vacation. You can expect that once this is all cleared up, there will be lawsuits all around, and I have a feeling that the primary focal point of my legal ire will be you, Ms. Hunt."

Jessie wasn't sure what to make of Booth's reaction. Did she really think that her best move was to feign cluelessness about all of this? She couldn't possibly imagine that her choice to go on a Mexican vacation the day after her ex-husband was murdered would be viewed without suspicion.

As Jessie turned all this over in her head, she saw Ryan running down the concourse in their direction, looking even more winded. She knew that although he was almost completely recovered from his stabbing and subsequent coma last summer, the two things that still posed a challenge for him were climbing multiple flights of stairs and sprinting short distances. In the last two days, he'd had to do both. As he walked over, she pretended not to notice his struggle.

"Captain Hernandez from LAPD," she said by way of introduction, "these are officers Lorenzo and Beatts of the airport police. They apprehended Mrs. Booth and have been keeping her company until our arrival. I thought we could take her off their hands, go for a drive, and see if she'd be interested in answering a few questions."

"I'm not going anywhere with either of you," Booth announced dramatically. "I am going to Mazatlán, if not on this flight, then on the next one, and I expect a round of apologies prior to that."

Ryan, still unable to speak, looked at Jessie incredulously, also stunned that this was the tack Gwendolyn Booth was choosing to take. Jessie knew what he would say if he could get the words out and decided to do it for him.

"Mrs. Booth," she began, doing her best to avoid sounding patronizing, "you're ex-husband was murdered yesterday. You're relationship with him was notoriously rocky. We have a number of questions for you. You can't just up and leave the country."

"Why not?" Booth demanded. "I can answer your questions just as well from Mazatlán. Phones work there too, don't they?"

"Yes ma'am, but extradition can get tricky, and we wanted to chat in person," Jessie replied calmly. "Besides, what if Louisa needs you? Aren't you her primary caregiver now?"

She watched closely to see how Gwendolyn reacted to that question.

"I am," the woman answered without hesitation. "That's why she's supposed to meet me in Mexico tomorrow. How am I supposed to care for her if I'm not there?"

Jessie and Ryan shared a surprised glance.

"I guess the solution is to cancel her flight too," Ryan huffed, now finally somewhat able to speak.

"Wait," Booth said, increasingly horrified, "are you saying that we won't be able to go on this trip *at all* now?

"I've pretty much lost patience on this one," he said to Jessie before turning his attention back to the seemingly inebriated, self-righteous woman in front of him. "Gwendolyn Booth, you're under arrest for the murder of Lowden Booth. We can continue this conversation back at the station."

CHAPTER TWENTY SIX

Kat knew she was close.

Hank's directions from his most recent call were brief but specific. He asked where she was.

"Still headed west on the 10 freeway approaching the split with Highway 111," she replied.

"Good," he said. "You're almost there. Keep going west on the 10. Get off at Tipton Road and go north from the freeway toward Whitewater Preserve and Red Dome. Once you pass an A-frame cabin on your right, you'll see a large grove of trees off to the right. Pull off the road out of sight and take the nearby unmarked trail east toward the Painted Hills. That's where I'll be waiting with Violet. Don't you or your little sidekick try anything stupid."

"Just keep Violet safe," Kat said, "and by the way, it'll just be me. You didn't really think I'd bring a kid to something like this, did you?"

There was silence on the other end of the line for a second, before Hank finally replied.

"That's too bad," he said. "I was looking forward to meeting both of you in person. Maybe I'll run into her another time."

"Let's just make this a 'one and done' encounter, shall we?" Kat suggested. "Now before I come out there, I need to hear from Violet again."

After a couple of additional seconds, she heard her client's familiar voice.

"Kat?"

"Yes, it's me, Violet," she said. "Don't worry. This is almost over with. Are you okay? Has he hurt you?"

"No more than usual," the woman said bitterly.

"Hang tight," Kat replied, her blood boiling.

"That's all for now," Hank said. "You can gossip all you like on the drive back. But for now, you just come with that money and zero surprises. Got it?"

"Yes," Kat agreed as she pulled off the freeway at the Tipton Road exit.

Hank's directions had taken Kat from the mountains to an isolated desert outpost, far from the help of any of her friends in L.A. She was on her own, where someone with his training and experience would have all the advantages.

It was only half a mile north to the cabin from the exit. Kat passed it and saw the grove of trees where Hank had instructed her to park. Instead, she continued north for another quarter mile until she found a large rock outcropping next to the side of the road. She pulled off to the side and parked behind it so that her car couldn't be seen from either the road or the hills in the distance.

Then she got out, checked her gun, and texted Hannah that she was going to the meet. She noted that the reception was weak out here and it took several attempts for the text to go through. She put her phone on silent and started walking toward the Painted Hills along a parallel line to the trail Hank had told her to use.

The map on her phone indicated that the trek to her destination was only about a mile and a half, although the terrain appeared to be pretty rugged. A hundred yards into walking, the image froze completely, indicating that she no longer had any connection at all. She'd have to use her old school military training the rest of the way.

After twenty minutes of hiking up and down over multiple small hills and valleys, without coming across another soul, she reached a crest and immediately dropped to her stomach. In the basin below her, about a hundred and fifty feet away, was the pickup truck from the video at Mitch's cabin. Next to it, seated in a metal folding chair, gagged and with her hands and feet tied up, was Violet. She was still barefoot and wearing the white t-shirt and jeans from this morning. Hank was nowhere in sight.

Kat stayed where she was for several minutes, studying the scene, watching for additional movement, listening for any sound. But other than Violet's soft cries and her intermittent, ineffectual attempts to tug free of her restraints, the desert was quiet.

Kat knew that Hank Keene was probably out there somewhere, watching and waiting for her to make a move but she didn't have much choice. She couldn't stay like this forever. Once it was dark, it would be even harder to defeat Keene out here, especially with a frightened, potentially injured woman.

Against her better judgement, she wriggled up over the crest and crawled down toward Violet's location. When she was about halfway there, she got to her knees, removed her gun, and squat-walked to a large, nearby boulder. Still, she couldn't see or hear any sign of Keene.

She waited until Violet lifted her head briefly, then gave a quick flutter of a wave to get her attention. The woman's tear-stained eyes opened wide. Kat held a finger to her lips. Violet nodded almost imperceptibly. Kat held out her hands questioningly and mouthed the word "Hank?"

Subtly, with both her head and her eyes, Violet motioned backward over her shoulder, as if to indicate that he'd gone over the hill behind her. Kat nodded and carefully moved around the boulder. She wanted to hurry over and free Violet right away but needed to be careful. It was entirely possible that Keene had booby-trapped the sandy area around the chair she was sitting in.

So instead, she took a wide arc, going around the pickup and being careful to only step on rocks jutting out from the ground. She was about to approach the grateful but terrified looking Violet when she noticed men's sized boot prints in the sand off to the right. She wondered if it might be wiser to follow them and try to take out Keene rather than attempt to free Violet first, potentially leaving them both exposed.

Following the path of prints, she noted that they seemed to stop about fifteen feet off to the right. Had he removed his boots to make himself untraceable? It wouldn't be unheard of. She gripped the gun tighter as she moved in that direction, unsettled, sensing that despite her caution, she was playing into the former covert operative's hands.

As she got closer to the where the boot prints ended, she noticed something else. The tracks ended at a sort of sand dune, but an unconventional looking one, smaller than usual, not particularly windswept. If she didn't know better, she'd say that it looked less like a sand dune and more like…a shallow grave. That's when she noticed the dark, thick drops in the sand—lots of them.

As she spun around, lifting her gun hand, one thought flashed through her head.

I have been played. But not by Hank.

CHAPTER TWENTY SEVEN

Even as she raised the gun, Kat knew she was too late.

Violet Sheridan was already standing directly in front of her, a knife in her hand, slicing down toward Kat's right forearm.

Kat managed to twist her arm at the last second so that the knife mostly hit the ulna bone just below the outside of her elbow, but the pain was still excruciating, and the gun fell from her hand immediately. Violet kicked it away. They both watched it slide off and disappear into the sand before staring at each other.

Kat couldn't believe what she was looking at. The woman in front of her bore no resemblance to the meek woman who had come into her office yesterday morning. Her brown eyes, so weepy and scared-seeming just moments earlier, were now steely and cold. Her pale skin, angular face, and arched nose no longer seemed porcelain and frail but sharp and menacing. Her black hair, worn in a messy bun yesterday, was now tied in a tight, utilitarian ponytail. She looked confident—and dangerous.

Kat didn't know exactly what was going on, why Hank was dead in the sand beside her, or who Violet really was, but now wasn't the time to ask. Right now, she just had to survive. And considering that she was unarmed and bleeding profusely from her right arm, while Violet had a hunting knife, that seemed like a dicey proposition.

So she did two of the things she was best at: stay calm and play dirty. She took a big step backward, while simultaneously sucking in a deep breath. Then, when Violet took an inevitable step toward her, she kicked a big pile of sand in the woman's face.

She saw Violet close her eyes and heard her cough, but rather than use the moment to try to attack her, she chose to retreat and darted off toward the bed of the pickup, looking for anything she could use to defend herself. The only thing she could find was a rusty tire iron but it was better than nothing, so she grabbed it just as Violet had regrouped and was advancing on her again.

"Wouldn't you rather talk this out?" Kat asked, wincing as she swung the tire iron to keep the smaller woman at bay.

But Violet deftly ducked under the iron, popped up, and swiped the knife horizontally at the taller woman's shoulder. Kat flung herself backward, her back slamming into the side of the pickup truck, but she still felt the blade's sting as it cut through the skin just below her left collarbone. Two inches higher and it would have been her neck.

The other woman was older than Kat, but she was clearly quicker and more agile. The one thing Kat had working for her was that she was bigger and, hopefully, stronger.

Violet was already swinging the blade back in the other direction, but Kat caught her forearm with her right hand and since they were in such close quarters, snapped her head forward and headbutted Violet in the nose. For the briefest of moments, the woman looked surprised.

But then she smiled, even as blood poured down her nose into her teeth. Without warning, she tossed the knife from her right hand to her left, caught it cleanly, and swung it down, jamming it into Kat's right shoulder blade.

Kat let out a scream as she felt a searing pain more intense than anything she'd experienced since the day she was nearly blown up by that IED in Afghanistan. The agony started in her shoulder but radiated outward from there, consuming her whole body. She knew she'd dropped to her knees but couldn't actually feel the contact with the earth below. Her eyes were watering so badly that it was hard to see Violet clearly.

The woman was saying something, but she couldn't make out the words. It didn't really matter anyway. They were almost certainly something about how she was about to die. She wasn't interested. Inhaling deeply despite the anguish it caused, she reached back with her left hand and managed to throw an open-palmed blow at Violet's ribcage, making nice contact that ended with a satisfying "oof" sound.

But she paid the price a few seconds later when Violet gave her an open-palmed punch of her own, but hers was to the face. Kat felt her nose go sideways and knew it was broken, though that was the least of her concerns right now.

"Can you hear me, Kat?" Violet said. "Nod for yes."

Kat nodded.

"Good," Violet said. "Please don't hit me again. As I was trying to tell you when you punched me in the rib, me holding this knife in your shoulder might be the only thing preventing you from bleeding out. I can't guarantee that I didn't nick an artery. So what we're going to do is move over to the chair I was sitting in. I'll remove the knife and you'll put pressure on the wound while I restrain you. Then we'll get on with things."

"Get on with things?" Kat said, feeling a little woozy but trying to fight it. "What does that mean?"

"I'll explain everything in a moment," Violet said, "but first, stand up."

Kat got to her feet slowly and followed instructions as the woman sat her in the metal chair, handed her a towel, then, all in one quick motion, removed the knife and placed her hand and the towel over her bloody shoulder. Despite her best efforts, Kat screamed a second time, gasping and fighting not to pass out as she pressed hard against her pulsating injury.

By the time her head had stopped swimming, she realized that both her hands and ankles were zip tied to the chair and a towel was duct-taped to her leaking shoulder. Apparently there was only one available towel because the knife wound near her elbow was being staunched only by the duct tape.

Violet stepped toward her, sheathed the hunting knife, and slowly raised her hand with her palm open. Kat thought she was about to punch her again, and despite her best efforts, twitched slightly.

"Made you flinch," Violet said, chuckling before waving smelling salts under her nose.

Kat's head bolted back, and her eyes watered as she coughed. All her wooziness was gone.

"You're probably confused, Kat, and I get that," Violet said as if they were chatting amiably over brunch, "so I'm going to lay this out for you in a straightforward manner. I don't have the time to mess around anyway because I promised someone this would make the news tonight. My name isn't really Violet Sheridan and that guy in the ground over there isn't actually my husband, although he really is a scumbag."

"I don't follow," Kat said.

"I know," the woman who was apparently not Violet said. "That's by design. But you will soon. That's part of the plan too. Some of this I'll tell you off camera. Then we'll record the rest for the people. My real name is Ash Pierce. I used to be an element leader for a Marine Special Operations Team. Hank was a critical skills operator under my command before he eventually washed out because he couldn't stay on the right side of the law. Is any of this biographical history sounding familiar to you, Kat?"

"A little," Kat said, hoping she sounded sarcastic, "but I feel like it got somewhat mixed up by the time I read it."

"Yeah, sorry about that," Ash said. "I messed with Hank's personnel file a bit and leaked a doctored version of it that incorporated some of my service history as his own. You know, the part about facilitating coups while in the military, performing covert assassinations while on leave for the CIA—all that was me, not Hank. He was just a screwup who got drummed out of the Marines, ended up holding up jewelry stores, and beating up his common law wife. But that made him the perfect patsy for my grand plan."

"Grand plan?" Kat said, chuckling at ridiculousness of the phrase, even though the movement made her whole body throb.

Ash noted the chuckle with a tight smile, then walked over to the pickup truck, opened the passenger's side door, pulled out something that Kat couldn't see, and walked back over. Then, she showed Kat the item. It was a baton, like one the police might use. In one swift motion, she swung it backward like a baseball bat and then forward, connecting with Kat's left kneecap.

"Probably not a good idea to laugh at me," Ash said sharply.

Katherine Gentry refused to make a sound, but she couldn't stop herself from doubling over in anguish. She stayed that way for a good ten seconds before sitting upright again and staring back at her tormentor.

"You were saying?" she asked, her voice even.

"I cannot tell you how much I admire your toughness, Kat," Ash said, sounding almost sincere. "When I read your personnel record, your bravery nearly brought a tear to my eye, if I was capable of tears anymore. Just watching you gut this out is inspiring. It's times like this that that my job engenders real mixed emotions. But back to your question: my grand plan?"

Kat was listening to Ash, but she was also looking around, searching for any way out of this situation. Was there perhaps a rattlesnake slithering close to her torturer? Or if she could somehow trip the woman, was there a rock outcropping with a jagged point nearby that she might fall on? But Kat saw nothing. Meanwhile Ash happily shared the grand plan.

"Like I was saying, Hank was the perfect patsy. He was about to get out of prison. He lived in the same city as you. He was an abusive bastard, so I knew that when I came to you with my sob story about needing to escape from him, you'd be suckers for it, which you were."

Kat understood that she'd been manipulated but she didn't still have the first clue as to why a former CIA assassin would be targeting her.

"Once he got out," Ash continued, "I convinced him and the real Violet to sign on to the plan. It wasn't hard when I promised them $30,000. They didn't ask too many questions. All Violet had to do was make herself scarce and leave for Mexico where she'd wait for him until everything was done. His job was a little harder. He had to earn his money."

Ash smiled, apparently relishing the memory of how she'd manipulated the Marine she used to lead into battle.

"He had to play along with my elaborate ruse," she recalled. "That meant beating me up a little to make me look like a convincingly abused spouse. The bastard didn't mind that. It also meant performing a convincing cabin kidnapping for Mitch's cameras. Finally, it required him to make a few phone calls on one of the burner phones we'd been using to keep in touch *and* recite a prepared script that I wrote for him to get you to drive out here. But he was game if it meant he could take that money and join Violet south of the border for a life of beaches and margaritas."

"But Violet never made it to Mexico, did she?" Kat guessed.

"Of course not," Ash acknowledged with what could only be described as glee. "She couldn't be trusted to keep her mouth shut. I told Hank I'd take her to the airport myself when I sent him off to lie low for a few days, but she never made it on any flight. Let's just say that she had an appointment with a bone saw and a metal oil drum of boiling lye solution."

"Oh God," Kat muttered.

"Rough, I know. I was much more merciful with Deputy Coolidge. That was me, by the way. Hank was just a bystander when I dispatched your boyfriend's buddy. Used the same knife that's making your shoulder seep blood right now. Anyway, before the real Violet met her bubbly end, I was able to make sure all the little intimate touches were just right, in case you looked at her ID real close. I mean, it worked out that we had the same general size and build—we were within one inch and five pounds of each other. But the rest was harder to fake. I'm normally blonde so I had to dye my hair black to match hers. My real eyes are blue. These are brown contact lenses. I guess I can take them out now."

She did exactly that, removing the lenses, tossing them into the wind, and then batting her blue eyes dramatically. After that, she walked over to the pickup truck, opened the door, and grabbed several items from the center console. They included a gag, a sheet of folded up paper, a black ski mask, and a phone with a small tripod.

"But why do all this?" she asked, as if she was an instructor teaching a class of trainees, something Kat suspected she may have once been. "Why this elaborate scheme?"

She set up the phone and tripod on the hood of the car, put the ski mask on her face, and walked back over with the gag.

"Why the hell do I care?" Kat asked belligerently, hoping her combative tone would renew the strength she found waning.

"What do you mean?" Ash demanded, clearly not expecting that response.

"I mean, you told me your real name and what you used to do. You admitted to murdering three people. You obviously have no intention of letting me live. Why should I listen to another word you have to say?"

Even though she was masked, it was clear that Ash was frowning. She walked over and stared down at Kat. Brown or blue, her eyes were icy and merciless. She stuffed the gag in her mouth.

"First of all, that is incredibly rude," she said picking up the police baton again. "Secondly, you are really spoiling my fun!"

Then, without warning, she pulled the baton back and took another swing, smashing it into Kat's left knee for a second time. The pain was terrible, but because her knee was still throbbing from the first blow, it didn't have the same impact as her tormentor probably intended. Kat didn't even bend over this time. Ash, untroubled, elaborately flung the baton in the air, watching it spin endlessly before it landed in the sand near a patch of brush. Then she walked over to the pickup truck.

"It's a good thing I'm being paid three million dollars to put up with your crap," she said.

The she adjusted the phone on the tripod, unfolded the piece of paper, and hit record.

"Hello everyone, out there in TV land," she said, using a curdled take on an announcer voice as she read from the paper, "I'm here with Katherine Gentry, private detective, one-time failed head of security at the Non-Rehabilitative Division of Norwalk's Department State Hospital for crazy killers, and former decorated Army Ranger. More importantly, she is the best friend of famed criminal profiler Jessie Hunt, who you all know and love. Well, almost all of you. It turns out that Jessie was *not* loved by one Andrea Robinson, who she wronged and deceived. But since Andy is no longer here to exact her revenge, she has left it to her dutiful servant, Zoe Bradway to pursue vengeance on her behalf.

"Now, I am not Zoe, but these are her words. Zoe has achieved vengeance on behalf of Andy Robinson through the majesty of Operation Z. The first part of the operation, as you may recall, was poisoning your fellow Angelenos as they went to the movies a few months ago. That didn't go quite as intended, but at least the practice run took out twenty-seven of you. Part two of the operation is much more targeted. It is directed specifically at those closest to Jessie, those she loves the most. This is one of those people."

Kat felt the bile rise in her throat and fought hard to choke it back down. With the gag over her mouth, she found it suddenly hard to breathe. Her eyes stung with hot, angry tears.

"Over the next little while, I will slowly torture Katherine Gentry, or Kat, as she likes to be called. Then, when she is beyond feeling pain, I will kill her. The video will be sent directly to Jessie and to the fine folks in the news media. It will serve as punishment to Jessie for her betrayal of Andy Robinson. She will always know that it was her failures that led to the suffering of those she cared for the most. She will have to live with that. It will be her cross to bear."

Kat tried to swallow but her mouth was too dry. Ash approached her. When she got close, she leaned in so that she couldn't be heard on the phone's microphone.

"It's a bummer that Hannah didn't come with you," she whispered. "I was supposed to do you both together. But I get paid as long as I get the job done. And since I won't be sending this video out to Jessie and the media for a few hours yet, I'll still have more than enough time to head back up to the cabin and pay her a visit. Maybe I'll do Mitch too, gratis, as a lucky strike extra."

Kat wriggled in her chair, praying that she could get close enough to butt Ash in the nose again, but it was useless. The woman smiled down at her nastily. When she spoke again, she was back to using the announcer voice.

"It's time for you and me to have some fun, knifey-style!"

CHAPTER TWENTY EIGHT

Jessie made sure not slam the door as she left the interrogation room.

She didn't want Gwendolyn Booth to think that she'd gotten the better of her and there was no more surefire way to give the woman that impression than to storm out of questioning her and bang the door closed. Besides, it didn't matter if Booth had gotten under her skin. They had more than enough for the D.A. to indict her for her ex-husband's murder. They didn't need a confession.

As she walked down the hall to the research office, she tried to put her finger on what was gnawing at her. Why was she so unsettled when everything seemed so certain? Was it Gwendolyn's unshakeable confidence that she would walk away from this? The woman was either truly as dense as she'd first appeared back at the airport or a master at creating that impression. Either way, Jessie couldn't read her, which is perhaps what scared her the most.

"Hey," Ryan called out as he chased after her down the hall, "why the rush?"

"I just needed to get out of there," Jessie muttered. "She was driving me up a wall."

"Don't let her get to you," he said. "She can play up her clueless, *Real Housewives* persona all she wants, but it doesn't change the fact that everything points to her guilt."

"I know, Ryan," Jessie said as they rounded the corner and stepped into the research office where Jamil and Beth looked up from their screens, "but it's that cluelessness that's making me nervous. I can't tell whether it's real or an act. She's so cool in there, I worry that she's just setting us up, waiting to pull the rug out from under us. I feel like we're pawns being manipulated in some larger game."

"Anything's possible," he conceded, "but she didn't have good answers for most of the questions we asked. When we pointed out that because of her daughter's minor trust, she was about go from getting about $25,000 a month in alimony to over $100,000,000, she had no good response."

"She said that it would all go to caring for Louisa and that the funds would be constantly monitored," Jessie countered. "Even if those funds end up including a beachside home in Malibu and limo service everywhere they go, that might hold up as legitimate. Unless she starts bathing in caviar or something, I'm not sure a court will say she doesn't have the authority to spend it as she deems appropriate."

"That's not the point though," Ryan countered. "However she uses the funds, the trust is a clear motive for murder. And don't forget that she was fleeing the country."

"She had a good answer for that one," Jessie reminded him. "Whether she was being dense or sneaky, she said she wanted to get away from all the media attention about Lowden's death. That was also why she was having Louisa leave her New York cousins early and meet her in Mazatlán: to do a detox from the crush of press attention and just be with each other. True or not, it was a compelling explanation. A jury might buy it."

Ryan shook his head adamantly.

"In a vacuum, that might sound credible, yes," he admitted, "but not when you add it on top of everything else. Don't forget that whoever she hired for this hit job knew where to go in the mansion. Gwendolyn has been there many times and knew her way around. And the hitman didn't kill Devon Booth, which makes sense too because that wasn't his assignment. It looks like she got in the way, so he simply knocked her out. But he let her live, which left her as a possible suspect for a while, conveniently drawing attention away from Gwendolyn."

Jessie sat down heavily on the research office sofa. Jamil and Beth were both staring at her, waiting to hear her response. Everything Ryan said made sense, and yet she couldn't shake the feeling that she was being played somehow.

"When is Decker's news conference announcing the arrest?" she asked.

"It's tentatively planned for a half-hour from now," Ryan said. "They're going to send out the media alert five minutes beforehand. He wanted to give us as much time as possible to lock down a confession before going on the record."

Jessie shook her head, more in frustration with herself than anything else.

"Can we do anything to help?" Jamil asked.

She thought for a second. There was actually.

"Can you pull up Gwendolyn Booth's recent financials?"

Jamil nodded, typing away at the keyboard.

"What do you need?" he asked.

"Do you see any major outflows recently, other than the Mexico trip? Anything that could mask a payment to a hitman?"

Jamil scanned the screen for a several seconds, then shook his head.

"I don't know what the going rate is for assassins these days, but I don't see a purchase or cash withdrawal by Gwendolyn Booth in the last six months totaling more than $4300."

Jessie turned to Ryan, who was leaning against the office door. He was clearly itching to give Decker the go-ahead to proceed with the news conference but knew from experience not to do so if she wasn't on board.

"Does this feel right to you, Ryan?" she asked. "Killing Lowden Booth on his private, security-heavy estate, isn't like knocking over a liquor store. You need either someone you can trust unconditionally or a real professional, preferably both. That doesn't come cheap. But where would Gwendolyn get the money for this? She couldn't pay up until after the deed was done and she got access to the trust funds. But is a hired killer going to take payment on layaway? Even then, how would she explain a giant expenditure without anything tangible to show for it to the trust's lawyers? Wouldn't that seem suspicious to them? To us?"

"Maybe by then it would be too late," Ryan suggested. "The evidence would be gone. The killer would be in the wind."

"Maybe," Jessie agreed, "but it doesn't explain her going to Mexico. If she's guilty and thought she was going to get away with it, the last thing she'd do is take a trip out of the country the day after her husband was murdered. Why draw attention to herself when there are so many other potential suspects? If she's conceived this elaborate plan, why be so clumsy at the end? No, if this is a set-up, I feel like it's someone else moving the pieces around. I just don't know who."

Ryan slumped down next to her on the sofa.

"Do I need to call Decker and tell him to cancel the news conference?" he asked glumly.

Jessie shook her head.

"It hasn't been a half-hour yet," she replied. "We just need to find someone who has as strong a motive as Gwendolyn but is better at manipulating the big board. Let's remember, this is a woman who basically got straight-up robbed during her divorce. It's hard to believe that she could have put together some big set-up."

Something about hearing herself say the phrase "set-up" sent a shiver down Jessie's spine. Though she couldn't explain why, she felt a sudden urge to call Hannah and Kat. She pulled out her phone as she tried to pin down what was bugging her. Was there some element of their abusive former assassin case that had the earmarks of a set-up too? She was just about to dial Hannah's number when another phone rang, and Beth waved at her frantically.

"It's Buckley Taverner's office," she said excitedly, "finally calling back. What should I do?"

"Put it on speaker," Jessie said, shoving her phone back in her pocket.

"LAPD Homicide Special Section, Research Office, this is Beth." she said, after she hit the speaker button.

"Beth, this is Sienna returning your call on behalf of Buckley Taverner. He's available now to speak to your investigators."

Beth looked at Jessie and Ryan questioningly. Jessie pointed to her cell phone, which she removed from her pocket again. Beth nodded.

"That's great, Sienna," she said. "I'll transfer you to them now."

She transferred the call. Jessie's phone rang. She answered right away.

"This is Jessie Hunt. I'm here with Captain Hernandez."

"Please hold for Mr. Taverner," Sienna said.

The phone buzzed. Jessie saw that there was a video call option and picked that. The screen was filled by a trim guy with shaggy blonde hair who couldn't have been out of his late twenties. He had the tanned skin of a regular surfer and wore a Hawaiian shirt. He was seated at a desk that looked to be made out of multiple surfboards. The ocean was visible in the background through a window. Part of her wondered if he'd kept them waiting to talk this long because he'd been catching waves all day.

"Hey guys," he said with a twang that suggested that he was from Texas or Oklahoma, "glad we were finally able to make this work. I assume this is about Lowden's panic room."

"It is," Jessie said. "We had a few questions about it, and it seems that no one in the mansion knew it existed other than him, so we thought you could help."

"Yeah," Taverner said, "he was pretty hardcore about keeping it secret, which I respect. I mean, what's the point of having a panic room if everyone knows it's there, right?"

“So when did he have it installed?” Ryan asked. “And how did he manage to keep it from everyone?”

“It was about six years ago,” Taverner said. “He was pretty clever about it actually. It was after his divorce but before he got remarried so he was alone in that bedroom, which made it easier. He said he was having the closet remodeled and that we were the closet company. We even wore fake uniforms and had a van with a fake logo. He paid for all of that. It was kind of awesome. Anyway, he had the whole residential wing closed off. I’m sure some of the staff thought it was weird but who was gonna question this guy, right?”

“Right,” Jessie said.

“We had the thing done in three days, working sixteen hour shifts,” Taverner continued. “It was one my earlier jobs, and he was paying serious bucks, so I was willing to do whatever it took.”

“I guess that explains why the room looked so bare bones, “Jessie noted. “I was surprised that it wasn’t more elaborate, considering his resources.”

“Exactly,” Taverner said. “I begged him to let us do more, but he just wanted it finished—quick and dirty—so we could get out of there fast with as few questions as possible. Anyway, I had to sign a nondisclosure agreement, so I couldn’t promote it, but it was worth it to be in tight with Lowden, you know? By the way, that’s why it took so long to get back to you. I had to get the all-clear from my lawyers before I could say a word. So what else do you want to know?”

“Yeah, I have a couple more questions,” Jessie said. “First, are there any cameras inside the panic room itself?”

“I’m afraid not,” Taverner said. “Lowden expressly prohibited that and I’m not a fan anyway. It’s not likely but there’s always the remote chance that an intruder could somehow gain access to them and use what they saw against the people inside. What else?”

“Why did you set up the panic room with an automatic alarm that was audible throughout the house?” she asked. “Wouldn’t that alert the intruder as well and let them know that there *is* a panic room? Why not go with a silent alarm instead?”

Taverner looked confused.

“I don’t get the question,” he said flatly.

Jessie didn’t understand his confusion and tried again.

“I guess I’m asking: why spend so much time hiding the existence of the panic room only to announce its presence with a blaring alarm? The Booth’s head of security heard it down in the kitchen.”

"Ms. Hunt," Taverner said, leaning forward in his chair. "The alarm is designed to be ear-splitting and scare off any potential intruder, yes. But not until the time of Lowden's choosing. It's not automatic. That would be ridiculous. What if he just wanted to go in there for the hell of it? He wouldn't be able to without alerting the entire estate. No, the alarm is manually activated using a button inside the room."

Jessie looked over at Ryan to make sure he'd heard Taverner say the same thing she had. His stunned expression told her that he had.

"Wait, just to be clear," she said, "you're saying that there's no automatic alarm for that panic room—that it has to be turned on by a person pushing a button *inside* the room."

"That's what I'm saying," Taverner said with certainty.

"Mr. Taverner," Jessie said, "we have to go, but do you think I can get your direct cell number in case we have any more urgent questions?"

"Sure, I'll text it to you," he said. "I feel like something big might have just shifted here. Can you fill me in?"

"I'm afraid I can't," she said. "But hopefully, it'll make sense tomorrow."

She hung up the phone as she popped up from the sofa. Her whole body was tingling as she tried to rein in her instincts, which were threatening to gallop ahead of what she actually knew.

"What?" Beth asked.

"Someone lied to us," Jessie said slowly, "and I'm trying to decide if it was an innocent mistake or an intentional attempt to mislead."

She turned to Ryan to see if he was on the same page as her.

"Devon Booth?" he asked.

She nodded.

"Yeah," she confirmed. "She told us that the alarm went off when she and Lowden entered the panic room. Now maybe she got mixed up in all the confusion with running in there. Maybe Lowden hit the button right after they got inside and it all got jumbled in her head after she got knocked out, but I have my doubts."

"Why?" Jamil asked.

"Because Grover Nix got up to that room in about three minutes. If the alarm really went off just after the panic room doors opened, he almost certainly would have gotten up there in time to see the intruder. Remember, according to Devon, she was tied up and there was the scuffle that knocked her out. That alone would have taken a couple of minutes. What makes more sense is that the alarm button was pressed *after* the intruder had been in there for longer than two minutes."

"Okay," Ryan said, "so let's play this out. Assuming Devon's in on it, she has this intruder tie her up, maybe threaten her to get Booth to open the safe, which is what she claimed the guy did. But somehow it goes wrong."

"Possible," Jessie agreed.

"But if Devon and the intruder were working together, I don't get why the intruder would kill Lowden and knock Devon unconscious," Ryan said. "Did they have a falling out or was that part of the plan? And why activate the alarm at that point? It only made Grover come up quicker, meaning the intruder was more likely to get caught."

"I don't know the answers to any of those questions," Jessie admitted. "And I'm starting to realize that I don't know very much about Devon Booth either. Because she's been married to him for five years, we didn't do much digging into her life before they met. I think we should remedy that. Can you get on that, Beth?"

"Right away," the junior researcher said.

"And Jamil, I'm wondering if Mr. Booth's lawyers might be a little more forthcoming with the documents you've been trying to secure for the last two days if they got a call from Chief of Police Decker. Do you think you could coordinate that?"

"Sure," he said. "What would the chief be asking for?"

"The terms of any prenuptial agreement," she told him. "We still don't even know if they had one, much less what it might have said. That needs to change."

"Okay, but I worry that they might still hold onto those details kind of tight," Jamil warned.

"Not if their client was murdered to get at his billions," she countered.

"I'll join you on the call with the chief, Jamil," Ryan said. "Once we make it clear the significance of getting this information, he'll reach out. And in my experience, when Roy Decker wants something, he usually gets it."

"I think you'll have to join him on that call from the road," Jessie said. "We should get moving."

"Where to?" Ryan asked.

"The home of Devon's sister, Tricia," she replied as she headed out the door. "Remember, the other security guy, Rufus, said that's where she'd be staying for a while. Can someone text us that address?"

“On it,” Beth called out as Jessie and Ryan started down the hall.

They hurried to the door leading to the parking garage. As Ryan opened it, another thought popped into Jessie’s head.

“Better have them cancel that news conference,” she said. “We should probably be sure who the killer is before we announce a name on television.”

CHAPTER TWENTY NINE

Hannah pulled up next to Kat's car and jumped out.

She had missed it completely the first time she drove by because it was hidden behind a large boulder off to the side of the road, but using the AirTag locator she'd hidden under the passenger seat, she found it on the way back. Looking at the phone location app on her phone, she saw that Kat had walked about a mile to the east into the desert before she disappeared completely, likely a sign that her signal was too weak out here in this isolated stretch of land.

The text from Kat saying she was leaving her car and going to the meet with Hank Keene was from twenty minutes ago. That meant that Hannah had to move fast. The only problem was that once she eventually got a mile east of this spot, she would have no idea where to go.

I'll solve that problem when the time comes.

A sharp wind tore across the desert, giving her a shiver. She threw on Mitch's bulky tan parka and zipped in up. Even though it was June, and it was still a little warm now, evening would be arriving soon and she knew it could get chilly fast here once the sun started to set.

As she left the road and stepped onto the hard-packed dirt, she considered texting Jessie. She felt guilty for sending that earlier message as she was leaving Lake Arrowhead asking how her sister's case was going and saying that she and Kat weren't having any luck with theirs. Technically she hadn't lied when she'd texted: *Still don't know where he took her. Palm Springs FBI will be on the scene soon to help,* though the spirit of the message hadn't been entirely forthright.

But she knew that if she hadn't fired off a pre-emptive text, Jessie would have eventually reached out to find out how things were going, and she would have had to lie to avoid violating Hank's rule about not informing anyone about the situation. Better to communicate on her terms and avoid raising suspicion.

She'd only been off the road for about ten yards when the dirt gave way to softer sand, and she saw a set of footprints that she chose to believe were Kat's. She broke into a jog as she followed them up one hill, back down, and then up a second one.

After fifteen minutes and what she suspected was about a mile, she lost the footprints completely as the sand gave way to a stretch of brush and rocks. She had no idea which way to go next. She wasn't even sure if she could maintain a straight path without the footprints as a guide.

As she stood there, debating what to do, fully aware that each passing second put both Kat and Violet in greater danger, she heard a sound that was unmistakable: someone screamed in pain. She immediately began running in that direction. The rocky terrain again gave way to sand. Less than a minute later, a second scream told her that she was on the right track as she sprinted up a steep dune, trying not to lose her balance in the shifting sand.

When she got to the top, she looked down into a vale and noted movement about fifty yards ahead of her. She squinted, holding her hand up to block the sun, and was horrified by what she saw. For a second she thought she was having a waking nightmare.

Kat was tied to a metal folding chair. Her face was bloody, as was her shirt. There was a white towel, slowly turning red, duct-taped to her right shoulder. More duct tape covered her crimson forearm. She was groaning softly. Standing over her menacingly, holding a hunting knife, was Violet Sheridan. Hank Keene was nowhere in sight.

Hannah stood there, frozen in place, barely able to comprehend what was right in front of her eyes. Everything she'd believed to be true ten seconds ago was wrong. She didn't understand what any of it meant but apparently Violet wasn't a victim at all.

The woman—carrying herself with a confidence she'd never shown in Kat's office—sheathed her knife and held her hand up to Kat's face, causing her whole body to shake in revulsion.

"Made you flinch," Violet said.

In that moment, Hannah realized that the person in front of her wasn't just deceptive, she was a dangerous sociopath and that standing atop this sand dune, completely exposed, wasn't the best move. She scurried back out of sight behind the lip and listened as the woman talked.

"My name isn't really Violet Sheridan and that guy in the ground over there isn't actually my husband, although he *really* is a scumbag."

Hannah pulled out her cell phone to try to call Jessie, anyone. But there were no bars. The top of the screen read "no service." There was no time to run back to the car. There was no time to go anywhere. Besides, no one would be able to find this place in time to do anything even if she could contact them. She was on her own.

Hannah poked her head back over the dune and tried to focus on the words of Kat's tormentor, whose real name, if she was to be believed, was apparently Ash Pierce. As she listened, she slid down the sand dune and hid behind a large rock about thirty yards from where the two women were. She didn't have the first clue what she intended to do now that she was closer, but it was clear that Ash had no intention of letting Kat survive this experience, so Hannah had to *do something*.

Meanwhile Ash was going on about what an idiot Hank was, seeming to get great pleasure out of describing how easy he was to control.

"...that made him the perfect patsy for my grand plan."

"Grand plan?" Kat repeated, with a laugh.

Ash clearly didn't like that. She went silent and walked over to the pickup truck. Hannah used the distraction as an opportunity to scurry to another boulder fifteen yards closer to Kat. She was safely concealed behind it when Ash returned to Kat holding a baton, which she violently slammed into her left kneecap, before spitting, "probably not a good idea to laugh at me."

She went on, talking about how she admired Kat's bravery, but the detective's attention seemed to be focused elsewhere, as if she was looking for an escape route. Hannah considered trying to get her attention but decided it was too risky. If Ash somehow noticed her, then it would all be over.

So she stayed put, listening to Ash happily describe how she manipulated Hank and the real Violet, how she dissolved Violet's body in an oil drum filled with lye, and murdered Deputy Coolidge. She seemed especially proud of how she managed to recreate Violet's look enough to fool them.

"My real eyes are blue. These are brown contact lenses. I guess I can take them out now."

As she did exactly that, Hannah peeked out and noticed an ideal spot to get closer to them. There was a hollow at the edge of the clearing where they were situated that was overgrown with heavy brush. If she could get to that without being seen, she would be within a dozen feet of Kat.

She got her chance a moment later when Ash went to the pickup again to retrieve some additional items. Dashing out right as the wind picked up, Hannah used its howl to cover her footsteps. She made it with time to spare as Ash was busy setting up a phone and tripod on the hood of the truck.

"But why do all this?" the woman asked loudly. "Why this elaborate scheme?"

"Why the hell do I care?" Kat retorted with a confrontational tone that Hannah both adored and feared. She knew Ash wouldn't respond well to it.

Sure enough, she walked over and stared Kat down icily.

"First of all, that is incredibly rude. Secondly, you are really spoiling my fun!"

Then she struck Kat in the same knee again, though she didn't get anywhere near as satisfying a response this time around. Apparently bored with the weapon, she tossed it high in the air. It hit the sand and came to a stop just feet from the patch of brush in front of the hollow where Hannah was now crouched.

"It's a good thing I'm being paid three million dollars to put up with your crap," Ash said as she walked back to the pickup truck.

Hannah barely heard the words as her eyes focused laser-like, on the baton, less than a hammock's length from where she was currently huddled. There was no excuse now. It was as if fate had placed a gift in her lap. She had no choice but to use it. If she didn't, how could she ever face herself again?

"Now, I am not Zoe, but these are her words," Ash pronounced in an absurdly dramatic faux anchor voice. "Zoe has achieved vengeance on behalf of Andy Robinson through the majesty of Operation Z."

As Hannah listened, she slid off her shoes, hoping that when she made her move, being barefoot might offer her some extra advantage as she tried sneak up on Ash quietly.

"Over the next little while, I will slowly torture Katherine Gentry, or Kat, as she likes to be called. Then, when she is beyond feeling pain, I will kill her," Ash continued.

Hannah got as close to the edge of the brush as she could without risking being seen, Right now, she was particularly grateful for Mitch's tan parka, which blended in nicely with the desert landscape.

"The video will be sent directly to Jessie and to the fine folks in the news media. It will serve as punishment to Jessie for her betrayal of Andy Robinson. She will always know that it was her failures that led to the suffering of those she cared for the most. She will have to live with that. It will be her cross to bear."

Hannah's heart seemed to stop beating for a moment. She had been focused on Kat but now she turned to stare at Ash. The fear she'd been feeling at trying to take on a former special operations Marine and CIA assassin didn't disappear completely, but another emotion rose up and took a seat beside it: fury.

CHAPTER THIRTY

The idea that this mad woman had spent all her time planning a mission with the primary goal of making Jessie suffer filled Hannah with a rage that almost made her vision blur.

It was all she could do not to run out and grab that baton right now. She clutched at the sand in the hollow, squeezing it tight as it slipped through fingers. She reminded herself to breathe.

We'll see who suffers.

Ash walked back over to Kat and whispered something in her ear. Then she stood upright again and turned so that she was facing both Kat and the camera on the hood of the truck. Her back was to Hannah.

"It's time for you and me to have some fun, knifey-style!" she shouted like a ringmaster at a circus.

Then she removed the hunting knife from its sheath and held it up above her head. It glimmered in the sunlight.

"Should we maybe start with the pinkie finger?" she asked Kat, "Or perhaps the ring finger, not that you'll need that one. Neither will Mitch once I catch up to him in a few hours."

Ash laughed at her own joke as she reached down and grabbed hold of Kat's left hand, which was zip-tied and immobile. She moaned in horror. The wind howled too, as if in shared protest. Hannah knew it was now or never.

She slid out of the hollow, crawled over to the baton, scooped it up, raised it above her head, and darted toward the two women. She was only steps away when the wind gust suddenly died out. She heard the squish of her own bare feet on the sand and knew that Ash did too by the way her shoulders suddenly tensed up. The CIA assassin spun around with shocking speed, swinging her knife arm in a wide arc as she turned.

But it was too late for Hannah to stop and, besides, she had no intention to. She continued with her own swing of the baton but dug her heels into the sand, slowing her momentum moving forward so as not to run right into the blade that was slicing in her direction.

Ash Pierce was a former special operations Marine and CIA assassin with years of hand-to-hand combat training. Hannah Dorsey was a recent high school graduate who had taken a few self-defense classes at her sister's insistence. But there was one thing their vast difference in experience couldn't account for: Hannah was very tall, and Ash was not.

Hannah's long arm reached out and the baton acted like an extension of it, resulting in a clean, sharp thwack on Ash's left temple. Ash's swipe, despite the quickness of her reaction, couldn't compensate for her shorter arm, smaller weapon, and the distance between her and Hannah. The hunting knife ripped through the outer layer of Mitch's parka but didn't make contact with Hannah's body.

For a second after the exchange, neither of them moved. Hannah stared at Ash, who had a stunned, glassy-eyed expression on her face. But she hadn't dropped the knife. Seeing that, Hannah raised the baton again, ready to take another swing, but as she did, she lost her grip and it slipped from her sweaty fingers to the ground below.

She looked up at Ash, who still appeared a little off, but less so than a moment ago. Blood was pouring from the spot on her head where the baton had made contact, and running down the left side of her face. She already had another streak of blood extending down from her nose, into her bloody-toothed mouth, and dripping off her chin. She looked like a zombie who'd just fed on a whole family. Behind her, in the chair, Kat's eyes bulged in horror.

"Hi Hannah," Ash said, taking a step forward and raising the hunting knife as she smiled widely. Her teeth were goopy and viscous red.

Out of the corner of her eye, Hannah saw Kat lean back in her folding chair and then, with violent force, lunge forward, slamming into Ash. Her upper body collapsed hard, crashing into the back of Ash's legs, taking out the woman's knees and knocking her to the ground face-first.

Hannah didn't hesitate. She grabbed the baton from the dirt and in one continuous motion smashed it down hard on Ash's right forearm. She heard a loud crack and a sharp gasp from the woman as her grip on the weapon loosened. Hannah didn't take any chances and swung at her knife hand like it was a golf ball, and the baton was a driver. The knife came free and skidded off across the clearing.

Groaning, Ash slid her left, undamaged hand under her chest and began to push herself up, trying to get to her knees. Hannah watched her for a second, not sure whether to be impressed or scared.

This bitch is like a human Terminator.

She decided to go with pissed off. Taking a step forward, she reared back and swung the baton hard, landing it right on the crown of the woman's head. Ash immediately collapsed back to the ground and lay still. Hannah took a step closer and saw blood-stained saliva dripping out of the side of her mouth. She was out cold.

Hannah gripped the baton as she stood over her. Then she looked at Kat, lying helplessly on her stomach, zip-tied to a folding chair. She looked back at the woman who put her there and intended the same fate for Hannah, who wanted for Jessie to see the video of it happening, for her to relive the memory endlessly, for her to suffer forever.

Hannah gripped the baton even tighter, shaking with renewed rage. She imagined lifting it up high and bringing it down on Ash's head in the same spot as before, again and again, until the skull cracked open, until the brains oozed out.

Then she blinked, and it seemed to break the spell. She followed that up with a deep breath. After that, she shook her head forcibly from side to side, jettisoning the image from her mind. She felt her grip on the baton loosen.

That's not who I am. I'm better than that. I have to be.

Kat groaned. Hannah rushed over to her and slowly rolled the folding chair over so that she was on her back. Then she removed the gag.

"Zip ties," Kat muttered.

"Right," Hannah said. "I'll get the hunting knife and cut you free."

"No," Kat said hoarsely. "More zip ties in truck. Secure her."

"I have to free you first," Hannah insisted.

"CIA assassin," Kat warned sharply, "Too dangerous. Could wake up anytime. Drag her to truck's front grille. Tie wrists. Top priority. Then me."

As bad as Kat looked and as much help as she seemed to need, she was insistent and she made sense, so Hannah did as she was told. Once Ash was secured, she grabbed the knife, freed her boss, and set her comfortably on the desert floor, where she carefully poured some water into her mouth.

"We've got to get you to the hospital," she said. "I got the truck keys out of Ash's pocket. We can be in Palm Springs in fifteen minutes."

"First warn others," Kat insisted.

"What do you mean?"

"She said she was paid $3 million," Kat told her.

"I know," Hannah said, "I overheard everything she said."

"Think!" Kat said, rasping. "We know Andy Robinson wanted you, me, and Ryan killed. But how do we know how much Zoe paid Ash for each hit? Was it $1 million for each of us? Or was it $1.5 million each for just you and me? Did Zoe hire someone else entirely to take out Ryan? If so, wouldn't it make sense for that person to do it at the same time as the hit on us, so he couldn't be warned?"

"Oh God," Hannah muttered.

"Just in case," Kat insisted, "we have to warn them!"

Hannah checked her phone again.

"There's no service out here, Kat," she said. "We have to get closer to civilization."

"Then go! Hurry!"

"There's no way I'm leaving you here. I have to load you in the truck."

"No time," Kat objected. "Have to warn them."

Just then, they heard a groan. Hannah looked over and saw that Ash was starting to regain consciousness. Suddenly, an idea occurred to her. She looked back at Kat.

"I may have another way."

CHAPTER THIRTY ONE

"You ready for this?" Ryan asked.

Jessie nodded although she wasn't sure if she was.

A half-hour ago they had accused Lowden Booth's ex-wife of hiring someone to kill him. Now they were walking up the path to Devon Booth's sister's house in Ladera Heights, potentially about to make the same accusation against the man's widow. They were either going to solve a billionaire's murder or embarrass themselves and possibly the entire LAPD.

"Just remember," he said as he rang the doorbell, "let's wait until we get a response from Jamil before making any formal accusation."

"I know," Jessie said. "Truthfully, I don't love the idea of even going in there without knowing if there was a prenup, but we're out of time. Word is going to get out that we don't buy Gwendolyn as our killer. If the feds hear that and take over, we may not get to question Devon again, or anyone else for that matter."

"Don't worry," Ryan said. "If anyone can get Booth's lawyers to spill about what their financial arrangement was, it's Decker. Have a little faith."

Jessie preferred to have faith in herself and scanned the neighborhood, hoping she might see a stray Lamborghini on the street that would give away the fact that Devon was already spending her dead husband's money without restraint. But there was nothing like that in this decidedly upper-middle-class neighborhood. Instead it was all hybrid SUVs and sensible sedans.

The closest thing to a flashy sports car was the twenty-year-old red Camaro just down the street. The driver, with his carefully cultivated five o'clock shadow, Ray-Ban sunglasses, and cigarette dangling from his lips, looked anything but sensible. In fact, he looked like an extra from an old episode of *Miami Vice* that he was still hoping might re-air one day.

Jessie was about to offer a snarky comment about the guy when the door opened. They were greeted by a woman who was clearly related to Devon. Tricia Barry was four years older, but she had many of the same features that made her little sister so attractive: the big, brown eyes, full lips, and the button nose.

She also had the same voluptuous figure, tan skin, and wavy brown hair. She was shorter and heavier than her sister but then again, unlike Devon, she'd given birth to two children, both of whom Jessie could hear yelling in the background.

"Can I help you?" she asked with a friendly smile.

"Hi," Ryan said, holding out his ID. "Sorry to bother you in the evening but we're here to see Devon Booth. I'm Captain Hernandez with the LAPD and this is Jessie Hunt. We actually spoke to her yesterday, and we need to follow up on some questions."

"Okay," she said, opening the door, "I'm Devon's sister, Tricia. She's in the family room with the kids. Why don't you come on back?"

They followed her down the hall, dodging nerf footballs and assorted Lego pieces that littered the floor.

"I'm sorry," Tricia said as they walked, "I wish I could say this is unusual, but the place always looks like this. When you've got two boys who are seven and four, it's impossible to keep a floor clean for more than ten minutes straight, so I gave up trying."

"Don't worry about it," Jessie said as they arrived in the family room, where the two boys were wrestling on the floor while Devon sat on a nearby sofa, watching them with detached amusement. When she saw Jessie and Ryan, her expression changed to one of mild surprise.

"Your friends are here," Tricia told her with less coddling than Jessie would have expected from an older sister helping a grieving sibling through the loss of a spouse. Then again, having grown up as an only child who only learned that she had a sister two years ago, she wasn't an expert on those dynamics.

"Is something wrong?" Devon asked, standing up. She was dressed in lounge-style yoga pants and a ribbed t-shirt that seemed casual but probably cost a combined $500. Somehow she still looked impossibly chic despite her injuries.

The bruise on her right cheekbone was starting to turn yellow and her split lower lip was pinched with a small suture strips. She had another dressing on the side of her head and wraps on both wrists where the ropes had been tied.

"We just have a few additional questions that have come up since we spoke to you last," Ryan said. "Do you have a few minutes?"

She looked at the kids rolling around on the floor and then at her sister, apparently unsure how to respond.

"That's okay," Tricia said. "Since school's out now, their bedtime schedule is completely shot. I was thinking of taking them for pizza and a movie anyway to give you a break from all the screaming and shouting for a few hours. I'll tell Dan to meet us there when he gets off work. We'll go now so you can talk freely."

"You sure?" Devon asked.

"Not a problem," Tricia replied before turning to the kids on the floor and bellowing in a voice that would impress a drill sergeant. "Boys, shoes on and out the door in two minutes if you want pizza and a movie!"

The children immediately stopped wrestling, scrambled to their feet, and ran down the hall to where their shoes presumably were.

"That was amazing!" Jessie marveled.

"That's not all," Tricia said, holding her index finger in the air expectantly. "Wait for it."

"Ready," the boys said in unison five seconds later.

Tricia smiled.

"It's all worth it for moments like that," she sighed.

"She truly has a gift," Devon said with real affection.

Jessie was impressed with how relaxed the new widow was, considering that the LAPD had shown up unexpectedly in her adopted living room. Either she was innocent or that rare breed that could truly separate work from family. Only in this case "work" would theoretically be murder.

"It seems only fair to give you a break," Tricia said, walking over and giving her sister a hug, before addressing Jessie and Ryan. "Seriously, the girl comes over here to get away from all the pain and madness of the last thirty-six hours and her supposed safe space has two psychotic rabblerousers knocking into each other all afternoon. I thought she was going to have to hang out in the panic room. Did you know my baby sister had a panic room built for us?"

"No," Ryan said. "We had no idea. That's very generous."

For the first time since they'd arrived, Jessie noticed Devon look uncomfortable.

"We want pizza!" the boys screamed from the other room.

"I should go," Tricia said, heading for the door.

The moment that she was gone, the house became instantly quieter and to Jessie, more tension filled. Before either she or Ryan could speak, Devon launched in.

"I know it seems weird, me having a panic room built for them, but it's really not," she said. "Lowden was the one who suggested it after they were robbed a couple of years ago. Luckily they were out of town at the time. But he said they should have a safe place to go if it ever happened when they were here, so he gave me the name of this guy and he paid for the whole setup. Looking back, it's kind of weird that he never told me that *we* had one of our own. It seems like that would have been the perfect time to mention it."

"Yeah, that is odd," Jessie agreed. "Actually, the questions we had were about the panic room, but before we get to that, how are you feeling?"

She made a circle around her own face to indicate that she was asking about Devon's injuries.

"Oh, they hurt worse than they look," Devon said bitterly, before adding, "just kidding. They have me on some medication that takes the edge off the physical injuries, and you know, the whole dead husband thing. So if I seem a little loopy, that's why. They call it Vicodin. I call it my 'pain, pain, go away, I know you'll be back another day…to rip my heart out but until then this will keep you at bay' pill. I never was much of a poet. Also, did I mention that they think I have a concussion?"

She did a little twirl, nearly losing her balance before recovering. Ryan looked over at Jessie with his patented "profile this lady" expression but she had nothing for him. At this point she didn't know if they were dealing with murder-induced guilt, head trauma, drug intoxication, plain old crazy, or some combination of all of it.

"Do you want to sit back down?" she asked.

"I do," Devon said, "but do you mind if we do it in the back den? The kids aren't allowed to bring toys in there so there's a vastly reduced chance that I'll step on something plastic and pointy. Plus the couches there have fewer ice cream stains."

"Lead the way," Ryan said.

They followed her down the hallway, past the bedrooms to what looked a combination home theater, poker room, and bar. Jessie could see why Devon wanted to come here. Compared to the rest of the house, it was an oasis.

"Make yourselves comfortable," she said. "I just need to visit the water closet. I won't be but a minute or two."

She stepped into the bathroom just across the hall, but neither Jessie nor Ryan made any move to sit down. It was a tired old trick to invite law enforcement to relax while the suspect being questioned snuck out a bathroom window. Considering that Devon was barefoot, injured, and potentially drugged up, it seemed like an ill-advised move, but they'd both seen dumber choices, so they waited by the entrance to the den, trying to seem casual.

But true to her word, after two minutes, a flush, and a running faucet, she came back out. When she opened the door, she appeared startled to find them both still standing there and stumbled slightly. Ryan grabbed her arm to steady her.

"Thanks," she said, regrouping and leading them into the den. "You took me by surprise there. Either you were worried that I was going to trip and accidentally drown in the toilet, or you thought I might make a break for it and crawl out the window."

"The options are limitless when someone is on heavy painkillers," Ryan replied diplomatically.

Devon sat down in an easy chair facing the big screen TV on the far wall and Jessie and Ryan sat on the adjoining sofa.

"So what is this about the panic room?" Devon asked, rocking back and forth in the chair. "You said you had more questions."

"Right," Jessie said, deciding to be direct and see if it would generate a reaction. "We were just a little confused because yesterday you said that when you and Lowden ran into the panic room the alarm sounded immediately."

Devon looked at her blankly for a second, as if she didn't totally get that the chatty portion of the visit was over. But after a moment, she seemed to register that she was expected to either confirm or deny her earlier statement.

"That's right," she said. "It started blaring really loudly."

"Yeah," Jessie replied, "that's where we have the issue, because we spoke to the guy who designed the room, and he informed us that the alarm doesn't turn on when the door to the room is opened. It has to be manually activated by pushing a button inside the room."

Devon scrunched up her face, perplexed. Then she pulled her feet up under her.

"Huh," she said. "Are you sure? Because I could have sworn it went on when we ran in."

"Well," Ryan said evenly, "this guy *did* build the room, so we are sure. You can see why we came to you because that's quite an odd discrepancy."

Devon nodded slowly.

"I guess," she said slowly, before her eyes lit up, "but is it really that odd? I mean, everything was happening so fast. We had a guy with a mask chasing us. Maybe I got it wrong. I suppose it's possible that we ran in, and Lowden pushed the button right after we got inside, and I got confused about the timing. I was really scared and then I got tied up and punched in the face and had my head slammed against a wall. It's possible that I'm not as reliable a witness as I thought I was. Does this mess things up really badly? Is it going to make it harder to catch the guy?"

Jessie looked over at Ryan to see if he wanted to press her harder, but he looked frustrated, and she understood why. Devon's answer could interpreted as either deceptive or a sincere admission of prior confusion. What had seemed like a "gotcha!" moment felt much weaker all of a sudden. Jessie tried a different tack.

"We're not sure yet," she said. "Every discrepancy complicates matters, so we always like to tie up as many loose ends as possible. Speaking of tying things up, we did a little more digging recently and I was interested to learn about your career back in Las Vegas before you met Lowden, when you were Devon Pike, single gal about town."

"You mean when I was a waitress at the joint where we met?" she asked.

"No, before that."

Devon shook her head uncertainly.

"I had a lot of jobs," she said. "I was a showgirl for a while. I was a blackjack dealer. I don't know which one you mean."

"I'm talking specifically about your time as a magician's assistant," Jessie said. "You did that for about seven years, right?"

"Yeah," Devon acknowledged wistfully, shifting positions in the easy chair. "I worked with Zanzibar the Magnificent for a long time. He was great. Unfortunately, he had a heart attack and died, right on stage actually. I had to get a new job after that. Bounced around quite a bit. No one was as good to me as Zanzibar. His real name was Zane by the way. Very sweet man but he loved his cinnamon rolls and his cigars. In the end, I think that was the combination that did him in. He was only forty-seven when he died."

"I'm really sorry for your loss," Jessie said. "I actually watched some videos of his act on YouTube and was fascinated by how involved you were in it. I was especially intrigued by the section with all the rope tricks, how you got out of being tied up in ropes, but particularly how you got *into* them. That's a real skill, to be able to tie yourself up with ropes, don't you think, Devon?"

The woman shrugged modestly. Something about it didn't seem genuine.

"It's not exactly the sort of thing you put on your LinkedIn profile," she said.

"Yeah, but it could be handy in specific circumstances," Jessie pressed, pausing briefly before deciding that she been noodling around long enough. She knew she was supposed to wait for a call from Jamil with word about a possible prenup. She knew that going down this road without evidence was a huge risk.

But she could sense a vulnerability in Devon, one that she wasn't sure would ever be present again. She might never get another chance to exploit it. She could feel Ryan's eyes on her but didn't look over for his approval. Instead, she just went for it.

"Can I throw a scenario out to you and see what you think?" she asked.

"Sure," Devon said, though the hesitation in her voice suggested she might not be all that enthused by the idea.

"What if someone wasn't happy with the state of her marriage and was looking for a way out, but wanted what she felt was hers too, what she was owed? And what if she found out that her husband had a panic room? What if she had someone break into her mansion, gave the guy all the details to evade security on the way to the bedroom, and then tricked her husband into opening that panic room? What if she made sure the intruder got in, had him subdue her husband and punch her in the face, but then had him leave right away? What if she activated the panic room alarm after that so that the intruder had time to escape? What if she *killed* her husband herself, taking him completely by surprise, smashing his head into the safe, which she never intended to open in the first place? What if she tied herself up using the skills she'd learned as a magician's assistant all those years ago so that she looked like an innocent victim? What if she further cast suspicion elsewhere by slamming her own head against the wall, concussing herself, maybe even knocking herself out? What if the whole robbery was a charade, part of some larger plan? What do you think of that scenario, Devon?"

The whole time that Jessie had been talking, Devon's jaw had gotten more and more slack until, by the time the monologue was complete, it was wide open. She looked dazed and blinked several times, as if walking out of a dark room into the sunlight. Then she unfurled her feet from under her and planted them squarely on the floor. When she spoke, her voice was quiet but clear.

"Setting aside how mean-spirited what you just suggested is, why would you think that I would do any of that?" she demanded. "I've been married to Lowden for half a decade. I have an amazing life. You yourself pointed out that I used to be a magician's assistant. I told you that I was a showgirl, a blackjack dealer, and a waitress. But what I *didn't* tell you was that I didn't work at the Bellagio or the Venetian. I worked at low rent places. It was a grubby life. Lowden saved me from all that. The idea that I would ever put that at risk is ridiculous. And that's on top of the fact that I loved him. Do you have any reason, or what do you call it, *motive*, for me to do what you described?"

This was the risk Jessie had taken. She glanced over at Ryan to see if he'd gotten a text from Jamil saying that Decker had come through for them with the proof they needed from Lowden Booth's lawyers. But her husband and boss, who knew exactly what she was silently asking, shook his head. He'd heard nothing. She looked back at Devon, who was staring at her expectantly, with hurt in her eyes.

"You are taking these random little things," the woman said intensely, leaning forward in her chair, "and turning them into a conspiracy that isn't there. So I got confused about when the alarm went off—big deal. And yes, I was a magician's assistant who also happened to get tied up by an intruder. Is that really enough to accuse me of killing my husband? I feel like you should have more than that. Or did you just decide that it *has* to be the younger, gold-digging wife and figure you'd make the evidence fit your theory, even if it doesn't make sense? And while we're at it, have you ever considered that maybe whoever did this wanted to make me look bad? That this could be some kind of set up and the person who murdered Lowden has some other motive that none of us can see yet?"

Jessie had asked herself that question repeatedly for the last two days and always came up empty. It didn't feel great to have it thrown back at her now by Devon Booth. But was she right? Could all of this really be a set up? If so, who would do such a thing? Who even had the resources to plan such an involved undertaking? And to what end?

Just then, both her phone and Ryan's buzzed simultaneously. She was about to reach for hers when the lights in the den suddenly went out.

They were in total darkness.

CHAPTER THIRTY TWO

Devon let out a scream.

Jessie would have clamped her hand over the woman's mouth if she could have found it.

"What the hell?" Devon said a moment later, her voice cutting through the blackness. "There's no way this is an accident, right? Do you think it's connected to Lowden? Is the guy who killed him coming for me too?"

"Be quiet," Ryan whispered.

"Oh God, I should never have come here," Devon muttered. "I've put my sister's family in danger. I should have just stayed at the Estate like Grover recommended."

"Devon," Jessie said, making sure to keep her voice quiet and calm as she unholstered her gun, "we need you to stop talking now. This is probably nothing, just a blown fuse or something. But freaking out won't help. So just back up toward the big screen on the wall, crouch down, and wait there. Okay?"

"Uh-huh," Devon mumbled. "You're not going to leave me, are you?"

"No," Ryan said, "just do as you were told and stop talking."

They heard rustling as Devon finally did as she was asked. Jessie reached out, found Ryan, and leaned in close to his ear.

"There's only one way in here," she whispered. "If this is some kind of attack, do we want to wait it out?"

"I'm texting it in now, just in case," he whispered back. "Backup should be here in less than three minutes. But I don't want to just wait in here. If this *is* an attacker and he's heavily armed, we're sitting ducks. I can see a dim light coming from a window somewhere in the hallway area. Cover me while I get closer to the door. When I whistle, shine a light in that direction."

"Please be careful," Jessie pleaded quietly as he moved away.

"I will," he whispered back.

Jessie could hear the soft swish of his slacks as he moved away from her. She pulled out her phone and prepared to shine its flashlight in the direction of the doorway while she pointed her weapon there too. After about thirty seconds, she heard a soft whistle.

She pushed the button and a cascade of light emanated from her phone, lighting up the entire section of the den near the door. To her shock, there was a man already inside the room, halfway to the sofa and her. She recognized him.

The cigarette and Ray-Bans were gone but the five o'clock shadow was still there. It was the guy from the Camaro across the street. Only now he was holding a revolver in his right hand, which he was pointing off to Jessie's right. The light seemed to blind him, and he lifted his left hand to shield his eyes. As he did, he fired the revolver.

Jessie heard the bang as she felt a whoosh of air whiz by, uncomfortably close to her right ear. Instinctively, she dove to the ground. For a moment, she lost her grip on the phone and the room slipped into darkness. Just seconds later, she heard another shot go by somewhere several feet above her head.

She saw the dim light of the facedown phone, snagged it, and shined it back in the direction where she thought the man was. He was still there, wildly swinging the weapon around in front of him.

Ryan, who was now behind the guy, took a giant leap and whacked down on his hand, knocking the gun to the ground. As the guy turned around, Ryan clocked him in the jaw with his left fist, sending him sprawling to the floor.

Jessie leapt to her feet, still shining the light on the man, trying to keep it steady as Ryan pulled out his handcuffs. Then she felt a sharp, unexpected pain at the back of her skull, as if she'd been hit with something. The phone slipped from her hand, though she managed to hold onto her gun, as she fell forward onto the sofa.

"Jessie, are you okay?" Ryan called out.

"I don't know," she replied, feeling the back of her head. "I think I just got—."

Suddenly the house lights came back on. Jessie could see but felt mildly disoriented as she pushed herself up from the sofa. Ryan had the man with the stubble pinned to the ground in handcuffs.

"Dammit," the man muttered, "the lights were supposed to stay off for five minutes. That was barely two. I got ripped off."

"That's the least of your problems, buddy," Ryan told him before looking up at Jessie. "What happened to you?

"I got hit in the head with something," she said, glancing around behind her. On the carpet was an empty ice bucket. Notably *not* behind her was Devon Booth.

"Where the hell is Devon?" she asked.

"She's not there?" Ryan said, standing up and pulling the stubble guy to his feet as well.

A thought began to percolate in Jessie's aching head as she steadied herself, took a few steps, and peeked around behind the bar. She turned back around to face the two men.

"There's only one door out of here and you were blocking it," she said as she rubbed her sore skull, "which makes me think one thing: that panic room is in here somewhere."

She felt a mild wave of nausea pass over her and reached out for the bar to steady herself.

"Jessie?" Ryan said, concern in his voice.

"Yeah, I know," she told him, "once this is done, we should go to the hospital and get me checked out. Apparently now ice buckets are weapons and I was on the receiving end of one. So that's not great."

"Maybe you should lie down," he suggested.

"Maybe," she said, "but you know I'm not going to. As long as we're here, let's see if we can find Booth's killer. And I feel confident calling her that now. She was damn convincing there for a while, but innocent people don't generally smash criminal profilers in the head. I'm willing to bet that Sonny Crockett over here is our friendly neighborhood mansion intruder, isn't that right?"

"I don't know what you're talking about," the guy grumbled sourly.

Jessie looked the guy over, fully taking him in for the first time. He was a total poser. He'd come in here with a cheap revolver and no expertise in how to use it. She wasn't sure if he was Devon's lover or just her lackey, but it was clear that he wasn't the brains behind this operation. Maybe she could use that. Ignoring the dull throb she felt, she took a step toward him.

"You *do* know what I'm talking about," she growled at him, "and you're about to go down for some serious crimes, pal. I saw you outside earlier. Were you waiting for your payoff? For your next assignment, little lapdog? That's what she was doing in the bathroom—texting you with orders to eliminate us. She had you do the dirty work that she wouldn't do herself. Made you put yourself at risk. And now look at you, about to go down for attempted murder of two law enforcement officers. Just like you're going to be her patsy for her husband's murder. I'll bet that when you left that panic room yesterday morning, Lowden Booth was alive. But later you found out he'd been murdered, right? She did that, but when you're both on trial, who are they going to believe? She might still get off scot-free while you rot in prison. Do you really think that a woman capable of what she did is going to be loyal to you when it comes down to it? Your best bet is to spill everything before she does because only one of you is getting a deal, Mr.…what's your name?"

"Walters," he said with a defeated tone in is voice that told her she had him, "Roscoe Walters."

"How do you know Devon, Roscoe?"

"We used to see each other from time to time back in Vegas, when she was a showgirl," he said. "She called me up a while back and said she had a proposition for me."

"Maybe I should read Roscoe his rights before we go any further," Ryan suggested.

"Good idea," Jessie said. "While you're doing that, I'll see if I can find out how to access the panic room in this place."

As she listened to Ryan read Roscoe Walters his Miranda rights, she stepped around behind the bar top to the display rack, where the Barry family had an impressive array of hard liquor lined up along an old-timey mirror.

Considering that Devon had used an ice bucket to attack her, Jessie was fairly certain that the entrance to the panic room was somewhere behind the bar's display rack. She just had no idea how to access it. There could be a hidden button placed anywhere. The room might be opened with a fake bottle that one could lift or twist or push down.

She could stand here for hours and never figure it out. Or she could simply call Buckley Taverner, who she suspected did the job, and ask him directly. She was about to pull out her phone and dial the number he'd texted to her earlier when she noticed something that had escaped her attention earlier.

"Hey Ryan," she said, "do you want to hold off on questioning Roscoe for a moment?"

"Okay," he replied, "why?"

"Why don't you cuff him to something and come over here?"

The Captain of Central Station and head of Homicide Special Section followed his wife's request. When he joined Jessie, she pointed out the intricate woodwork designs at the four corners of the display rack. In one corner was a turtle. In another was a dolphin. In the third, a rowboat. And in the back left corner was a surfboard.

"Are you thinking what I'm thinking?" she asked him with a smile.

"It's worth a shot," he said.

Jessie reached over, put her left thumb on top of the surfboard, and pressed down firmly. The board gave way, sinking a quarter inch as they heard a soft clicking sound. A moment later, the display case hinged inward revealing a narrow hallway that led to a larger room about six feet away.

"Take a step back," Ryan instructed Jessie in a quiet, firm voice.

Jessie wasn't sure what he intended but she'd learned that when he used that tone, it was better not to ask questions. She took a step back. He stood in front of her and pointed his weapon down the hallway.

"Devon Booth, you are under arrest for the murder of Lowden Booth. I will read your rights in regard to that charge momentarily. But let me warn you. You might not get that chance. You assaulted my partner. More importantly, you attacked the woman I love. You need to come out here with your hands up right now. If you don't, I'm coming in. And I will shoot first and ask questions later, maybe never. You will not get a second chance. I'm giving you five seconds. One, tw—."

Devon appeared in the hallway with her hands above her head. She walked toward them slowly. Jessie handed Ryan her cuffs and sat down on the sofa as he formally arrested Lowden Booth's killer.

They could hear the sirens approaching in the distance and walked both Devon and Roscoe Walters outside to meet the approaching squad cars. As they stood on the Barry' front lawn, Ryan leaned over and whispered, "Remember, straight to the hospital to get checked out."

"I haven't forgotten," she promised, squeezing his hand. "Don't worry, I think I'm going to be fine. I think we're both going to be fine."

CHAPTER THIRTY THREE

"How many targets did Zoe pay you to kill?"

Hannah stared down at Ash Pierce, waiting for the response that she knew was inevitably coming.

Ash glared back up at her, seemingly oblivious to having both her wrists zip-tied to the front grille of a pickup truck in the middle of the desert. Then she broke into a vicious smile.

"Screw you," she said.

"That's what I figured you'd say," Hannah admitted. "Actually it was kind of what I was *hoping* you would say, so now we're going to have a little fun."

"Hey," Kat called out from the passenger seat of the pickup, where Hannah had managed to maneuver her after several slow, arduous, painful minutes, "be smart about this, Hannah. The camera is still on."

Hannah looked at the camera on the hood, still affixed to the tripod, with its red light burning bright. She pushed the button to turn it off.

"No it's not," she said, bending down so that her face was just inches from Ash's. "Shall we get started?"

"Don't try to scare me, little girl," the woman said with a smirk. "What you're attempting to do, I did professionally for over a decade. You are so out of your depth; you don't even know that you're drowning."

Hannah stood back up and walked over to get the hunting knife from where it still rested by the folding chair, after she'd used it to cut off Kat's zip ties. She picked it up and returned, casually sitting down cross-legged five feet in front of Ash.

She knew time was precious, but she couldn't give that impression to the other woman. She had to make her think she had all night. She had to make her think that she'd let this go on forever.

"Do you really think I'm out of my depth, Ash?" she asked, tracing the sand in front of her with the tip of the knife. "If you do, that tells me that maybe you don't deserve that $3 million Zoe Bradway is paying you, because clearly you're not as good as you claim to be. If you were, then you would have done the proper research on me."

"Don't insult me, Barbie," Ash spat. "I did a complete work up on you."

"Barbie?" Hannah said, feigning offense. "Just because I'm blonde? I thought you said that you were a natural blonde too and dyed your hair for this job. Or is it because I'm *tall* and blonde and you're pissed that those extra inches are the reason you're tied up right now instead of me?"

Ash looked like she had a comeback, but Hannah barreled ahead.

"No matter. If you really did a complete work up on me, then you'd know that my mother was murdered by my serial killer father when I was a baby. You'd know that my adoptive parents were slaughtered right in front of me by that same serial killer daddy. You'd know that an entirely different serial killer who considered my daddy his personal hero kidnapped me and tried to brainwash me into becoming a serial killer myself. He even tried to get me to make Jessie my first kill. I've touched the darkness."

"Yeah, but it didn't take," Ash taunted. "Guess you were soft."

"It didn't take?" Hannah repeated, uncrossing her legs, getting onto her knees, and crawling slowly towards the woman. "Are you sure about that?"

Hannah stared at her unblinkingly from two feet away and could tell that the Ash *wasn't* entirely sure. She was about to have even more doubts.

"Ever hear of the Night Hunter?" Hannah asked. "Of course you have. Everyone has. Legendary serial killer. Murdered hundreds. No one is sure of the final tally. Quite elderly by the time he decided to come after Jessie, Ryan, and me. But still incredibly dangerous. Got us holed up in a snowy, mountain cabin, not unlike that one in Lake Arrowhead where you snuffed the life out of Deputy Coolidge. We barely survived. I had to shoot him in self-defense. At least that's the official story."

She was right up close to Ash now, only inches apart, and could smell the blood on the other woman's breath. Ignoring it, she kept going.

"That was a lie. What really happened was that Ryan and Jessie took him down, had him in custody. But that wasn't enough for me. I wanted him dead for what he'd done to us, what he might do to us in the future if I let him live. Does he sound like anyone you know?"

She got off her knees and sat cross-legged again, only now she and Ash were so close that she only had to whisper to be heard, which is what she did. But in the silence of the desert, every word seemed to echo.

"And something else, Ash. Something I don't tell many people. I wanted to know what it was like to kill someone, just for the hell of it. This was a bad guy. No one would miss him. So I shot him dead. With the cuffs on, when he was defenseless. An old man. And it felt good. It was such a rush."

"What are you doing, Hannah?" Kat shouted from the passenger seat. "You shouldn't be telling her this."

"But I feel like she gets me, Kat," Hannah said, smiling at the zip-tied woman in front of her, who was no longer smiling back. "I've never met a person who got me who wasn't on the FBI's most wanted list."

"You're full of it," Ash said, though she lacked the conviction of a few minutes earlier.

"Anyway," Hannah said, ignoring her comment, "I checked myself into an in-patient psychiatric rehabilitation facility after that, officially for self-harm tendencies— that's probably what you read in my file. But the real reason was to try to stop my addiction to pursuing that rush I got when I killed the Night Hunter. You see, until I went to rehab, I kept looking for ways to recreate it, trying to find people who were bad enough that I could justify taking them out and getting that thrill again. I spent a lot of time in that facility and did some real work. And when I left I was in a good place. I was moving forward. Until you came along."

Hannah stood up and walked back over to the folding chair. This time she picked up the baton that she'd left there. When she returned to the pickup, she held it in one hand and the knife in the other.

"Now here I am," she said softly, "trying to find out if my sister's husband is in danger. I asked you a simple question earlier: how many targets did Zoe pay you to kill? I just want to know if you have the contract to take out Ryan Hernandez or if someone else does. But you're not answering me. So I have to ask you a different question, Ash, what's the point in letting you live if you can't help me?"

"I don't understand," Ash said.

"Let me make it clear then," Hannah said. "I was going to beat your skull in earlier, after I knocked you out. I wanted to see your brains mix with the sand, but I held off. I told myself that I wasn't like that anymore. But I think I still am. And since you won't help me, I have no reason to hold back. I figure you've given me another bite at the apple.

Now I can recapture that feeling that I've been craving all this time and there won't even be any consequences."

"Don't do this, Hannah," Kat called out.

"I mean, who's going to question it?" Hannah asked Ash, paying Kat no mind. "When the authorities investigate, they'll find that I was rescuing my friend over there, my mentor. You're a former CIA assassin, a hitwoman. I had no choice but to fight. And when I got the advantage with the baton, I had to hit you with it again and again to make sure you wouldn't get up. After all, I'm just a teenage girl and I was scared and I didn't know that you were dead. And even though Kat's begging for your life right now, when the cops ask her about it later, she'll have my back."

"You're better than this, Hannah," Kat pleaded. "There might not be legal consequences, but if you do this there will be consequences to your soul. You won't ever be able to come back from it."

"I think it's too late for that anyway, Kat," Hannah replied. "I want to watch the ants eat her brains. I've been daydreaming about it this whole time. There's no coming back from something like that."

"You're bluffing," Ash said.

Hannah looked down at her.

"There was a time there when everybody I ever cared about died," she said. "And tonight you made a video announcing that you were going to torture me and my new family and leave my sister to suffer forever. You think I'm bluffing?"

"Yes," Ash said without any confidence.

"You know what?" Hannah replied, her voice rising in the still desert air. "I've changed my mind. I'm not going to kill you. I'm going to hold off with that baton, just one blow short of death so that you're still alive, out here, alone, in pain, brain damaged, begging for the coyotes to come, and put you out of your misery."

She tossed the knife to the side and gripped the baton with both hands.

"Last chance, Ash or Violet or whatever the hell your name is," she said, returning to a harsh whisper, "otherwise you won't even get a sand dune for a shallow grave."

She lifted the baton and focused her attention on a spot just above the woman's left eyeball. She started to bring it downward.

"It was just me!" Ash yelled. "I had the contracts for all three of you. $1 million apiece."

Hannah stopped her momentum but kept the baton in place.

"Keep going," she snarled.

"Zoe told me to do you two first," she said. "She warned that that I might not be able to get to Hernandez once I finished with both of you because he'd have too much protection after that. She said that I might have to just be satisfied with a guaranteed $2 million for your deaths. She said she might have to be satisfied with that too and that she would be, because they'd be destroyed anyway. Their marriage would be ruined, ripped apart by the loss of both of you."

Hannah listened to all of it, turning it over in her head, trying to decide if there were any holes in the story. It sounded credible. She noticed that Ash was still flinching and realized that her hands were still gripped tight on the baton, held above her head. She lowered it, letting it rest by her side.

"Now that wasn't so hard, was it?" she said.

"Are you okay?" Kat asked from the front seat.

Hannah walked around to where she was. The detective was in bad shape. Her shoulder was seeping blood, the duct tape had completely slipped off her gooey, burgundy-tinged forearm, and her face was chalky-white.

"I'm okay," she said. "How are you feeling? We need to get you to the hospital ASAP."

"We will. But Hannah, how are you really? That was a lot."

"Really, I'm good, all things considered," she promised. "Pretty convincing though, huh? I'm starting to wonder if I missed my calling. Should I still pursue a career in investigations? Maybe I should have gone into acting. I'm young. Is there still time to apply to Juilliard?"

Kat made a sound that was half-laugh, half-moan.

"I know we planned this out in advance, but even so, you had me convinced."

Hannah smiled back, hoping it was reassuring, as she kept her thoughts to herself.

You and me both.

CHAPTER THIRTY FOUR

Mark Haddonfield was glad about one thing: the Goodsen kids wouldn't hear their mother's screams.

As luck would have it their father, Nicholas, was taking them to San Diego for a short trip. His sister lived in La Jolla, and both families were going to Sea World and the Zoo Safari Park.

But as it turned out, Janet Goodsen hated her sister-in-law, so she made up an excuse—a fake fundraising meeting on Friday that she couldn't miss. As a result, she'd have to stay in L.A. while the rest of the family went south.

That was doubly advantageous. It meant that the children's nightmares wouldn't forever be haunted by the curdled shrieking of their dying mother as acid melted her body. But it also meant that Mark wouldn't have to contend with anyone else in the house tonight. It was like it was meant to be.

He took the same route he'd used during yesterday's practice hike, only this time he was dressed slightly differently just in case any other evening hikers were the type who paid close attention. Maybe someone would have thought it odd that, rather than wearing a more reflective color, his hiking pants, shirt, boots, cap, and the thin jacket around his waist were all black. But it wasn't that hot a day, plus the sun was beginning to set and the temperature in the hills was cooler than down below, so it wasn't that unusual.

The combination of the cap, long sleeves, and sunglasses masked his blonde hair and fair coloring, though there was no way to hide his enormous height. Unlike yesterday, he was wearing contact lenses instead of glasses. They weren't his preference, but for tonight's task, they were a necessary concession. He was confident that no one would pay any mind to the metal thermos attached to the carabiner on his belt, which contained the acid. It looked like any other fancy water bottle.

He waited until he was sure no one was anywhere in sight before going off trail and climbing the hill that overlooked the Goodsen home on Cardwell Place. He settled in there, just out of sight, and pulled the peanut butter and jelly sandwich he'd made earlier out of his backpack.

He watched the scene down below as he took tiny bites and sipped at his Gatorade, making sure he was properly hydrated.

Before it got too dark, he pulled the trigger sprayer he'd brought out of the backpack. It was a challenge to find the right model because it required components that were all resistant to the acid. He took off the cap, put on his goggles and gloves, then carefully poured the requisite amount of acid from the thermos into the sprayer. He didn't fill it up completely. From his research, it seemed that sixteen ounces would be more than enough. He'd only brought a full thermos's worth just in case there was a hiccup.

When that was done, he removed the goggles and gloves, then put on the protective coat that looked like a hiking jacket. He wrapped up the thermos and put it in the backpack, which he left on the crest of the hill. Then he put on the ski mask, followed by the goggles and gloves again. He took the trigger sprayer and the taser and began to walk down the hill. He really hoped he didn't have to use the latter. That felt like it would be cheating.

Cheating wasn't his style. He wouldn't have cheated if he had taken Jessie Hunt's UCLA seminar and he wouldn't cheat now. That was the difference between them—he had honor. Now that he was the professor, and she was the flailing student, he wouldn't reject her for some arbitrary reason. He wouldn't rip someone's dream away from them as she had done. He wouldn't just quit in the middle of teaching the course, like she had. He wouldn't abandon her. Unlike Jessie Hunt, he'd give his nemesis an opportunity to learn from her mistakes. He would *instruct* her.

"At least I'm giving you a goddamn chance, you self-righteous bitch!" he snarled.

Mark stopped in his tracks halfway down the hill. He realized that he'd spoken those words out loud rather than just thinking them, and that he'd said them far louder than he should have. His voice echoed through the canyon before fading into the early evening air.

He bent into a crouch and glanced around. There was no one in sight but he waited several minutes in case anyone appeared over the crest of the hill. Eventually, he felt confident enough to continue, though now he instructed himself to stay focused on the assignment at hand. He could not afford to lose himself like that again. Jessie would learn the lesson he was teaching through his deeds, not his vitriol.

Once he got to the spot where the hill met the wooden, latticed fence surrounding the Goodsens' yard, he hopped down and walked quietly along the edge of the property, careful not to get too close to the pool deck. He didn't know if the wood planks might creak and didn't want to chance it.

He could hear the television playing as he approached the house, though he couldn't identify the show. It sounded like one of those competition programs, maybe one where people sang or danced, and judges eliminated them or let them move on. Mark didn't really watch much TV, other than the news. There was lots of cheering, which he liked, because it covered up any possible missteps he might make, though so far, he'd been error-free.

He reached the sliding side door that led to the kitchen and could already see that the latch wasn't locked. He had assumed that the security system wouldn't be set this early in the evening, if at all, but to not even have the doors locked when she was home alone? Janet was just courting danger.

Before he went inside, Mark looked up. It really was quite beautiful out, just past dusk, when the sky was passing from blue into an inky purple. Even in a giant city like this, he could see the faint twinkle of what he thought might be a distant star. Or maybe it was just a high-flying airplane.

He felt a little ache as he realized that Janet Goodsen would never get to see any of these things again. He didn't know if she ever cared to look up. He didn't know if she ever came out in the morning with a mug of coffee and marveled at the snow on the distant eastern peaks near Big Bear and Lake Arrowhead. He didn't know if she liked to watch the sun set over the Pacific Ocean, which was visible from here on clear days.

He didn't know what mattered to her. The listening devices he'd planted in the home a while back had told him about the trip to San Diego and the spat with the sister-in-law. But that didn't mean he really understood her.

He knew she read to her kids at night but didn't know if she liked it or if it was a chore. He knew that she and Nicholas made love about twice a week but couldn't gauge whether she enjoyed that or whether it was chore. He didn't know if she ever thought about the second chance that Jessie Hunt had given her when she'd saved her life six months ago.

Mark didn't know any of these things. All he knew was that she was a difficult person, but not a truly despicable one, like his first victim, Woody Garnett, had been. Janet Goodsen was petty and entitled and self-involved. But she read to her kids and made love to her husband and as he could now more clearly tell by the sound of the TV, she liked at least one show in which regular people sang for judges, hoping to become stars. She didn't deserve this.

But it wasn't about "deserve." There was a higher purpose involved here. There was a strategy at work—The Strategy, in fact. Jessie Hunt had to be taught a lesson. And if Janet Goodsen had to suffer along the way, then so be it. Everyone had a role to play. Janet's role was to be the next "survivor to surrender." Mark's role was to move the pieces on the board so that all the players ended up where they were supposed to be.

He hated being the bad guy. He hated what he was about to do. But he didn't have a choice. Jessie Hunt had given him no choice. And soon the time would come when she would be the one backed into a corner, trapped, alone, begging him to be *her* angel of death.

But that was a matter for another time. Right now he had a job to do. He carefully slid open the Goodsens' kitchen door with one hand while he held the trigger sprayer in the other.

When he closed the door after him, he made sure to lock it.

CHAPTER THIRTY FIVE

"What are the results?" Jessie demanded the second Ryan walked in the hospital room at Cedars-Sinai Medical Center.

"Don't you remember?" he asked, concerned. "Dr. Varma was just in here a few minutes ago giving us her initial evaluation."

Jessie shook her head, reminding herself to be patient with him and not get frustrated.

"No, babe, that's not what's I meant," she said carefully, adjusting the scratchy hospital gown she wore as she used the button to raise her bed to a fully upright position. "I remember the evaluation. She said it looks like I got lucky: that the preliminary tests show no obvious concerns, but that she wants me to return tomorrow for a follow-up evaluation, take a week off from work and all high-intensity physical activity, even running, and get another MRI in exactly seven days. Does that sound about right?"

"That's actually a better summary than I could give," he replied, impressed. "So what results were you talking about?"

"From the interrogations with Devon Booth and Roscoe Walters?"

"Oh right, those."

"Yeah, don't tell me you forgot about those!" Jessie said in mild disbelief. "Maybe I'm not the one who should have their head checked."

Ryan had insisted that Jessie allow the rest of the HSS team to question the suspects while she got evaluated and she'd reluctantly agreed. So while Dr. Varma was doing her battery of tests, the other detectives—who were all available after recently closing their own cases—had been busy with Booth and Walters.

"I didn't forget," Ryan assured her. "I was just hoping you'd want to rest and not ask. But of course, that was silly of me. I just got off the phone with Karen Bray, who gave me an update. You want the good or the bad news first?"

"How long have you known me, husband?" Jessie asked.

"Right then," Ryan said, "here's the bad news: Karen was questioning Devon and apparently she hasn't said a word. Completely clammed up and is waiting for her lawyer. The good news is that

Susannah Valentine and Sam Goodwin have had much more success with Roscoe Walters. As chatty as he was about to be with us, he's been way more so with them."

"What has he told them?"

"He pretty much confirmed your theory," Ryan said, pulling up a chair next to her hospital bed. "Devon hired him to break in, gave him all the details on how get onto the property and into the mansion, avoid detection, and get out. She told him that she and Lowden would run to the panic room in the closet. Apparently Lowden mentioned it to her in passing once when he was drunk. That's how she found out about it. Roscoe said she told him that once they were in the panic room, he was to threaten them, demand they open the safe, beat her up a little if necessary, and then, on her signal, leave."

"So he didn't know that Lowden was going to be killed?" Jessie asked.

"He swears that he thought it was just a robbery," Ryan explained. "He said that he assumed that Booth would open the safe and that Devon would give him the signal to leave with whatever was inside after that. But she never even had him try to open the safe. She just gave the sign for him to punch her, then had him leave seconds later. Roscoe said he was surprised but figured that she knew what she was doing so he followed her instructions and left. He didn't learn about Lowden Booth's death until later that day. Or about Devon hitting her head. But when he confronted her later, on their burner phones, she promised to double his payday when the will became official."

"The will?" Jessie asked.

"Yeah, your hunch was right about that too," Ryan said. "I figured you'd be gloating about that by now. Didn't you see your messages?"

"They took my phone when they did the MRI," Jessie reminded him. "I haven't seen any messages."

"Oh, I'll get it back for you," he said, "but do you remember that text message we both got just before the lights went out in the back den at the Barry house?"

"Yeah."

"That was from Jamil," Ryan explained, "passing along that Chief Decker got Booth's lawyers to reveal the existence of a prenup and its terms. It was valid for exactly five years after the date of their wedding, which was in May, one month ago. After that, she got almost everything, despite his attorneys repeated warnings against that plan."

"Wow," Jessie said, "so she was slated to get all of his billions?"

"Correct," Ryan said, "but apparently the prenup's term was adjusted down from an original sunset clause of ten years. You want to guess when that happened?"

"When?" Jessie asked.

"Three and a half years ago," Ryan said, "after Devon 'saved' Lowden's life when he had a heart attack in their screening room. As it turns out, Lowden's most trusted housekeeper, Vera Przekop, saw the rescue and later told Lowden that she'd never trusted Devon until that moment. After that, she did, and it seems that was enough to make Lowden change his will."

"That's awfully convenient," Jessie mused. "Knowing what we know now, it sure seems like Devon may have manufactured Lowden's heart attack specifically to win Vera's trust and get the terms of the prenup altered. Maybe we should have someone go back through the medical records from the cardiac incident to see what was in his system at the time. I wonder if there was some way for Devon create a drug cocktail that could mimic the symptoms of a heart attack."

"Jamil and Beth are on it as we speak," Ryan said, beaming like a kid who had just won the spelling bee.

"Aren't you a proud young man," Jessie said, amused by his self-satisfaction.

"Anyway," Ryan continued, ignoring her playful teasing, "to hear Roscoe tell it, Devon was not as enamored with Lowden as she let on. Apparently the bloom was off the rose after about a year. She complained that Lowden was too lovey-dovey, constantly in her personal space, not to mention expecting sex all the time. According to Roscoe, she said that he was sloppy and boring in bed. He claims that she even admitted that she wanted to sleep around but knew Lowden was always checking up on her and that it would violate the prenup. Of course, being implicated in her husband's murder would also violate the prenup."

"So that explains why she came up with an incredibly long con that ended in a murder that couldn't be tied to her," Jessie said. "It also explains leaving the safe in the panic room alone too. No need to go after the contents when what you're really after are the billions in his bank account."

"Right," Ryan agreed. "And she made herself seem the victim in the attack."

"She was great at it," Jessie said. "She was found tied up and knocked out. Legitimate suspicion is cast elsewhere. There's video of an intruder looking to rob the safe, maybe on behalf of an ex-wife in desperate need of the money, who stood to gain a windfall of her own if Lowden died. Devon had the staff snowed. To be honest, if she hadn't ordered Roscoe to come in after us, I probably would have walked out of her sister's house giving her the benefit of the doubt too. She was good."

"She wasn't *that* good, Jessie,' Ryan countered. "I think the very reason she called Roscoe was because she was worried about the questions you were about to ask. She was about be interrogated by the renowned criminal profiler Jessie Hunt and she panicked."

"So you're saying my reputation made her screw up? Because I don't think it was the actual questioning that did it."

"Whatever gets the job done," Ryan said with a grin. "And please don't give her too much praise. She is a sociopath who apparently waited nearly four years to kill her husband. That's cold. Not to mention the fact that she was willing to let her flunky gun us down in the same home where she was happily watching her nephews wrestle minutes earlier."

"That's actually a skill I'm hoping to take from her," Jessie said.

"Um, what?" Ryan asked, uneasily. "Do I need to get Dr. Varma back in here?"

"Don't worry," Jessie said, giving him a little slap on the hand. "I just mean that even though she had all this intense stuff going on in her life—admittedly that 'stuff' was trying to get away with murdering her husband and locking down his billions—she still seemed able to sit back, relax on her sister's couch, and genuinely enjoy watching two little boys beat the crap out of each other."

"I don't get it," Ryan said.

"What I'm saying is: she didn't let the big picture at work prevent her from enjoying the simple pleasures of family," Jessie clarified. "I need to do a better job of that. We both do. I don't know that there's a perfect solution to the conflicts that we've been having. But I think a good start would be genuinely choosing to separate our work lives from our home lives."

"Okay," Ryan said. "How do we do that?"

"I'm not saying we never talk about one at the other place," Jessie replied, "but making sure that the roles—husband, wife, captain, profiler, boss, employee—don't bleed from one space into the other too much is essential. I think that's infecting our personal relationship *and* our professional one. And if we want both to thrive, we need to know how to create clear boundaries. It won't be easy, but it has to be done. What do you say?"

Ryan squeezed her hand.

"Of course I say 'yes.' When it comes to you, I always say 'yes.'"

"Thank you," she said, leaning over to give him a kiss. "See all the progress we're making here? Now I just need to do better at not pushing you away when you get worried about my health."

"You're already doing better," he said, "And I still need to work on being more transparent with you, instead of trying to protect you like I did when I didn't tell you about Zoe's threats."

Jessie lowered her head and nodded. She wanted to let him off the hook for that, but it was still raw, especially since the threat was still out there.

"Speaking of her," she said, "aren't you concerned that the other shoe hasn't dropped on that yet?"

Ryan shrugged.

"Maybe I was right, and she really was just messing with you the whole time," he said. "Regardless, Chief Decker told me that he convinced the administrator at Western Regional PDC to allow to two undercovers inside. One is an orderly who starts on tonight's overnight shift. Another will be a new patient transferred in tomorrow. I know it's late, but hopefully one of them will pay dividends."

"Maybe," Jessie said, "I just don't think that Zoe Bradway is the type to open up to some random person. It will take weeks to build that kind of trust—."

Ryan's phone rang and he pulled it out. The screen showed Hannah's name. He hit "accept' and put the call on speaker.

"Hi Hannah, what's up?"

"I've been trying to reach Jessie on her phone repeatedly and it keeps going to voicemail," she said with an intensity that immediately had Jessie on guard. "Do you know where she is?"

"Her phone is in another room," Ryan said, smoothly covering for the fact that they were in the hospital, "but she's here with me. You're on speaker."

"What's wrong, Hannah?" Jessie asked.

"I'm okay," her sister said.

"But something's very wrong. I can hear it in your voice. Tell me."

"I'm going to," she said. "But I need you to promise to let me get through this and not interrupt. You have to stay calm and not get angry.

I will answer all your questions. Just know that I'm okay and that Kat will be too."

"*Will be*?"

"Listen to me," Hannah said, her tone suddenly changing, becoming less amped up and more restrained. "Hank Keene wasn't the former CIA hitman. Violet was. Her real name is Ash Pierce. It was all a set-up. She was part two of Zoe Bradway's Operation Z. She pretended to be a client and get kidnapped as part of an elaborate plan to lure me and Kat out to an isolated spot in the desert near Palm Springs. She killed Deputy Coolidge. She murdered the real Violet and Keene too. She was supposed to torture and kill both of us while recording it and send the video to you and the news media. She was also supposed to go after Ryan if she could get to him."

Jessie felt like her mind and body were separating from one another. The only thing tethering her to reality was Ryan's hand, holding hers tight. She desperately wanted to interrupt her sister, to ask a thousand questions, but she stayed quiet, and let her go on.

"We didn't know any of this," Hannah said, speaking in quick, crisp sentences. "Kat went to rescue 'Violet' and told me to stay in Lake Arrowhead, but I followed her anyway. Kat was captured and hurt pretty badly. I managed to sneak up on Pierce and disarm her. Then I got her to admit that she had the contracts on all three of us and that no one else is out there hunting us. After that, I drove us all to a hospital in Palm Springs. That's where we are now. Pierce is under armed guard, in FBI custody. Kat is in surgery. She has multiple injuries, the worst of which is a deep stab wound to her shoulder. She lost a lot of blood. The doctors say that the blade missed any major arteries and that her life isn't in danger anymore but that if we had arrived an hour later, she might not have made it. They say that the surgery will probably last another couple of hours. I know you're working on that billionaire case, but I figured that if you left L.A. now, you could be here when she woke up."

Jessie looked at Ryan, who nodded silently. She gave his hand a little squeeze, then responded.

"Are you sure you're okay?"

"Positive," Hannah said. "I'm not injured at all. Just worried about Kat."

"Okay, listen," Jessie said. "I'm not mad at you. I'm just glad you called and that you're safe. I'm also incredibly proud of you. Kat was lucky to have you there. We will wrap things up here as quickly as we can and try to be there before she wakes up. Do you think you can nap a little?"

"No way."

"Okay, then get yourself a bite to eat and book a few rooms at a nearby hotel. Keep yourself busy. We'll be there as soon as we can. And Hannah?'

"Yeah?" her little sister said.

"I love you."

"I love you too."

Jessie hung up and looked over at Ryan, whose eyes were filled with guilt.

"Don't," she said.

"I'm so sorry," he whispered. "I didn't take this threat seriously, and people you love almost died because of it."

"Listen to me," she said sternly, "do not beat yourself up over this. I love you and I promise that I will not let this come between us. Now hug me."

He leaned over and wrapped his arms around her. As he did, Jessie tried to push away the thought that snuck into her head.

I hope I can keep that promise.

EPILOGUE

"How did it go in there—lots of laughs?"

Jessie smiled as she shook her head at Ryan's question, amused by his overtly lame attempt to inject a little levity into a heavy situation.

She and Hannah walked over to the car where he was parked on the side of the road outside the hospital, waiting to pick them up after their first survivor's guilt group meeting.

"You know I can't tell you about the session," she said faux disapprovingly. "That's only for people in the group."

"What about you, Dorsey?" Ryan asked, turning his attention Hannah. "You have a good time?"

"Stop trying to get us to violate the sanctity of group," Hannah instructed him, wagging her finger for effect, "or I will report you to our moderator, who will have a thoughtful word with you and make you see the error of your ways."

"Okay, okay," Ryan said, holding up his hands in surrender, "I give up. I was just curious."

Just then, Jamil walked outside.

"Don't say a word to him," Hannah said, startling the poor guy.

"What?" he asked, confused.

"Captain Hernandez over there is going to try to ask you how our group session went," she explained, "but you're not at work right now. Out here in the real world he's just Ryan and you don't have to tell him a thing. Just stick your tongue out at him and walk away."

"I'm not sure that I'm going to do that," Jamil said nervously.

"She's just messing with you," Jessie said, before moving closer so that no one else could hear her, "but how do you feel? It seemed like you really opened up in there."

"Yeah," he said quietly, "I think it really helped to know everyone in there could relate to what I was experiencing. I didn't feel so lonely."

"So you'll go back?"

"I think so," he said. "The pit in my stomach feels…smaller somehow right now. I like it."

"Cool," she said. "I think I may have a positive way to fill that pit. We were actually going to get some ice cream. You want to meet us?"

"Sure, but I'm lactose intolerant, so I'll just hang out with you guys."

"This is L.A., Jamil," Jessie teased. "They'll have options for you. We'll see you there."

She and Hannah got in the car. She refrained from asking her sister how the session had gone for her, in part because of Ryan's presence. But it was also because she was afraid the answer might not be as encouraging as Jamil's. Besides, she was still working out her own feelings about her experience.

"We should bring something back for Kat," Hannah said, pulling her back into the now. "If she's going to be stuck in the guest room of our house for the next few days, at least she should have something to look forward to. And who doesn't look forward to ice cream?"

"Sure," Jessie said, "text her to see what flavor she wants."

"I should also tell her that she's paying," Hannah said, with a wicked grin, "considering that she has a money belt with $30,000 in it."

"You know that she already turned that in to the FBI, right?" Jessie said. "She couldn't just keep it."

"No!" Hannah replied, disappointed. "Doesn't she even get a reward?"

"She did and it's pretty respectable," Ryan said. "She told them to apply it to her medical bills, which is why I still think she should have stayed in the hospital for one more night."

"I'm not surprised that she didn't," Hannah replied. "Getting out of there fast was her way of reminding herself that she's a badass, not a victim. She knows that her recovery is going to be tough, and she doesn't want to let self-pity sneak in when she's not looking, you know? Ever vigilant, those Army Rangers."

Jessie shook her head in amazement.

"When did my baby sister become so insightful?" she marveled.

They'd only made it half a block when a call came in on both Jessie and Ryan's phones simultaneously. Jessie immediately recognized the ring as Chief Decker's. She and Ryan exchanged a look. If the chief of police was calling them both at 2 p.m. on a Saturday afternoon, it couldn't be good.

"Hi Chief," Ryan said. "You're on speaker with me and Jessie. What's going on?"

"I'm sorry to bother both of you on your day off but I wanted you to hear about this from me before you got the news elsewhere. Do you remember Janet Goodsen?"

"Of course," Jessie said. "She was the last intended victim of Sloane Baker before we managed to catch her."

"That's correct," Decker said. "Unfortunately, she's dead—murdered. She was found in her home today when her husband and children returned from a trip to San Diego."

Jessie felt a strange shudder run through her body at hearing the words.

"Oh God," Ryan said.

"I'm afraid that's not all," Decker said.

"Let me guess," Jessie interrupted. "She was killed using acid, just like Baker's other victims."

"Exactly," Decker said, "so you can see the problem. Sloane Baker is safely locked away, which means it looks like we've got a copycat killer on our hands."

The shudder Jessie had felt earlier gave way to deep pit of dread.

"I think it's much worse than that, Chief," she said. "A few weeks ago, Woody Garnett, the final intended victim of Harper Grey, was murdered—stabbed to death—just like all her prior victims were. Now this. That's two near-victims of serial killers from previous cases I investigated, murdered in the exact same way as the original serial killers did it."

"What exactly are you suggesting, Hunt?" Decker demanded.

"I'm saying there's a new serial killer out there, Chief," Jessie explained. "But this one is not just killing people. This one is sending a message—to me."

NOW AVAILABLE!

THE PERFECT PEOPLE
(A Jessie Hunt Psychological Suspense Thriller—Book Twenty-Seven)

When the hostess of a decadent Malibu beach party is found dead in her home, it seems clear that a killer is stalking these parties and looking for his next victim. But as Jessie digs deeper and enters this killer's mind, she realizes there is more than meets the eye: these murders are personal. And if she doesn't stop him soon, another woman will be dead.

"A masterpiece of thriller and mystery."
—Books and Movie Reviews, Roberto Mattos (re Once Gone)

THE PERFECT PEOPLE is book #27 in a new psychological suspense series by bestselling author Blake Pierce, which begins with *The Perfect Wife*, a #1 bestseller (and free download) with over 5,000 five-star ratings and 1,000 five-star reviews.

A fast-paced psychological suspense thriller with unforgettable characters and heart-pounding suspense, the JESSIE HUNT series is a riveting new series that will leave you turning pages late into the night.

Future books in the series are also available.

"An edge of your seat thriller in a new series that keeps you turning pages! ...So many twists, turns and red herrings… I can't wait to see what happens next."
—Reader review (Her Last Wish)

"A strong, complex story about two FBI agents trying to stop a serial killer. If you want an author to capture your attention and have you guessing, yet trying to put the pieces together, Pierce is your author!"
—Reader review (Her Last Wish)

“A typical Blake Pierce twisting, turning, roller coaster ride suspense thriller. Will have you turning the pages to the last sentence of the last chapter!!!”
—Reader review (City of Prey)

“Right from the start we have an unusual protagonist that I haven't seen done in this genre before. The action is nonstop... A very atmospheric novel that will keep you turning pages well into the wee hours.”
—Reader review (City of Prey)

“Everything that I look for in a book... a great plot, interesting characters, and grabs your interest right away. The book moves along at a breakneck pace and stays that way until the end. Now on go I to book two!”
—Reader review (Girl, Alone)

“Exciting, heart pounding, edge of your seat book... a must read for mystery and suspense readers!”
—Reader review (Girl, Alone)

Blake Pierce

Blake Pierce is the USA Today bestselling author of the RILEY PAGE mystery series, which includes seventeen books. Blake Pierce is also the author of the MACKENZIE WHITE mystery series, comprising fourteen books; of the AVERY BLACK mystery series, comprising six books; of the KERI LOCKE mystery series, comprising five books; of the MAKING OF RILEY PAIGE mystery series, comprising six books; of the KATE WISE mystery series, comprising seven books; of the CHLOE FINE psychological suspense mystery, comprising six books; of the JESSIE HUNT psychological suspense thriller series, comprising twenty-eight books; of the AU PAIR psychological suspense thriller series, comprising three books; of the ZOE PRIME mystery series, comprising six books; of the ADELE SHARP mystery series, comprising sixteen books, of the EUROPEAN VOYAGE cozy mystery series, comprising six books; of the LAURA FROST FBI suspense thriller, comprising eleven books; of the ELLA DARK FBI suspense thriller, comprising fourteen books (and counting); of the A YEAR IN EUROPE cozy mystery series, comprising nine books, of the AVA GOLD mystery series, comprising six books; of the RACHEL GIFT mystery series, comprising ten books (and counting); of the VALERIE LAW mystery series, comprising nine books (and counting); of the PAIGE KING mystery series, comprising eight books (and counting); of the MAY MOORE mystery series, comprising eleven books; of the CORA SHIELDS mystery series, comprising eight books (and counting); of the NICKY LYONS mystery series, comprising eight books (and counting), of the CAMI LARK mystery series, comprising eight books (and counting), of the AMBER YOUNG mystery series, comprising five books (and counting), of the DAISY FORTUNE mystery series, comprising five books (and counting), of the FIONA RED mystery series, comprising five books (and counting), of the FAITH BOLD mystery series, comprising five books (and counting), and of the new JULIETTE HART mystery series, comprising five books (and counting).

An avid reader and lifelong fan of the mystery and thriller genres, Blake loves to hear from you, so please feel free to visit www.blakepierceauthor.com to learn more and stay in touch.

BOOKS BY BLAKE PIERCE

JULIETTE HART MYSTERY SERIES
NOTHING TO FEAR (Book #1)
NOTHING THERE (Book #2)
NOTHING WATCHING (Book #3)
NOTHING HIDING (Book #4)
NOTHING LEFT (Book #5)

FAITH BOLD MYSTERY SERIES
SO LONG (Book #1)
SO COLD (Book #2)
SO SCARED (Book #3)
SO NORMAL (Book #4)
SO FAR GONE (Book #5)

FIONA RED MYSTERY SERIES
LET HER GO (Book #1)
LET HER BE (Book #2)
LET HER HOPE (Book #3)
LET HER WISH (Book #4)
LET HER LIVE (Book #5)

DAISY FORTUNE MYSTERY SERIES
NEED YOU (Book #1)
CLAIM YOU (Book #2)
CRAVE YOU (Book #3)
CHOOSE YOU (Book #4)
CHASE YOU (Book #5)

AMBER YOUNG MYSTERY SERIES
ABSENT PITY (Book #1)
ABSENT REMORSE (Book #2)
ABSENT FEELING (Book #3)
ABSENT MERCY (Book #4)
ABSENT REASON (Book #5)

CAMI LARK MYSTERY SERIES
JUST ME (Book #1)
JUST OUTSIDE (Book #2)
JUST RIGHT (Book #3)
JUST FORGET (Book #4)
JUST ONCE (Book #5)
JUST HIDE (Book #6)
JUST NOW (Book #7)
JUST HOPE (Book #8)

NICKY LYONS MYSTERY SERIES
ALL MINE (Book #1)
ALL HIS (Book #2)
ALL HE SEES (Book #3)
ALL ALONE (Book #4)
ALL FOR ONE (Book #5)
ALL HE TAKES (Book #6)
ALL FOR ME (Book #7)
ALL IN (Book #8)

CORA SHIELDS MYSTERY SERIES
UNDONE (Book #1)
UNWANTED (Book #2)
UNHINGED (Book #3)
UNSAID (Book #4)
UNGLUED (Book #5)
UNSTABLE (Book #6)
UNKNOWN (Book #7)
UNAWARE (Book #8)

MAY MOORE SUSPENSE THRILLER
NEVER RUN (Book #1)
NEVER TELL (Book #2)
NEVER LIVE (Book #3)
NEVER HIDE (Book #4)
NEVER FORGIVE (Book #5)
NEVER AGAIN (Book #6)
NEVER LOOK BACK (Book #7)
NEVER FORGET (Book #8)
NEVER LET GO (Book #9)

NEVER PRETEND (Book #10)
NEVER HESITATE (Book #11)

PAIGE KING MYSTERY SERIES
THE GIRL HE PINED (Book #1)
THE GIRL HE CHOSE (Book #2)
THE GIRL HE TOOK (Book #3)
THE GIRL HE WISHED (Book #4)
THE GIRL HE CROWNED (Book #5)
THE GIRL HE WATCHED (Book #6)
THE GIRL HE WANTED (Book #7)
THE GIRL HE CLAIMED (Book #8)

VALERIE LAW MYSTERY SERIES
NO MERCY (Book #1)
NO PITY (Book #2)
NO FEAR (Book #3)
NO SLEEP (Book #4)
NO QUARTER (Book #5)
NO CHANCE (Book #6)
NO REFUGE (Book #7)
NO GRACE (Book #8)
NO ESCAPE (Book #9)

RACHEL GIFT MYSTERY SERIES
HER LAST WISH (Book #1)
HER LAST CHANCE (Book #2)
HER LAST HOPE (Book #3)
HER LAST FEAR (Book #4)
HER LAST CHOICE (Book #5)
HER LAST BREATH (Book #6)
HER LAST MISTAKE (Book #7)
HER LAST DESIRE (Book #8)
HER LAST REGRET (Book #9)
HER LAST HOUR (Book #10)

AVA GOLD MYSTERY SERIES
CITY OF PREY (Book #1)
CITY OF FEAR (Book #2)
CITY OF BONES (Book #3)

CITY OF GHOSTS (Book #4)
CITY OF DEATH (Book #5)
CITY OF VICE (Book #6)

A YEAR IN EUROPE
A MURDER IN PARIS (Book #1)
DEATH IN FLORENCE (Book #2)
VENGEANCE IN VIENNA (Book #3)
A FATALITY IN SPAIN (Book #4)

ELLA DARK FBI SUSPENSE THRILLER
GIRL, ALONE (Book #1)
GIRL, TAKEN (Book #2)
GIRL, HUNTED (Book #3)
GIRL, SILENCED (Book #4)
GIRL, VANISHED (Book 5)
GIRL ERASED (Book #6)
GIRL, FORSAKEN (Book #7)
GIRL, TRAPPED (Book #8)
GIRL, EXPENDABLE (Book #9)
GIRL, ESCAPED (Book #10)
GIRL, HIS (Book #11)
GIRL, LURED (Book #12)
GIRL, MISSING (Book #13)
GIRL, UNKNOWN (Book #14)

LAURA FROST FBI SUSPENSE THRILLER
ALREADY GONE (Book #1)
ALREADY SEEN (Book #2)
ALREADY TRAPPED (Book #3)
ALREADY MISSING (Book #4)
ALREADY DEAD (Book #5)
ALREADY TAKEN (Book #6)
ALREADY CHOSEN (Book #7)
ALREADY LOST (Book #8)
ALREADY HIS (Book #9)
ALREADY LURED (Book #10)
ALREADY COLD (Book #11)

EUROPEAN VOYAGE COZY MYSTERY SERIES

MURDER (AND BAKLAVA) (Book #1)
DEATH (AND APPLE STRUDEL) (Book #2)
CRIME (AND LAGER) (Book #3)
MISFORTUNE (AND GOUDA) (Book #4)
CALAMITY (AND A DANISH) (Book #5)
MAYHEM (AND HERRING) (Book #6)

ADELE SHARP MYSTERY SERIES
LEFT TO DIE (Book #1)
LEFT TO RUN (Book #2)
LEFT TO HIDE (Book #3)
LEFT TO KILL (Book #4)
LEFT TO MURDER (Book #5)
LEFT TO ENVY (Book #6)
LEFT TO LAPSE (Book #7)
LEFT TO VANISH (Book #8)
LEFT TO HUNT (Book #9)
LEFT TO FEAR (Book #10)
LEFT TO PREY (Book #11)
LEFT TO LURE (Book #12)
LEFT TO CRAVE (Book #13)
LEFT TO LOATHE (Book #14)
LEFT TO HARM (Book #15)
LEFT TO RUIN (Book #16)

THE AU PAIR SERIES
ALMOST GONE (Book#1)
ALMOST LOST (Book #2)
ALMOST DEAD (Book #3)

ZOE PRIME MYSTERY SERIES
FACE OF DEATH (Book#1)
FACE OF MURDER (Book #2)
FACE OF FEAR (Book #3)
FACE OF MADNESS (Book #4)
FACE OF FURY (Book #5)
FACE OF DARKNESS (Book #6)

A JESSIE HUNT PSYCHOLOGICAL SUSPENSE SERIES
THE PERFECT WIFE (Book #1)

THE PERFECT BLOCK (Book #2)
THE PERFECT HOUSE (Book #3)
THE PERFECT SMILE (Book #4)
THE PERFECT LIE (Book #5)
THE PERFECT LOOK (Book #6)
THE PERFECT AFFAIR (Book #7)
THE PERFECT ALIBI (Book #8)
THE PERFECT NEIGHBOR (Book #9)
THE PERFECT DISGUISE (Book #10)
THE PERFECT SECRET (Book #11)
THE PERFECT FAÇADE (Book #12)
THE PERFECT IMPRESSION (Book #13)
THE PERFECT DECEIT (Book #14)
THE PERFECT MISTRESS (Book #15)
THE PERFECT IMAGE (Book #16)
THE PERFECT VEIL (Book #17)
THE PERFECT INDISCRETION (Book #18)
THE PERFECT RUMOR (Book #19)
THE PERFECT COUPLE (Book #20)
THE PERFECT MURDER (Book #21)
THE PERFECT HUSBAND (Book #22)
THE PERFECT SCANDAL (Book #23)
THE PERFECT MASK (Book #24)
THE PERFECT RUSE (Book #25)
THE PERFECT VENEER (Book #26)
THE PERFECT PEOPLE (Book #27)
THE PERFECT WITNESS (Book #28)

CHLOE FINE PSYCHOLOGICAL SUSPENSE SERIES
NEXT DOOR (Book #1)
A NEIGHBOR'S LIE (Book #2)
CUL DE SAC (Book #3)
SILENT NEIGHBOR (Book #4)
HOMECOMING (Book #5)
TINTED WINDOWS (Book #6)

KATE WISE MYSTERY SERIES
IF SHE KNEW (Book #1)
IF SHE SAW (Book #2)
IF SHE RAN (Book #3)

IF SHE HID (Book #4)
IF SHE FLED (Book #5)
IF SHE FEARED (Book #6)
IF SHE HEARD (Book #7)

THE MAKING OF RILEY PAIGE SERIES
WATCHING (Book #1)
WAITING (Book #2)
LURING (Book #3)
TAKING (Book #4)
STALKING (Book #5)
KILLING (Book #6)

RILEY PAIGE MYSTERY SERIES
ONCE GONE (Book #1)
ONCE TAKEN (Book #2)
ONCE CRAVED (Book #3)
ONCE LURED (Book #4)
ONCE HUNTED (Book #5)
ONCE PINED (Book #6)
ONCE FORSAKEN (Book #7)
ONCE COLD (Book #8)
ONCE STALKED (Book #9)
ONCE LOST (Book #10)
ONCE BURIED (Book #11)
ONCE BOUND (Book #12)
ONCE TRAPPED (Book #13)
ONCE DORMANT (Book #14)
ONCE SHUNNED (Book #15)
ONCE MISSED (Book #16)
ONCE CHOSEN (Book #17)

MACKENZIE WHITE MYSTERY SERIES
BEFORE HE KILLS (Book #1)
BEFORE HE SEES (Book #2)
BEFORE HE COVETS (Book #3)
BEFORE HE TAKES (Book #4)
BEFORE HE NEEDS (Book #5)
BEFORE HE FEELS (Book #6)
BEFORE HE SINS (Book #7)

BEFORE HE HUNTS (Book #8)
BEFORE HE PREYS (Book #9)
BEFORE HE LONGS (Book #10)
BEFORE HE LAPSES (Book #11)
BEFORE HE ENVIES (Book #12)
BEFORE HE STALKS (Book #13)
BEFORE HE HARMS (Book #14)

AVERY BLACK MYSTERY SERIES
CAUSE TO KILL (Book #1)
CAUSE TO RUN (Book #2)
CAUSE TO HIDE (Book #3)
CAUSE TO FEAR (Book #4)
CAUSE TO SAVE (Book #5)
CAUSE TO DREAD (Book #6)

KERI LOCKE MYSTERY SERIES
A TRACE OF DEATH (Book #1)
A TRACE OF MURDER (Book #2)
A TRACE OF VICE (Book #3)
A TRACE OF CRIME (Book #4)
A TRACE OF HOPE (Book #5)

Made in United States
Orlando, FL
27 June 2023

34560763R00136